Synopsis

It's the year 2130 and Kendal Benz, a competent, up-and-coming New York attorney has been assigned the world's highest profile case; the theft of a deepliner spacecraft, stolen by communication specialist Sedge Nile on a mad quest to be the first human to reach the Centauri System - our solar-system's nearest neighbor. Unable to communicate with her client and unaware if he's even alive, Kendal begins to cleverly unravel the reality behind the profound sequence of events that have led to the perfect crime, events that run as deep as the stolen ship itself.

Alluring Echoes is an action-rich story of survival, discovery, human connection, obsession, and raw sanity.

Alluring Echoes
Across a Sea of Time

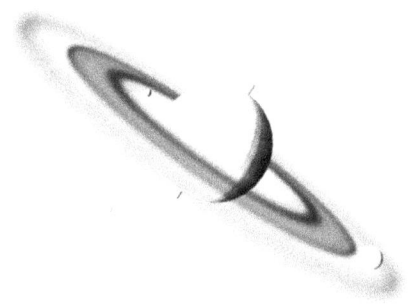

Moonliner: Book 2

Donald Hanzel

Part 1: Jan 02, 2130

New York City

Snow begins to fall outside the windows of the Midtown Manhattan law firm of Thacker & Walcott. Kendal watches the floating flakes drift softly downward and wonders how long it will take them to reach the sidewalks fifty-four stories below. It's a welcome distraction from the perpetual mental replay of the fight she had with Brice only thirty-six hours ago. Their three-year relationship hasn't survived into the new year. She wonders if it stands any chance of doing so as she again checks her messages to see if he has called. He hasn't of course. It's not his way. She knows his pride won't permit him to make the first move and she's tired of being the one to step up. It's a familiar cycle and she has to really ask herself this time, this year, this decade, if she wants to go around again.

Kendal also wonders why she's sitting in Phil's office, the office of senior law office partner Philip Thacker; her boss. Her caseload is already more than she can bear and for some time she's had half-a-mind to quit the firm and find another avenue in life. Back in law school, she used to dream of more purpose, more adventure, more meaning to the job. So far, she has only helped highly affluent people keep the legal deck stacked in their favor.

"Good morning," Phil says, somewhat startling Kendal as he swiftly enters his office, looking like he's got a lot on his plate. "How were the holidays?" he asks.

"Relaxing," Kendal answers. "Good morning to you too."

"Thank you," Phil replies while taking a seat at his desk. "I'm rather busy," he tells her; "so I'm not going to waste our time. I'll cut right to the chase," he says with a serious look on his face. "Do you remember Sedge Nile?" he asks.

"Sedge Nile? A.K.A *Joy Rider,* the guy who stole a spaceship several years ago from the Sultan of Oman and took off to another planet?" Kendal asks. "Who doesn't?"

"Yes," Phil answers. "It's now becoming a high profile legal case and it has fallen on our lap. He's facing a litany of charges and I want you to look into them."

"Isn't he dead?" Kendal asks.

"That's a good question," Phil answers. "Some interesting new developments have indicated otherwise," he tells her.

"Like what?" she asks.

"Well for starters, he's not actually off to another planet," Phil tells her. "Luna Nuevo is a moon, orbiting a planet in the Centauri System. If it takes light over four years to get there from here, his chances of making it there alive really depend on his ability to achieve a speed nearing the speed of light. A few days ago, NASA received a signal sent from a deep space probe over two light years from Earth. The probe spotted an object traveling at over three quarters the speed of light on a trajectory to the Centauri System. Since radio signals travel at light speed, this fly-by occurred over two years ago, meaning that if Mr. Nile is still alive, he is now nearing Centauri, Luna Nuevo, or wherever the crazy bastard is going," he says shaking his head with a chuckle.

"I haven't heard anything about the spotting," Kendal says.

"It hasn't been published yet," Phil answers; "but it soon will be, so expect a lot of public attention to be given to the matter. NASA likes to double check its data before jumping to conclusions. This kind of press could be good for our firm and is frankly one huge reason why I've agreed to look into the case. It was over five years ago when he stole the spacecraft and you remember what a big story it was back then. Just wait until the world hears he may be alive."

"How did you hear?" Kendal asks.

"His common-law partner, a guy by the name of Holden Grant called us," Phil tells her. "He has a friend at NASA. Anyway, he swears up and down that Sedge is innocent of a lot of the charges filed against him and he wants to clear his name. I've pulled his case number from the court docket and am having the paralegal team assemble a file. It will be ready in a day or two. I'd like you to assess it and determine if he actually has a case. In the meantime, if you'd like to get started you could begin by contacting this guy Grant and seeing why he thinks Sedge is so innocent. Tina, the new temp at the front desk is now getting his contact info for you and has agreed to help you with whatever else you need."

"Fascinating," Kendal replies. "I suppose even spaceship thieves are entitled to representation."

"Yes," Phil answers; "as are spaceship owners, which is why you can expect to be up against a team of lawyers should this go to trial. The Sultan has unlimited resources."

"Minus one ship," Kendal replies with a laugh. "I'm on it," she confidently states as she gets up and makes her way to the door.

"Oh Kendal," Phil says, just as she's exiting the office.

"Yes," she replies.

"Happy New Year," he tells her.

"And a Happy New Year to you as well," she responds.

1:2

Kendal sits with her oldest friend Naya in the Riparian, their favorite restaurant at Sutton Square, overlooking the Riverview Terrace, the East River, and the endless stream of rush-hour pods flowing down FDR Drive. Naya grew up with Kendal in Bridgeport, Connecticut and followed her to the city a year after Kendal began law school at Columbia University. Aside from Kendal's first year in law school, the two have never really been apart.

Kendal checks her messages again, then stares out the large bay windows as Naya flirts with the waiter, a fellow Connecticuter from the town of New Haven. Naya, soon noticing Kendal's withdrawal, cuts her flirtation short to bring Kendal back into the conversation.

"Are you hungry?" she asks Kendal.

"Starving," Kendal replies. "I'll have the seared ahi tuna and a sparkling water," she tells the waiter, not needing a menu.

"I think I'll go with the bacon-wrapped sirloin medallion with a side of couscous," Naya tells him. "And can I get a Coke?" she asks.

"Certainly," the waiter answers before heading back to the kitchen.

"He's cute, don't you think?" Naya asks Kendal smiling.

"Yes he is," Kendal answers, trying not to let her busy mind dull Naya's playful mood.

"Happy New Year, by the way," Naya tells her. "You missed an awesome party on New Year's Eve. What were you and Brice up to?"

"Fighting," Kendal answers. "I wish I'd gone to the party. We haven't spoken since Monday night."

"Oh Kendal! I'm sorry," Naya responds.

"It's okay Naya, I'm fine," Kendal tells her. "It's a new year and a new chance to redefine myself."

"Does that mean this break-up is for good?" Naya asks.

"We'll see," Kendal responds. "Anyway, I don't want to dwell on Brice tonight."

"Good, then we won't," Naya says with a smile. "What else is new?"

"You won't believe this," Kendal tells her; "but I'm representing Sedge Nile."

"You mean Joy Rider, the guy who stole the spaceship?" Naya asks in amazement.

"Yes," Kendal answers.

"Is he alive?" Naya asks.

"I don't know," Kendal responds, not wanting to divulge the proprietary NASA signal, which doesn't answer the question anyway. "I'm meeting his partner for lunch tomorrow."

"That's so awesome," Naya says. "Remember what a huge news story that was? When was that?"

"Five years ago, in late 2124," Kendal answers. "If he is alive, he should be arriving at Luna Nuevo soon. It takes this long to get there."

"Yes, I remember the news reports," Naya says. "He has a lot of people cheering for him. I too hope he makes it. This could be huge for your career," she adds.

"Who knows?" Kendal says. "It's already a nice change of events. My cases are never this exciting and certainly not this high profile. I'm anxious to jump into it."

"You're going to rock this," Naya tells her. "I have a feeling this will be a real break for you."

Naya has never been a real fan of Brice and is happy deep down inside for Kendal, hoping this break-up sticks. Knowing Kendal too well, however, she knows not to push it. Kendal is a decisive woman who likes to make up her own mind. If she seeks advice, she'll ask for it. She usually just wants someone to listen to her and Naya's always willing to bend an ear.

The two end up reminiscing over old high school friends and teachers as the evening rolls by. Fine food and laughter lighten Kendal's mind. Eventually, they pay their bill and leave but not before Naya eagerly exchanges contact information with the waiter. Their year is off to an exciting start.

1:3

Soft, ambient music plays as Kendal enters Brice's office. The lights are on but nobody is in the room. She takes a seat and waits patiently. The office has changed dramatically from the way she remembers it. It's much brighter. She's late for work herself but knows she needs to speak with Brice. At last, a receptionist walks into the room and takes a seat behind the reception desk. She's wearing a white doctor's coat. This is odd. Brice is an accountant. Kendal approaches the desk and speaks to her.

"Hi, I'm Kendal Benz. I'm supposed to meet Brice Borrelli. Is he in?"

The receptionist keeps staring at her screen, seemingly ignoring Kendal altogether.

"Excuse me," Kendal says more loudly. "Is Brice Borrelli in?"

After an extended pause, the receptionist looks up at Kendal.

"Haven't you heard?" she asks. "Brice is gone. Everybody is gone."

"Gone," Kendal replies. "Gone where?"

"Luna Nuevo," she answers with a smile.

Kendal wakes to the gradually increasing sound of ambient music, her preferred alarm. She checks her messages to find only one from the office; it's her new casefile. This is now her third morning not waking in Brice's apartment and she's again growing accustomed to her own space. It's lonely but peaceful. She prepares and times a fresh pot of coffee to be ready for her upon her return from the building's gym, then dons her gym clothes and makes her way to the elevator for her morning workout. Once inside the gym, she gets on a treadmill and sets the screen to catch her favorite morning show.

"...the president will give his State of the Union address on January twenty-first as planned. We will be broadcasting the speech live on our network. Back to you Brenda.

"Thanks Steve, we'll be looking forward to that. Remember Sedge Nile, or Joy Rider to many, the guy making headlines five years ago for stealing a luxury spaceliner and disappearing to another star system? Well he's back in the news today. NASA has confirmed that what they believe to be Sedge's spacecraft, a deepliner DeepStream Series Nine, owned by the Sultan of Oman we should note, has been spotted by one of their deep space probes coming out of the Oort Cloud on course for the Centauri System, traveling at point seventy-six times the speed of light.

"The probe is now so far away from Earth that it took NASA's signal over two years to reach us, meaning that by now that ship should be nearing Centauri. This is good news for those fearing Sedge might not have attained the speeds necessary to reach Centauri during his lifetime. There is no way, however, for NASA to confirm if he is alive or what condition he or the stolen craft are in. Communicating with Earth while hurtling away from us at such a high rate of speed makes it impossible. Even if he does reach Centauri, or more specifically his likely intended destination of Luna Nuevo, we won't know for almost another five years. It will take over four years for any message he sends back to us to reach us. That's how vast space is. Mike.

"Thanks Brenda. Wow! What an amazing story. Snow is expected to fall again today in the greater New York area with..."

Kendal turns the news off, immediately cutting her workout short. This is all happening so fast. She feels her pulse pick up at the excitement of the story. For once, she finds herself in the center of the action, not Brice's world. She grabs her towel and quickly heads back to her condo.

Wasting no time, Kendal grabs a quick shower, gets dressed, puts her coffee in a to-go mug, and calls for a private pod to take her to work. Enroute, she decides to pass on her plan to begin reviewing the casefile to instead scan the dial for more news on her new client's spotting. It doesn't take long for her to find the story being discussed.

"...many people said five years ago, but it's not a suicide mission. He seems hell-bent on making it to Luna Nuevo," a voice says.

"Yeah but keep in mind, nobody knows if the guy's alive..." another voice adds.

"Either way, he's already gone faster, and further from Earth than anyone in history..." the first voice remarks.

"Okay, but does that really count for anything if he's dead? You have to also keep in mind the guy needs oxygen, food, water, heat, and to slow way down once he arrives, if he arrives. We haven't even landed a probe in the Centauri System yet, let alone a human. It's incredibly dangerous on so many levels," a third voice adds to the morning show.

Kendal arrives at her office to find a stack of memos with links to her casefile. She's never been so eager to get started on a case. Where to begin? The most obvious reference point, she thinks, is the last video Sedge left just prior to leaving Earth. She closes the door to her office, sits back in her chair and lets it play.

"I don't know what I can really say except that I'm sorry," Sedge begins with a somber look into the camera. "I apologize to Sultan bin Saeed for commandeering his ship. I mean no harm to come to it and plan to leave it safely in orbit around Luna Nuevo. You have been a fair and generous employer and I want to do all I can to both keep your name clear of any illicit intent and to credit you for any benefit that may come of this mission. I want you to know that I had nothing to do with the navcom glitch, nor can I explain how it happened. The system I designed has multiple protections built within it to keep that from occurring. I have not deliberately damaged the system in any way, nor done anything to endanger anyone's life except my own. I simply can't bear to lose my security clearance and access to the very system I was an integral part of designing.

"To my friends and family, I want to thank you all. I'll cherish our precious memories for as long as I shall live. Finally, to Holden, I'm really sorry. I really am."

Kendal, usually cool and calculated, finds herself swallowing to hold back a tear. Sedge's message has put a human face and voice on this case. This isn't someone looking to exploit tax loopholes. Her client is now very real and facing the most unique struggle to survive she's ever encountered. His legal issues are the least of his problems. Nevertheless, his legal issues are with what she has the power to help him. She gets to work.

One of the first names from the casefile to jump out at her is Drew Brite, former military colonel now working for NASA's ground control. According to the file, he was operating the ground based laser system at the time Sedge launched to Centauri. Maybe he knew what Sedge was talking about with the navcom glitch, something new to Kendal. She gives him a call.

"This is Drew. How can I help you?" he answers the call.

"Hi Drew, this is Kendal Benz with the law offices of Thacker and Walcott. I'm representing Sedge Nile," she tells him.

"Good morning Kendal. It's a pleasure. I heard the news this morning and was delighted to hear Sedge's flight appears to be on course," he says.

"You didn't know before this morning?" she asks. "You work for NASA."

"We're a large organization," he answers. "Departments aren't always privy to each other's information."

"Well, Mr. Brite, I know your time is valuable, so I won't waste it. Can you tell me how the laser system works and why Sedge needed access to it to launch?" she asks.

"Of course," he answers. "It's a ground-based laser guide which is fired into space, directly aligned with laser boosters on spacecraft. It's a developed form of the *laser-sail*, an ancient concept of accelerating to speeds near the speed of light, which we can now achieve if we couple it with nuclear-pulse propulsion. Still in its infancy, the system we've developed has to be fired from the ground, into laser boosters attached to a fitted vessel for it to work. It's highly effective. Nuclear-pulse engines alone would still take us thousands of years to reach Centauri. Now, as Sedge hopefully demonstrates, we can safely send someone to another star within a few years."

"That's astounding," Kendal says. "So how did Sedge gain access?"

"He knew of our plan to test-fire the lasers as part of the *Cortes* mission. He took a ship modified with laser boosters attached, flew it outside of our radar, lined it up with the proposed laser path, and timed his ignition. When we fired the lasers, we didn't know what was blocking their path until he had already accelerated to speeds well beyond return."

"That's astonishing," Kendal adds.

"You know Ms. Benz," Drew says; "they wanted me to immediately shut the lasers down upon realizing they were obstructed. I didn't, and I took a lot of heat for it. That act may, however, have saved Sedge's life. Had I cut the beams early, he would have been on a non-reversible course at a lower speed that would take hundreds, if not thousands of years to reach Centauri. His ship would have eventually arrived but long after his engines had failed - long after he had perished. Now, at least he has some chance. I felt vindicated this morning hearing that he'd cleared the Oort Cloud."

"Do you think he'll make it?" Kendal asks.

"I really don't know," Drew answers with a negative tone. "I don't design life-support systems. I can tell you that NASA won't send humans to Centauri without first robotically constructing a similar ground-based laser system on Luna Nuevo, not only to launch people back to Earth, but also to slow approaching vessels down. We took a number of risks just putting the Conquistador Probes into orbit without the system in place - risks we wouldn't take with human lives.

"I don't know what compelled Sedge to do what he did, but I do wish him well, not only for his sake, but also the human race. We could glean a lot from anything he learns should he survive the trip."

"Sedge mentioned a navcom glitch on his last transmission. Do you know anything about that?" Kendal asks.

"No," Drew answers. "You might want to call Stan Satterfield at the Allied Forces Ground Control office for that. Tell him I referred you. He's the military's finest navigation and communication expert."

"Thanks," Kendal says. "You've' been extremely helpful."

"My pleasure," Drew replies. "Let me know if there's anything else I can do.

Kendal spends the rest of her morning perusing documents and taking notes, unaware of time and almost forgetting about her lunch appointment. What an endlessly fascinating case to acquire. She has never been this excited about her career.

1:4

Holden Grant works for the New York Public Library, also in Midtown just down 6th Avenue from Kendal's office. They've agreed to meet at *Samgyeopsal House*, a newly opened restaurant on the edge of Korea Town. The day is cold but dry, so Kendal chooses to walk. The sun peeks from the clouds for a few moments as she walks within the canyon walls of 34th Street, past the Empire State Building. She doesn't look up anymore, now immune to the magnitude that once drew her to this city. She simply lives, works, and functions in it, leaving the dreaming to others.

She finally arrives at the restaurant, where a young Korean man guides her to a quaint table with a gas grill embedded in its center. Holden is waiting for her. He stands to shake her hand, a kind of traditional politeness she hasn't experienced in a while. They both take a seat and engage in a little small talk before silently looking over their menus. The restaurant is packed, something to be expected of almost any Midtown restaurant during the noon hour. Soon, the waiter comes and they order.

"I'll have an order of bibimbap," Kendal tells the waiter.

"And I'll have the samgyeopsal course for one," Holden says.

"Certainly," the waiter replies. "Anything to drink?" he asks.

"Just water," Kendal answers.

"Same for me," Holden adds.

"I watched Sedge's last message this morning," Kendal tells Holden as the waiter walks away from the table.

"What exactly did he say?" Holden asks her. "I wasn't allowed to see it. The lawyers from GulfStar told me it was classified. They were so rude to me, treating me like I had stolen their ship. They wanted me to answer a lot of questions but wouldn't answer any of mine"

"I'm sorry to hear that," Kendal replies. "The message was short, mentioning that he didn't want to hurt anyone and basically apologizing to Sultan bin Saeed, his friends, family, and lastly to you."

"What did he say to me?" Holden asks.

"Just that he was sorry," Kendal answers; "really sorry."

"He's sorry," Holden repeats, now visibly shaken. "He didn't want to hurt anyone, my ass. He knew he hurt me."

"I'm sorry," Kendal says. "I didn't realize this was still a touchy topic for you.

"No, I'm sorry. I'm fine," Holden replies. "It's just that when I heard his ship was spotted, it stirred up a lot of emotions in me."

"It's okay, I understand," Kendal replies in a consoling tone. "Maybe you can help me understand more why he did it," she says.

"It all started as an amusing hypothetical," Holden says. "Sedge spotted a security weakness that he thought he was capable of exploiting. He realized that he was in a rare position with his security clearance, his navigation and security training, and his job with GulfStar. At first, it was just a joke that he would drop at dinner with friends, or at small parties. He began telling people that it was possible to steal a spaceliner. I thought he was joking about doing it, but he clearly knew that it was feasible."

"Did he tell people how?" Kendal asks.

"Only me," Holden tells her. "He used to tell me that private sector security regulations are more lax than with commercial liners. He said that with private liners, only two pilots are required to detach from a port, unlike commercial flights, which require three. He knew how to override this using his maintenance clearance, after first deactivating the alarm which he also did with his maintenance clearance. Once detached with the ship in maintenance override, no central command could take control even if alerted, which they wouldn't be."

"He sounds clever," Kendal says amused.

"He's extremely clever," Holden replies. "He became preoccupied with the idea. We live in a world where not many things are stolen anymore. Cameras are everywhere and almost everything is geo-tagged. I think this was a unique situation that nobody foresaw, other than Sedge of course."

"How long do you think he'd been planning to do it?" Kendal asks.

"I don't think he ever planned to do it, to be honest," Holden answers. "He just loved knowing it was possible, and dreaming up ways to make it more so."

"How so?" Kendal asks.

"After he realized he could steal a ship, he talked GulfStar into adding the laser boosters. GulfStar is the only private company that has installed them. An independent contractor made them for NASA. Realizing they were compatible with deepliners, Sedge recommended they be added to GulfStar's fleet even though they've never been used for interplanetary travel, only for NASA's deep-space probes. Sedge convinced the GulfStar buyers that eventually they would be used by everyone and that they should get ahead of the game."

"Wow," Kendal says.

"Yeah," Holden adds. "NASA didn't even know they were being sold on the open market. GulfStar is a rich company that likes to have the best of everything, whether they need it or not. They even have diamond controls throughout the bridge. They spare no expense, and if there's no regulation against adding laser boosters, who's to stop them from acquiring them?"

"I had no idea how elaborate this plan was," Kendal says.

"Nobody did," Holden says. "Nobody except for Sedge of course. He even talked them into adding atmospheric anchors, which are controversial."

"What are they?" Kendal asks.

"They're fired from a ship like missiles into the atmosphere of a planet or moon, only they remain elastically tethered to the ship. They're used to slow a high velocity ship down without the ship itself having to risk the chance of entering the atmosphere. If he's alive, I'm sure Sedge is planning to use them to put his ship into orbit around Luna Nuevo," Holden answers. "The only problem is that they've failed every test. They're still allowed to be sold on the market so long as they are not used as a primary deceleration system, only a last-ditch safety feature. GulfStar bought them simply because they can afford to do so."

"So why did he do it?" Kendal asks. "What made him actually go through with it?"

"I think when the Conquistador Probes discovered that Luna Nuevo is likely habitable, his hypothetical plans started to truly tempt him. He was growing angrier with the world," Holden answers; "more misanthropic by the day, and as you know, living in New York City is not the cure for that. He's always seen himself as a true navigator. His prized possession is an ancient sextant he bought at an auction. He said he could find his way anywhere with it. He hates how regulation often delays human progress. He has always been obsessed with ancient explorers, watching endless documentaries on Magellan; Shackleton; Marco Polo; the Polynesians sailing to Easter Island; Yuri Gagarin; Neil Armstrong, all of them. He always said that real risk takers truly advance our species."

"That sounds noble," Kendal says.

"That's the tough-guy side of him," Holden replies; "but I know him well and there's another side to him. He's capable of lapses in judgement, often ones he later regrets. It happened sometimes when we would argue. He puts up a masculine, male ego front, but down inside he's as fragile as a kitten."

The waiter arrives with a tray full of food. He first serves Kendal her bibimbap, served with four little sauce dishes on the side. For Holden, the waiter lights the propane grill and serves him a bowl of white rice with two plates full of sliced, raw meat cuts. He asks if they need any instructions, or anything else. Neither Kendal nor Holden are new to Korean dining. They decline. Holden gracefully puts a few cuts of beef tongue on the grill with chop sticks.

"So what was the straw that broke the camel's back?" Kendal asks. "What happened at the time that sent Sedge over the edge?"

"He was in trouble for something," Holden answers. "Something happened at work and he was being blamed. This is why I contacted your office. There was some kind of security issue. Now they're saying it was all connected to his plot to take the deepliner, but it wasn't. That's why they're trying to charge him with reckless endangerment as well as theft. They think the security issue has something to do with Sedge stealing the ship. I know it doesn't."

"How do you know?" Kendal asks.

"Sedge told me the day before he launched that he was in trouble, being blamed for something that was out of his control. He said they threatened to revoke his clearance and that his job was in jeopardy. It's why he took the ship. I know it."

"Do you know anything about a glitch?" Kendal asks.

"No, why?" Holden asks in return.

"He mentioned it in his message. It must have something to do with the security problem."

"Do you think you can help him?" Holden asks.

"I don't know yet," Kendal answers; "but I want to try. I need more time."

"There doesn't appear to be any rush," Holden replies. "At least time is on his side."

They raise their water glasses and toast Sedge, then exchange thoughts on several lighter topics over some savory Korean barbeque. Holden seems happier after getting his pent-up emotions out. Kendal is happy as well. Holden being gay makes it easier for her to let her walls down and talk freely, knowing chemistry is out of the equation. Her break up has left her fed up with masculinity and the male ego, and Holden is none of that. They hit it off well.

1:5

Kendal gets back to her office just as snow again begins
to fall. 2030 is off to a cold and snowy start. She wastes
no time delving back into the casefile. She's convinced
there was no endangerment on Sedge's part and knows
that if she can better understand whatever happened the
day before he launched, she may be able to at least get
that charge reduced to gross negligence. It seems like a
good starting point. She needs, however, to know more
about the glitch that occurred, and the information
GulfStar provided when they filed the charges is limited.
God knows they aren't going to share either.

Following the advice of Drew from NASA, she contacts
Stan Satterfield, the recommended expert on navigation
and communication. His credentials indicate he has a
similar skillset to Sedge's, so if anyone can explain what
may have happened, it should be Stan. Kendal knows
nothing of navigation or communication and has never
had to deal with the military. Feeling a little intimidated,
she makes the call.

"Allied Forces Ground Control, how may I direct
your call," a man answers.

"Hello, my name is Kendal Benz and I'm an attorney with Thacker and Walcott. I'd like to speak with Stan Satterfield if I may," Kendal says.

"Certainly, please hold a moment," the voice replies. Moments later, the call resumes.

"Hello Ms. Benz, this is Stan Satterfield," an older man's voice is heard saying, sounding relaxed and confident. "What can I do for you today?" he asks.

"I'm representing Sedge Nile," Kendal answers; "and I would like to ask you a few questions if I may."

"Sedge Nile," he replies surprised. "You mean the guy who took a deepliner for a joy-ride? I had nothing to do with that whatsoever," he says.

"Of course you didn't," Kendal replies. "To be honest, this case is a little over my head, technically speaking, and Drew Brite told me that you might be the guy to help me understand glitches."

"Glitches?" he asks. "I suppose. What do glitches have to do with Sedge Nile?"

"I'm not really at liberty to disclose everything, but I can say that he's being charged with some serious crimes. One of them is reckless endangerment."

"Reckless endangerment!" Stan says. "Sounds like they're throwing the book at him. I suppose I can understand their anger, but endangerment is likely a stretch of the imagination on their part. They may be reaching a bit."

"That's refreshing to hear," Kendal responds. "Why do you say so?"

"A glitch is a rare occurrence," he answers. "In theory, one could be dangerous if it happened at precisely the wrong time, say when someone is docking for example, but they usually don't last more than a split second when they do occur. The danger is considered minimal. Again, however, systems are designed to prevent them from naturally occurring. For that reason, when they do happen they're almost always the result of some careless human communication error. That may be why they're blaming your client."

"They are saying the glitch, which occurred the day before he took the ship, had something to do with his plot to take the ship, thus the endangerment charge," Kendal tells him, stepping a little outside of lawyer-client privilege lines but trusting a military commander, knowing she needs to pick his brain.

"That I doubt," Stan says. "Again, maybe it was a foolish error, like not turning off his transmission equipment before working on the system, but I would think that should set off an alert. I don't know. Who was he working for?"

"GulfStar," Kendal answers.

"I don't know GulfStar's system," Stan tells her; "but I do seriously doubt there was any connection between a glitch and the theft of that ship."

"I'm relieved to hear that," Kendal tells him.

"I tell you what," Stan says. "I may be able to find out a little more if you give me the exact time of the glitch. I can check our records. If a glitch showed up on our system at the same time, then it would be highly unlikely Sedge was responsible for it. They're usually localized. Can you tell me exactly when it happened? It would have been logged."

"You can do that?" Kendal asks. "It was five years ago you know."

"Sure, we keep everything on file," Stan answers.

"I don't have the time of the incident in the casefile," Kendal says; "and GulfStar keeps it under wraps. If this case ever reaches a discovery phase, I'll find out. For now, all I can tell you is that it happened on December 11, 2124."

"That's enough to go on," Stan replies. "Again, glitches are rare so if we do find one on that day, there will be a good chance it was from the same source. Keep in mind that it may not definitively, or legally prove anything," he adds; "but if we find one, I'd be convinced they were of the same origin. And if you were able to show that a glitch happened at the exact time on two separate systems, it would be an incredibly strong alibi for Sedge. It would show that he didn't sabotage his system, because it would show that the glitch very likely didn't originate with him. He wouldn't be the source."

"I can't begin to tell you how helpful you've been," Kendal tells him, now feeling like she's getting somewhere.

"It's my pleasure," Stan replies. "It's a really interesting case for you to get."

"I couldn't agree more," Kendal tells him.

"I've gotta say though," Stan adds; "at the risk of sounding pessimistic, I don't think he's going to make it."

"Oh," Kendal responds.

"Not that I'm not pulling for him," Stan says. "I'm a navigator too. It's just that no man is an island, and what he's trying to do goes way beyond the scope of navigation or communication."

"I suppose," Kendal replies, now sounding much less excited.

"Keep your chin up though," Stan tells her, realizing that he just brought her mood down. "Not many people thought he'd get this far."

"Thanks," Kendal says. "I will."

1:6

Kendal is a morning person and seldom sleeps one away. Even these dark, cold winter mornings don't phase her. It's Friday and she's up well before the sun, making coffee, working out, and catching up on news. She's eager for the city to catch up with her today, but has to wait. Ordinarily, she could just go into the office and get started early. Today, however, she has other morning plans; an appointment to meet Dr. Julius Reed, assistant director at the Haden Planetarium. She wants to learn more about Luna Nuevo. She checks her messages; still nothing from Brice. Surprisingly, unlike previous break-ups, she isn't upset over this one. She smiles, now feeling like she's truly moving on with her life.

With almost two hours before her appointment, she decides to walk to the planetarium. She bundles up and steps out of her 42nd St. condo into the cold, brisk air. With a little extra time on her hands, she decides to stroll an extra block east so she can walk down 7th toward Central Park. As she makes her way through Times Square and down Broadway, she can't believe how different the scene appears than just a few nights ago. What a different perspective. The year no longer seems so new. It's now occurring. Time is lapsing. She can feel the excitement Friday brings to such a vibrant city, even this early in the day. She can see it on people's faces. When you start your work week on Wednesday, the weekend comes before you know it. It's a nice way to ease into the year, into the decade.

She eventually reaches Central Park and enters via a bridge-way at Columbus Circle. The sun is now out and warming the air. She hasn't been here in a while and has forgotten how beautiful the sycamore trees look, even in their leafless hibernation. The park sits so sheltered from time, between endless skyscrapers, in the middle of one of the world's biggest cities. She stays on the footpaths parallel to Central Park West, not wanting to veer too far from her destination, eventually taking Birdie Path past Strawberry Fields. The air seems so much fresher, but that could just be in her mind. Finally, she arrives at the 77th Street Stone Arch, where she exits the park and crosses Central Park West, thirty-five blocks north of her apartment. With her workout and the walk, she's done more exercise this morning than most people do in a week. She's proud and happy to have had such a different morning than her usual hustle. Waking early has advantages to those who find ways to spend their morning hours.

She enters the planetarium beneath the mighty Roosevelt Rotunda and makes her way to the information counter. She tells a man behind the desk that she's here to see Dr. Reed. He gives Dr. Reed a call and asks her to wait a few short minutes and he would be right with her. She looks around at a room filled with spheres and stunning displays of space. What a fun place to work.

Moments later a grey-bearded, dapperly dressed man approaches the desk. He has a certain distinguished, intelligent look about him. Kendal correctly assumes this to be Dr. Reed, but waits for him to introduce himself.

"Ms. Benz?" the man asks.

"Yes," Kendal answers.

"I'm Julius Reed, Assistant Director of the planetarium. I understand you've come to learn more about Luna Nuevo," he says.

"If it's no trouble for you to impart a little of what you've learned," Kendal politely replies.

"It would be my pleasure," Dr. Reed answers. "You've come to the right place. Why don't you come with me to where I can not only tell you about this intriguing moon, but also show you?" he says, extending his arm to guide her toward a long, circular ramp leading up the *Heilbrunn Cosmic Pathway.*

"What a great place," Kendal says as they work their way up the ramp around the edge of a massive sphere. "I'm embarrassed to admit it, but I've never been here."

"Not at all," Dr. Reed tells her. "I hope you enjoy your visit. Now I understand you're representing Sedge Nile."

"I am," Kendal replies. "It's why I need to get a better understanding of Luna Nuevo and its lure."

"Of course, we'd love to help. Please step this way," Dr. Reed tells her as they get off the path and enter an empty auditorium. "This room is our holographic universe. Here we can see a hologram of virtually anything in the known universe. Have a seat," he adds, motioning for Kendal to sit in the front row. Dr. Reed takes a seat just across a center aisle, close but appropriately distanced.

"Okay," Kendal says as she sits down. "I have to admit, I'm really stupid when it comes to astronomy. I wish I'd paid more attention in school."

"People often feel intimidated by astronomy," Dr. Reed replies; "it's a vast universe. Just remember, moons go around planets; planets go around stars, or suns for a more familiar word; and suns go around the centers of galaxies. As you can see with our moon, there's a lot of space between moons and planets, a lot more between stars, and a whole lot more between galaxies, which are seen as big islands in the sky.   Everything else is really just trivial."

"That helps," Kendal responds, feeling more at ease. "So our sun is a star?" she asks in a tone that reveals she's already learning something.

"Yes," Dr. Reed answers. "It's one of hundreds of billions that go around the core of our galaxy; the Milky Way."

"So, Centauri is a star in the Milky Way too then, I suppose," Kendal adds, maintaining a grasp on things.

"Centauri is actually three stars," Dr. Reed answers; "and the closest ones to us, except for our own sun of course."

"Really," Kendal responds.

"Yes. Most stars are binary stars, which means they are a pair of stars orbiting each other," Dr. Reed replies. "Alpha Centauri A and Alpha Centauri B, otherwise known as Beta Centauri, orbit each other. Further out, you have Proxima Centauri, sometimes called Alpha Centauri C, a smaller red star known as a red dwarf that orbits both of them. It's actually the closest star to our sun. To put its size and distance in perspective, if our sun was a grapefruit sitting here in New York, Proxima Centauri would be a cherry in California. The three Centauri stars and all of the planets and moons orbiting them make up the Centauri star system. Keep in mind, we use the word *system* in astronomy to indicate everything going around a celestial body, or set of bodies. Our solar system, for example, includes our sun, the eight planets, all their moons, and belts orbiting our sun."

"I'm still following you," Kendal tells Dr. Reed, appreciating his ability to simplify something she thought to be so complex. "So where does Luna Nuevo fit into the Centauri System?" she asks.

"Good question," Dr. Reed answers. "Let's take a look. To Luna Nuevo," he says out loud. The lights quickly dim and a system of lasers illuminates the room at the command of his voice. Earth suddenly appears but rapidly moves out of view as the hologram speeds them beyond our moon and to the Centauri System.

"For over a hundred years, NASA has had their eye on Proxima B, one of several known planets orbiting Proxima Centauri," he says as they approach the red dwarf. "The planet is in the star's habitable zone, otherwise known as the Goldilocks Zone, meaning it orbits in a narrow area not too close to or far from the star, an area warm enough for ice to become water but not too hot for it to boil. This is the first indication that a planet or moon can support life, because life as we know it depends on liquid water."

"I see," Kendal says.

"For almost a century, we've known about *Aureola*, a large planet orbiting just within the habitable zone of Alpha Centauri B. It's a ringed gas giant, much like Saturn with no solid surface, so it hasn't caught a lot of interest. Its moons, however, Luna Nuevo and Lunita were not discovered until a decade or so after Aureola because they're tucked away within the planet's rings. Being in the habitable zone as well, these moons drew our attention," Dr. Reeds says as a hologram of Luna Nuevo comes into view.

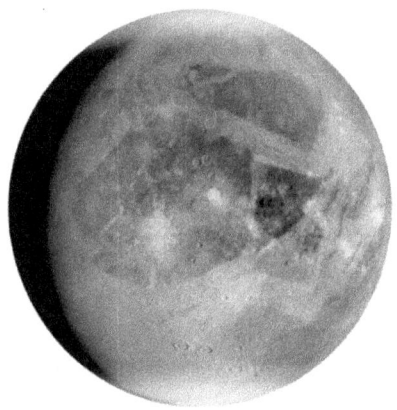

"Do they have solid surfaces?" Kendal asks.

"Yes, they do," Dr. Reed answers; "much like Mars' surface, reddish in color because of iron oxide, or rust as it's more commonly known. Lunita is too small to support a real atmosphere, however, causing all attention to shift to Luna Nuevo.

"There, we would weigh 9% more than on Earth. That's because it is slightly smaller in size than Earth, but denser, giving it more mass – more weight. It also has other features deemed necessary to support life; not only an atmosphere but an electromagnetic field generated from its large iron core, which moderates solar radiation and protects the atmosphere from solar flares. This gives Luna Nuevo spectacular auroras around its poles."

"Interesting," Kendal adds, jotting notes on her own holographic screen.

"Yes, but NASA quickly lost interest in the moon when it started getting its first atmospheric readings. Their original observations of the moon underestimated both the density and oxygen levels of its atmosphere, causing them to again turn their attention to Proxima B. It wasn't until their recent probes, the Conquistador Probes, sent back newer, more accurate readings that renewed both NASA's and apparently your client's interest in Luna Nuevo."

"Really?" Kendal asks, staring at brilliant auroras being generated by the hologram around Luna Nuevo's poles. "What did the probes find?"

"Oxygen," Dr. Reed answers; "a lot of it. Luna Nuevo is basically a two-tiered moon. It has an upper crust to it which comprises most of the moon's surface. Up there," he says pointing to the hologram; "is a very thin atmosphere largely devoid of oxygen. Prior to the probes, we were really only able to read that portion of the atmosphere using standard spectroscopy. The probes, however, revealed a lower level to the planet that we missed, a canyon system and valleys of collapsed lime and sandstone. Oxygen is heavy and the bulk of Luna Nuevo's oxygen lies beneath its upper-mantle, within this network of valleys and canyons."

"So, do you think there's any life on the moon?" Kendal asks.

"Great question," Dr. Reed replies. "The probes have sensitive instruments looking for it. Nothing seems to live on the upper crust. There appears, however, to be a great deal of plant life, likely ferns and possibly trees within the lower lands, but no animal life has been detected. The lower tier seems to be much like Earth prior to the *Cambrian Explosion* five-hundred and forty-one million years ago, when animal life seemed to explode, rapidly evolving around our planet."

"Fascinating," Kendal says. "Now I really want to go to Luna Nuevo myself."

"As do I," Dr. Reed tells her. "I'm quite jealous of Sedge, actually. I was really excited to hear the news this week and I really hope he makes it. I think that's why so many people are willing to overlook his crime and focus on his mission. Had he not done what he did, we would most likely never see a human make it to the Centauri System in our lifetime. He's given us a chance."

"Thank you for your help today," Kendal tells him, looking pressed for time. "I've really got to get back to the office."

"It's been my pleasure Ms. Benz," Julius answers. "Anything I can do to help, please don't hesitate."

1:7

Kendal checks the time as she walks out of the planetarium; a quarter past eleven. Neither in the mood nor having the time to walk all the way back from the Upper West Side to her Midtown office, she decides to save a few bucks and catch a public pod on Columbus Ave, knowing she can still beat the noon rush. Once aboard the number seven, she finds a seat, puts on a set of headphones, and scans stations hoping to hear anything she can of Sedge's story. It doesn't take her long to dial in a report.

"...Cortes Mission is the second phase of the Conquistador Probes. Though launched almost eight weeks after Sedge Nile's stolen deepliner, it should have reached a velocity of point eight-five times the speed of light and is thus going to arrive ahead of Sedge's voyage by several weeks. It should have been spotted by NASA's deep space probe coming out of the Oort Cloud just four weeks behind the GulfStar deepliner. Given the relative speed of the two vessels, the Cortes should be passing Sedge Nile's craft any time now. According to NASA, there is no expected danger of collision due to the differences in trajectories.

"NYPD detectives are still searching for the person who shot two people in Central Park on New Year's Eve. Both victims are in stable condition and are expected to recover, though there still seems to be no motive for the crime..."

Kendal's pod glides down Columbus and merges onto 8th for another ten blocks. She gets off a block and a half from her office. The midday rush is picking up.

Kendal gets back to her office shortly before noon. People are exiting the building for lunch, smiling and laughing, in Friday mode. Phil Thacker calls out to her before she reaches her office.

"Kendal, just who I wanted to see," he says. "Can you come in here for a minute?" he asks, waving her into his office. She enters and takes a seat.

"How are you Phil?" she asks.

"Great," he answers. "I'm off to the Hamptons in a few minutes and I'm glad I caught you before I left. My wife and I didn't get out of the city for the holidays, so I'm making it up to her this weekend."

"Nice," Kendal replies.

"Anyway, I'd like to hear how things are going," he says. "Have you made any headway yet?"

"I think so," Kendal answers; "at least I hope so. I may be able to get the reckless endangerment charge dropped if things go well."

"Wow!" Phil interjects. "That's huge. Getting rid of that would eliminate all the negligence and just leave us with the grand theft charges, which are pretty hard to get around."

"We'll see," Kendal says, pleased that her boss is pleased. "We'll see."

"I hate to drop this on you," Phil says, bringing the moment down; "but there may be an additional battle in this legal war with GulfStar."

"How so?" Kendal asks.

"Well, I don't know if you've heard this, but NASA has been doing all they can to help our client Sedge. They even went so far as to add additional supplies to the Cortes mission, a sort of care package if you will, to help him survive if he ever makes it to the surface of Luna Nuevo."

"Really?" Kendal asks, delighted to hear it.

"Yes," Phil answers. "They've stocked clothing, like footwear and outerwear to help him better deal with the climate and terrain, assuming of course he gets to the bio-dome. They've also stocked more provisions, like food and even some snacks."

"I didn't know that," Kendal says.

"Yes, they're really on his side. They've transmitted all news data and information feeds to the orbiters, which in turn will transmit to the Cortes when it arrives, so he can catch up on world events he's missed."

"That's really cool of NASA," Kendal says.

"Even better," Phil adds. "They've applied for a government grant of half-a-million dollars to cover additional costs incurred due to Sedge's private mission, arguing that we all stand to benefit from anything he discovers."

"That's awesome," Kendal responds.

"Yes, but that's where you come in," Phil says. "GulfStar has filed an injunction on the payout of the half-a-million dollars, claiming a legal right to the funds. They're doing so on the grounds that he cost them just over three billion dollars for the ship, which is six-thousand fold the grant money."

"Damn them," Kendal says. "Do they want him to die?"

"You know corporate lawyers," Phil responds, "They have to feel like they're pulling their weight when they're collecting those large retainer fees. Anyway, can you look into it, maybe work some magic?"

"I'll give it a try," she answers with a sigh, looking like the weight of the world just landed on her shoulders.

"That's all I ask," Phil responds, trying to cheer her up. "Oh, and one more thing."

"Yes?" Kendal asks.

"Tina Moran called, wanting to interview you if you're willing."

"Tina Moran from The Times?" Kendal asks.

"Yes, here's her voice line. It's up to you, but I'd love to see you do it. You're becoming a celebrity it seems," Phil says with a smile.

Phil heads out the door and Kendal back to her office grinning, flattered that The Times wants to talk to her. This case is giving her some real notoriety. Back in her office she sits down, takes a deep breath, and gives Tina Moran a call.

"Tina Moran's desk," Tina answers.

"Hi Tina. This is Kendal Benz with Thacker and Walcott. I'm ..."

"Yes Kendal, how nice to hear from you. Like a lot of journalists, I'm doing a piece on Sedge Nile. I've heard that you have been hired to represent him."

"Yes," Kendal responds. "That's true."

"Do you mind me asking you a few questions?" Tina asks.

"No, go ahead," Kendal answers.

"I've read that GulfStar has filed reckless endangerment charges against Sedge. Is that so and if yes, did he selfishly put people in danger in order to steal the ship?" Tina asks, getting down to brass tacks.

"I can't comment other than to say yes, reckless endangerment charges were filed, though at this point, we feel such charges to be baseless. Should this case get to a discovery phase, we'll know more about the specifics of such charges. For now I can say that there is no reason to suspect that Sedge Nile put anyone's life other than his own in danger."

"How can you represent him when you can't communicate with him?" Tina asks.

"It's certainly a unique case," Kendal answers. "All we can do is transmit updates to Sedge, but given the vast distance, any questions we ask him to answer will take almost a decade for us to receive a reply, given the amount of time it would take for the question to get to him and the answer to come back to us. We essentially have no two-way conversation capabilities."

"How interesting," Tina says, taking the time to make a note. "Is he alive?" she asks.

"Your guess is as good as mine," Kendal answers. "I certainly hope so. What he has done is, without question, highly controversial but undeniably daring. If he is alive, he's going to be the first human to achieve interstellar travel, and hopefully the first to set foot on a celestial body in another star system, that is if he touches down on Luna Nuevo."

"Amazing, isn't it?' Tina asks rhetorically.

"That it is," Kendal asserts.

Kendal decides to check her messages before calling it a week. She dials her voice-box.

- "Hi Kendal it's me," Naya's voice says after the first pong. "It's Friday! What are you doing tonight? Are you in the mood to do something? Give me a call." Another pong is heard.
- "Hello Kendal, Stan Satterfield with Allied Forces Ground Control. Can you give me a call when you get a minute? I have some interesting news." Another pong is heard, but followed by silence.

Kendal wastes no time getting back to Stan, hoping he has some good news.

"Stan Satterfield," he answers.

"Hi Stan. It's Kendal Benz calling back. What's up?"

"Kendal, glad I caught you before the weekend. I looked into the logbooks for the date you gave me."

"Yes," Kendal says in anticipation.

"There was no glitch detected by our instruments on December 11, 2124," he tells her.

"Oh," Kendal responds in disappointment.

"There was, however, an odd disturbance reported in the communication equipment on that day that could have easily been construed as a glitch."

"Really?" Kendal asks, now more excited.

"Yes," Stan answers; "but it wasn't a glitch. It was more like a failed signal. It lasted much longer than a glitch and had almost all the signatures of some kind of transmission, most likely narrow band. I can easily see why GulfStar may have thought it was a glitch, but our instruments are more sensitive than theirs. Our readouts indicate it was something much different."

"What was it then?" Kendal asks. "Why can't you simply classify it as a transmission?"

"It didn't have a time stamp," Stan answers. "We were able to document when the message was received of course," he adds; "just not when it was transmitted, information usually digitally embedded within the message. I've never seen that before."

"I see," Kendal says. "So Sedge may be responsible after all."

"No," Stan tells her. "At least I seriously doubt it," he adds.

"Why?" Kendal asks.

"Because the exact same phenomena happened three more times within the next several weeks, at the exact same frequency and apparently from the same source. How could Sedge be responsible for those interruptions if he was speeding away from the planet, incapable of transmitting any signals? That is unless he somehow pre-programmed the interruptions, which wouldn't make much sense," Stan replies.

"That's great news," Kendal says elated. "You've just made my day and my week."

"It's my pleasure," Stan tells her, excited for her.

"Would you be willing to sign an affidavit stating such?" she asks him.

"I don't have to go to court, do I?" he asks.

"No, I really doubt it, especially if you sign an affidavit. It looks like we may be able to get GulfStar to drop the reckless endangerment charges," Kendal answers, leaning back in her chair, looking out her window with a smile, watching a stream of pods glide down the street so far below.

Part 2

Wondering why the door to the little gate isn't locked, Sedge steps off the main spiral stairwell, onto a small platform that sits at the base of a separate, smaller spiral stairwell. He begins to ascend it into the arm. Within a few short minutes, he finds himself opening a little door and climbing out onto the 360-degree platform that encircles the torch.

"Whoa, I thought this thing has been closed for centuries," he says to himself, now hanging on tightly to the railing as he stares out over New York Harbor, back at the towering Manhattan skyline. He sits down to dampen his fear of heights, then watches boats cross the water below. He can see the Statin Island ferry slowing to dock at Whitehall Terminal. Low-flying aircraft are flowing in freeways across the sky. The sky is navy blue and becoming black as the last vestiges of daylight disappear into the thickening darkness. Sedge can just barely make out a few people sitting on the benches beneath the lamp posts in Battery Park, most likely looking back at him.

He begins to hear someone nearing the torch, coming up the stairwell behind him. The footfalls seemingly take forever to reach the top. He wonders who the hell else could be following him up here. Finally, the little door opens and Sedge's high school physics teacher, Mr. Holt, steps out onto the platform.

"Good evening Mr. Holt," Sedge says, but Mr. Holt doesn't answer him. "Am I in trouble?" Sedge asks him.

"What do you think Sedge?" Mr. Holt asks.

"They got really angry at me for something I didn't do," Sedge replies. "I didn't know what else to do. Besides, I didn't go. I just sent the ship as a diversion."

"They're going to figure it out you know," Mr. Holt replies. "Then what are you going to do? I think it's better if you tell them now."

"Look Mr. Holt, I've always listened to your advice," Sedge replies. "You've been my moral compass, but I can't tell them now."

"Why not?" Mr. Holt asks.

"Because I forgot my pants," Sedge answers, causing them both to look down at Sedges lower limbs. "I don't have any pants on."

Sedge suddenly awakens on a soft bench in the *Holo Café*, a charming little club built into the front gravity ring of GulfStar's deepliner. Just like in the dream, he isn't wearing any pants. In fact, he's stark naked from the waist down, wearing only a t-shirt. Unlike in the dream, however, he's very much on board, almost four light years away and moving further from our planet at just under two-hundred thousand kilometers every second. His greasy, untamed hair is almost ass-length and his beard is to his chest, an appearance that reflects his deep mental decay.

His first two years aboard were well balanced, spent in the solitude for which he'd long dreamt. The ship has plenty to keep a person's mind occupied. Though he can't keep up on recent earthly events, he has access to an endless database of information, as well as numerous exercise and entertainment options.

He had lived a loner's paradise, that is until his back went out on him; a periodic problem he's had throughout his life due to his *spondylolysis* - an underdeveloped fifth lumbar. That was when he first broke into the medicine cabinet in the ship's sickbay, where he discovered the powerful opiate pethidine. It indeed helped relieve his back pain, and so much more.

With no sunlight, there really are no days and nights. Yet Sedge initially kept the ship in Earth-mode, set to synch with New York, meaning the ship's lights would dim at the same time the sun would go down on the eastern seaboard, and increase in brightness as the sun would rise. This kept him in touch with the earth and patterns familiar to him.

When he began his pethidine habit, he would only take one 50 mg tablet on Friday nights. Before long, Saturday nights were included, then Thursday nights, Wednesday nights, and finally nightly. He eventually changed the ship's night-day mode to match Luna Nuevo's extremely long days and nights in a last-ditch effort to slow his habit down, but soon lost track of time altogether. His lucid dreaming, he correctly assumes, is another side effect of his self-medication.

He now faces, however, an unavoidable reality; he's running out of pills and will have to dry out. The Sultan is known to strictly abide by his Islamic ways and keeps no alcohol on board. Allah forbids it. That may be the only reason Sedge remains alive. Pills and alcohol aren't a good combination.

Sedge finds his shorts on the Holo stage. The last thing he remembers was playing guitar with his self-created holographic band in a stadium filled with exactly seventy-thousand holographic spectators. What a rush. He also remembers, however, seeing a bright star behind the ship, seemingly growing in brightness. This doesn't make sense. He turns on the rear-view cam to take another look. Sure enough, the star is even brighter than when he passed out. Could something be following him?

Sedge sits at a communication terminal, turns on the screen and begins recording another entry into his travel log:

"Something appears to be following me," he says, not bothering to state the date or time, knowing it's stamped into the recording. "Otherwise, I'm on course and doing well," he adds, though his appearance begs to differ. "The Centauri system has been getting brighter. Both Centauri A&B are visible now, though so small and faint. Soon the ship will begin its deceleration phase. My hope is to get it into a stable orbit around Luna Nuevo on a course I've carefully plotted. Granted, the maneuver is risky but my only alternative is to fly by the system, possibly using Centauri B's gravity to redirect the ship, but given my trajectory, that would kill any chances of me reaching any other system in my lifetime, leaving me to die on a hurtling ship. Besides, without slowing I have no hope of transmitting any messages, including this recording, back to Earth. My fate would never be known. So as risky as it may be, my aim is to slow this ship and eventually explore the surface of Luna Nuevo. I say eventually because should I succeed in setting this ship in a stable orbit around Luna, there are still enough supplies on board to last several more years, leaving me ample time to observe the moon from a safe orbit and calculate my precise touchdown on its surface.

"It's not that I really need the time, but the landing modules on this ship are calibrated for Earth's atmosphere, not Luna's thin upper highland regions, making the trip to the surface as dangerous as the slow down needed to achieve orbit. These moves are all physically feasible according to my calculations, but only within incredibly narrow margins of error. The slightest mistake anywhere along the way would very likely result in my death. Sometimes I wonder what I have done."

Sedge stands and starts walking through the ring, down its central path, or ringway. While walking past a chrome pillar, he spots his reflection. He stops to look at himself.

He's become so thin, so hairy; almost unrecognizable even to himself. He looks closely at his gaunt face, emaciated from the roller-coaster ride of emotional peaks and valleys on which he's managed to put himself. It, along with the pills, has aged him.

"I'm Neil Armstrong!" he yells at his reflection while flexing his scrawny chest. He can hear his voice echo down the ringway. "I'm Neil-fucking-Armstrong!" he yells once more.

2:2

Night has fallen again on Valles Grande, Luna Nuevo's renowned central canyon system. Sedge knows this because the cabin lights have dimmed throughout the ringway. He sits again in the Holo Café but not alone - he sits talking with Neil Armstrong. Neil is not a figment of his illusive imagination. He is a hologram, part of the onboard educational-entertainment system. Like songs in a karaoke book, patrons of the café can select from a long list of both living and historical figures to join them, anyone from Cleopatra to the Beatles. Each holographic character is uploaded into the system with a database of thoughts, facts, & even emotions based on what is known of their lives. They are even capable of associating new thoughts based on algorithmic parameters, giving them the ability to not only converse, but to offer advice on contemporary matters. Their use, however, has been met with a great deal of skepticism and legal limitations. They can't, for example, be used to offer testimony in a court of law, but they do make good friends for lonely people.

"How long did it take you to get to the moon?" Sedge asks Neil. "Four days?"

"Seventy-six hours," Neil answers.

"Do you know how long it would take to get from Earth to the moon at our current velocity?" Sedge asks.

"No," Neil answers. "How long?"

"Under two-seconds," Sedge replies. "It takes light about one and a quarter second. We're traveling at over three-quarters the speed of light. We'd get there in under two seconds."

"Fascinating," Neil responds, slightly nodding his head. "We're traveling at a truly remarkable speed."

"We can't even feel it," Sedge adds. "You and I sit here in a comfortably controlled environment - a little world protected from the cold, harsh universe that sits just a few meters away, through these thin walls. We're traveling from one thin bio-layer of atmosphere, gravitationally adhering to a planet's crust, to another one so far away that it takes light well over four years to reach it. That blows my mind."

"Yours and mine both," Neil replies. "Thanks for having me along."

"It's my pleasure. Have you heard of Maslow's hierarchy of needs?" Sedge asks.

"Yes, I've come across it in my academic courses," Neil responds. "I'm no expert on Maslow though. Why do you ask?"

"I think a lot about it," Sedge responds. "Your mission to the moon and this mission, they relate to Maslow."

"How so?" Neil asks.

"I used to argue to friends that oxygen was our most immediate need. Without it, billionaires would commit to spending their entire fortunes within seconds to get it back. That, however, is an earth-based assumption. Temperatures just outside these windows are so cold that were I exposed, I'd die before taking a single breath, placing heat back in the lowest, or most immediate spot on Maslow's hierarchy."

"Okay," Neil responds; "but oxygen is a close second."

"True," Sedge says in agreement. "I can think of no higher need, however, than the fulfillment of your mission to the moon, or my mission to another star, planet, and this far away moon. You know, and I soon will, true self-actualization. It's the tip of Maslow's pyramid."

"Interesting perspective," Neil says, sitting in thought.

"I question, however, the dimensions of Maslow's paradigm," Sedge adds.

"Oh, how so?" Neil asks.

"The closer you get to the top, the less you take for granted" Sedge tells him. "Our most basic needs are constant, perpetually needing to be met. Higher needs are only reached through an ongoing balance of lower ones, like air, water, and food. You can't move on to things like self-esteem or worth without them. They should never be taken for granted.

"In my case, I didn't bother to think of dentistry. I now have a tooth giving me minor sensitivity issues. I've also never taken better care of my teeth than I do now because there are no dentists where I'm going. Self-extraction seems to be my only option if or when my teeth go bad, and I don't know how to do that. If I break a bone, I won't be able to reset it. I'm really out on a limb here. This mission will very likely lead to my early death, all because I wanted to reach the top of Maslow's pyramid. Yet, the higher I go, the more I simply long for the basic essentials found at the base. To me, it's more circular than hierarchical, if that makes any sense."

"It makes perfect sense," Neil answers, leaving Sedge to wonder if he's actually caused a hologram to think. "Would you ever take your own life?" Neil asks, surprising Sedge that he would ask such a dark question.

"I would," Sedge answers. "In fact, my commandeering this vessel was somewhat of a suicide attempt. I knew the dangers when I launched, that I was killing a huge part of me, and that there was no going back."

"Well, it looks like for whatever its historical worth," Neil says; "you're about to be the first human to reach the Centauri System alive."

Cedric smiles as his mind drifts. Neil is right. He has come this far, something no human has ever done. Like Neil, he will live on in legacy, especially if he can slow this ship and transmit his journals back to Earth. Once the Centauri B orbiter has his transmission, he will truly be immortal.

"What could be following us?" Sedge asks Neil, now looking at the brightening object in the rear camera view.

"Whatever it is," Neil answers; "it obviously came from Earth. It's lined up too directly behind us to have any other origin."

"Yes, of course," Sedge says. "That's it. It has to be the Cortes. How could I have been so blind? The Cortes is catching up with us."

"That makes sense," Neil replies. "That makes sense."

2:3

Sedge catches a cross-tube elevator to the ship's central cylinder. He can feel his weight dissipate as the elevator approaches the ship's center, leaving the gravity ring. He's always thought *elevator* to be a poor label given that in space there really is no up or down. When he reaches the central tube, he begins making his way to the ship's stern, a place he hasn't been in over a year now, spending almost all of his time in the ship's gravity rings. They're his comfort zones, providing the amenities he needs to forget he is traveling through deep space, amenities like plumbing, running water, a gym - all things that rely on weight to function.

He finds being weightless exciting, but also a potential trigger for depression. He hasn't even been to the ship's bridge since launching. There has been no real need. After reaching its maximum velocity, the ship follows

Newton's first law of motion, remaining in motion until another force acts upon it.

He glides to the back of the ship using his arms and the handrails to guide himself, eventually reaching the rear viewing deck. He wants to get a better look at the Cortes. He spots it as he enters the viewing room. He aligns the room's telescope to take a closer look. It's still too difficult to see clearly but it's definitely brighter. Most of its light comes from its onboard lighting system, though some, Sedge thinks, must certainly now be reflected from Centauri. He finds Sol, our star, and notices that the Cortes is much brighter. To think, our sun is now that far away. After his eyes have a little time to adjust, he sees far more stars than when he entered the viewing deck. Interstellar space is so dark.

He takes another look at the Cortes. He can see that it's behind him, but not directly, obviously on a separate trajectory. That's good, Sedge thinks, not wanting to collide with it. It must be pointing to where Luna Nuevo will be in a matter of weeks. It will be Luna's first probe. The Conquistador Probes; the *Pinta, Nina,* and *Santa Maria* are already in orbit around the three Centauri stars, but incapable of reaching Luna Nuevo or its host planet Aureola. Their readings, however, are what has sparked Sedge's insatiable desire to reach this system. They have done their job. He stares for several minutes, feeling less alone with the Cortes in view. After five years, he'd almost forgotten it was out there.

Another reason it's good to see it pass him is that it's vital to his survival. He knows of its mission to place a bio-dome on Luna Nuevo's highland planes, somewhere near the canyon system. If only he knew where. Communication with the Cortes will be impossible until both vessels slow to a velocity beneath the transmission line. Only then can they exchange data, and then will he be able to transmit his journals, discover the Cortes' mission plans, and receive any earthly news updates the probes have received prior to both vessels' arrivals.

Transmissions travel slightly faster than both of these ships, so there should be a few months-worth of news waiting for Sedge upon arrival. If he can slow this ship down, he'll be able to learn what the world thought of his theft. The very thought of it sends a fearful chill down his spine. Is the world angry at him? He soon dismisses his concerns, however. Why care? This ship is his world now, and one day Luna Nuevo will be. Earth is a fading spec.

Back in the front ring, Sedge makes another stop at sickbay. He opens the last bottle of pethidine and counts the tablets. Only nine remain. He thinks again of his conversation with Neil Armstrong and his basic needs. When these pills are gone, he'll be left with nothing but ibuprofen to relieve any severe physical pain he might encounter, and for the rest of his life for all he knows. Again, he has compulsively errored in judgement and spotting the Cortes has also only reminded him that he's quickly approaching his time of action. Huge decisions soon have to be made - ones which may easily mean life or death. Is this really a time to be drugged up, walking around in circles? He puts the cap back on the bottle and heads back to the Holo for dinner.

2:4

Sedge wakes in a cold, opioid withdrawal-induced sweat. Prior to this point, his endless night had gone so well. After an extensive discussion on the topic of addiction with both Freud and Jung, which William Shakespeare later joined after the question of whether romantic relationships were considered addictions arose, Sedge lied down to sleep again on his favorite bench in the Holo. He was satisfied he had a handle on his addiction. He's now realizing, however, just how much his sleep had also become dependent on pethidine. The interior remains dimmed. It's still a long time until the next morning on Luna Nuevo. Without being medicated, Sedge wonders how he'll ever adapt to a sixty-three hour day. He'll either have to sleep in shifts, or maybe adapting simply isn't feasible. His biorhythms may forever be out of synch.

Luna Nuevo doesn't rotate around its axis. Like many moons, including Earth's, it's tidal-locked, meaning the same side is always facing its host planet. Night and day do occur, but due to the moon's orbital period around Aureola. The moon's close proximity to the planet means one orbit only takes one hundred, twenty-six hours and twelve minutes. The moon is moving at a high velocity. So, it does in fact rotate slowly in relation to its sun, Centauri B, but what is a one-day cycle on Luna Nuevo, is almost a five-day cycle on Earth.

Most of the collapsed region, or the moon's lowlands face Aureola, including the acclaimed Valles Grande, which sits on the edge of the exposed face. Sedge often imagines the impending view that awaits him, to have the ringed giant always in sight, day and night, on the horizon. How will it look through the canyons?

Oh how Sedge would like another tablet of pethidine, just one more to sleep. He knows, however, by raiding sickbay he'd only be delaying his withdrawal and of course depriving himself of potentially invaluable medication. Instead, he decides to check up on the Cortes. He turns on the ship's rear-view cam, but the Cortes isn't there. He quickly runs down the ringway to the elevator, summons it, and makes his way again to the ship's central cylinder. He glides weightlessly to a viewing deck on the ship's starboard side. Through large bay windows he spots it, the Cortes, flying alongside his deepliner. It's much closer now, but still hard to gage its distance. His eyes well up at its sight. Soon a tear streams down his face as he stares at it. It's the most beautiful thing he's ever seen.

For the first time since launching, Sedge feels accomplished. To see the Cortes way out here, light years from home yet just over there. That is something no human has ever experienced. He feels a connection with his home planet and the species he left so far behind. Here they are, his saviors, unified in purpose. If only he could signal the ship, communicate with it, or better yet get on a landing module and meet it, but there it goes. It's hard to believe that ship is moving so close to the speed of light, or both ships for that matter, like two photons across a dark, endless sky.

"Hey Newton," Sedge says excitedly to awaken the onboard computer system.

"Yes Sedge," Newton replies.

"Do you see the vessel passing us on the lower starboard side?" he asks.

"I do," the system replies.

"Can you take a spectroscopic analysis of it?" Sedge requests. There is a pause.

"It's giving a distinct chemical fingerprint," Newton answers; "clearly off-white silicone-oxide polymer signatures. It's a high heat and UV resistant paint commonly used by NASA."

Sedge watches for several minutes until the Cortes is well beyond the deepliner, still visible but just a fading dot into a diamond sky. The Cortes glides beyond the view of Sedge's starboard-side vantage point. Hoping to get another look at it and its direction, he moves weightlessly into the central tube, forward, toward the bridge. After a few minutes, he arrives there, the best place on board to get a view of what lies ahead.

He hasn't been here in years. In the G-rings, Sedge can simply be a passenger rather than the ship's commander, helping him forget the caliber of the choice he has made. There's a side of Sedge that's been growing since his departure, a side that doesn't want to reach Centauri. Staying in the G-rings has helped him foster that side, as well as hide from the reality of his decision, his plan; his mission. It's tempting to keep going and would certainly give him at least several more years aboard if he were to fly by Centauri. The ship is equipped with food for a thousand people to survive a year. Its nuclear engines provide all the warmth and light he needs. Nevertheless, the oxygen and recycled water would run out within a decade. Getting to the bio-dome on Luna Nuevo is his only hope of extending his life beyond that, as risky as it is. On the other hand, if he can't slow this thing down, he could die burning up in Luna's atmosphere.

Sedge thinks of Barry, the homeless guy who lives on his street in New York. He used to always wonder how long Barry would live. Is he alive today? Barry, he always thought, was not only a victim of circumstance, but also a product of the choices he made in life. Now Barry might outlive him.

Sedge spots the Cortes again out the front torus bay window. It's now well ahead of the ship, dimming by the minute.

"Farewell Cortes," he says aloud, laughing as he speaks. "We'll meet again."

He can see all three stars clearly, Centauri A, B, and the little red ball, Proxima Centauri further out, appearing like a really bright Mars. They've grown in size since he last saw them in the front-cam. The distance between them has also seemingly grown. They're much brighter than before, causing Sedge to squint to see them. It's now very evident to the naked eye that Centauri A&B are spherical in shape, no longer appearing as distant, twinkling stars. Sedge asks Newton to align the bridge's telescope with Aureola's location. He takes a look through the tube. There it is. For the first time, he's able to make out a pinhole light, much closer to Centauri B than A, clearly different than the faint, endless stars that comprise its backdrop. He can't see Aureola's ring system, nor can he see Luna Nuevo tucked within it, but it won't be long.

"I'll be damned," he says to himself. "That's where we're headed."

A chill runs down his spine, knowing the earth is so far behind him now that it can't even be seen with the ship's finest instruments. His potential new home, however, or at least its hosting planet can. He starts to tremble and his palms begin to sweat from fear and excitement, now realizing the mental weight of his discovery. To think, this vessel is on a course to, and has been for years, rendezvous with a really little pinhole going around that dot in the telescope. His only calming consolation comes from reminding himself that he just needs to get this ship into a stable orbit around it, after which he can relax and enjoy the view from above.

2:5

"One minute remaining," a woman's voice can be heard over the sound system as Sedge runs down the main ringway. He picks up his pace at the sound of her warning, jumping over a short flight of stairs, almost wiping out before rounding a large pillar. He continues to run with everything he's got as the voice continues her countdown.

"Thirty seconds," she says, causing Sedge to run even faster, now gasping for air as he leaps a sofa in the ringway's central waiting area, drenched in sweat, on his final stretch. "Ten, nine, eight, seven," she continues to announce.

"Time," Sedge yells as he crosses into the ship's gym. Gasping for air, he bends over, propping his upper body up with his hands on his knees, on the verge of collapsing.

"Congratulations Sedge," the voice says. "You've set a new course record."

Sedge grabs his towel and water bottle and guzzles from it, still well out of breath. He sits in front of a monitor while he catches it, proud of his new time record, a true sign that he's been getting stronger by the day. After he has his breath, he turns on the monitor and begins recording a new journal entry.

"It's been over seven weeks now since the Cortes passed me," he begins. "This ship entered Centauri's heliosphere last night, initializing phase one of deceleration. This technically means I've made it to Centauri, though still weeks away from entering orbit around Luna Nuevo. So far, every indication is that I'm on course. The main retro-thrusters fired on schedule and all lights are green on the timing indicator panel. The ship is now entering Centauri's frost zone, the circumstellar disc, or belt found in the star system's outer reaches. Assuming all continues to go well, I should soon be traveling slowly enough to transmit all data, including this entry to the Centauri B orbiter's relay station. From there, it can begin its four year, four-month journey back to Earth. Let it be known, I've entered the Centauri system," he finishes before turning off the monitor with a proud smile.

Sedge is now completely shaven, everywhere. He's strong and growing stronger as his confidence returns. The Cortes is most likely already in orbit around Luna Nuevo and the lander has probably touched down, meaning the bio-dome may already be operational, generating energy and converting hydrogen and oxygen to water. There's no way of knowing this, of course, until communication links can be established, but there's also no reason to think otherwise. Each flawless hour builds on Sedge's pride, now focused on his objectives like a hawk. His well-being seems to be back in balance. He's a new man.

He takes a shower, gets dressed, and heads to the Holo for lunch.

"What's new my friend? What's the word?" he asks Neil, his best friend, as he sits at his favorite table.

"Oh, not much I guess," Neil says with a laugh. "Word is that you set a new record on your obstacle course today."

"Word travels fast on this ship," Sedge answers.

"At light speed," Neil replies.

"Well, you heard right," Sedge tells him. "I suppose you've also heard we've entered Centauri's heliosphere?"

"I did hear that, yes," Neil answers. "Congratulations."

"Congratulations to you too Neil," you've been with me the whole way.

"Thank you," Neil kindly responds. "That's very nice of you to say."

"When night falls again on the canyon walls of Luna, we're going to celebrate," Sedge tells Neil. "We're going to have one huge party right here in the Holo."

"That sounds fun," Neil says with a smile. "I'm looking forward to it."

2:6

Sedge slowly depresses his wah pedal, making his guitar cry as he hits the highest note in his perfectly orchestrated rock solo. His holo-band is really laying the sound down tonight. The Holo is in club mode and packed with people, at least it appears, dancing, talking, and having a great time. The night is divine. The sound is tight. Sedge's guitar skills have vastly improved on this journey, for whatever that's worth. Their best tune, *Blown Away*, comes to a crashing halt with a perfectly synchronized stinger. The crowd cheers.

"Thank you all for coming," Sedge tells the house, now well into his role; "for coming to the first party ever thrown in the Centauri System!" The onlookers cheer even louder. "That is, to the best of our knowledge," he adds. "Anyway, we're going to take an extended break to join the party, but we may be back later in the night to do a few more songs for you. In the meantime, I'd like to introduce my friend Ludwig, who is going to perform a few piano numbers with his quartet. Ludwig," Sedge announces.

Donning a tuxedo, Beethoven makes his way onto the small stage, along with a contrabass player, a violinist, and a violist. The crowd cheers.

"This first number I call *Adieu au Piano*," he says into a microphone to a now quieted group. He sits upright at the piano with proper posture, interlocks his fingers to stretch them out, and softly begins playing a mood-shifting, beautiful piano piece. Within seconds, the bass blends in, then the strings. Sedge, recognizing the song to be in ¾ time, assumes a waltz position with his arms extended to an invisible partner and begins to dance. Soon, a laser-generated Ginger Rogers fills the invisible void, pleasantly surprising Sedge, who had no idea the holo-system, in dynamic-room mode, could improvise. They softly glide across the floor.

"I never knew you could waltz," Ginger tells Sedge.

"I took a ballroom dance class in college," Sedge answers. "Forgive me for not being a worthy partner."

"Oh," Ginger replies with a classic smile, "you're as worthy as anyone here."

"That's because I didn't invite Fred Astaire," Sedge replies with a smirk.

They dance until the song comes to a close, then finish with a bow & curtsey common two centuries ago. Sedge excuses himself to take a walk, really feeling like he's part of an enchanted party. If not the people, at least the occasion is real, very real.

Sedge walks out of the Holo and into the ship's ringway. The lights have all dimmed, indicating nightfall on Luna's lowlands. He takes a look at the ship's speed indicator on the wall, now showing point seventy-one times the speed of light. The ship is slowing. He walks over to a viewing window to watch the stars go round and round. Briefly, he thinks he sees something in the darkness - a momentary streak of light that looks like a laser beam, causing him to question if it was real or his eyes playing tricks on him. He stares out at the dark, endless sky. Within a minute, his eyes adapt to the low light. He can see the Cygnus-Orion arm of the Milky Way stretch all the way across the sky. To think, he's come so far and yet nowhere. He's traveled over four light years in a galaxy that takes a hundred and fifty thousand light years to cross, and this is only one galaxy. As he turns to go back to the party, he again swears he sees another quick laser beam, almost looking like a shooting star outside the window. He looks more closely but sees nothing. He rubs his eyes, shakes his head, and walks back to the Holo Club.

Sedge gets back to the party and takes a seat at a small table with Neil.

"Welcome back," Neil says.

"Thanks," Sedge responds. "Are you having a good time?' he asks the hologram.

"I am," Neil answers. "How about you?"

"I am too," Sedge replies. "I could use a glass of wine though. Do you drink?" Sedge asks.

"Oh, I was known to have a few back in my day," Neil answers. "In fact, the *Moonwalk Cocktail* was named for the first drink Buzz & I ordered after Apollo 11. You know, booze wasn't allowed in space back in our day," he adds with a wink and sly smile.

"That's what I want to do once we get this thing in orbit - I want to learn how to ferment. The sultan didn't pack any alcohol on board, but there's a decent supply of baker's yeast and grains. I'm going to be...' Before Sedge can finish his thought, Neil disappears along with all other holograms in the room. The house lights come on with a loud, steadily buzzing alarm.

"Warning, unknown objects encountered," the ship's onboard system announces. "Rear G-ring breached and losing atmosphere. Evacuate G-ring immediately. Damage to outboard engine three detected. Course correction required." Sedge stares like a deer in headlights as he can see the interior lights on the back G-ring dim and rotation stop. The alarm continues. "Warning, unknown objects encountered. Rear G-ring breached. Atmosphere at eighty-four percent and falling. Evacuate rear ring immediately."

"Newton, seal off the rear ring," Sedge yells.

"Rear ring sealing off," Newton replies, closing all air locks between the rear ring and the main fuselage.

"Warning, unknown objects encountered. Rear G-ring breached and losing atmosphere. Rear ring atmosphere at seventy-three percent. Damage to outboard engine three detected. Course correction required. Warning, unknown objects encountered. Rear

G-ring losing atmosphere. Rear ring atmosphere at sixty-six percent. Damage to outboard engine three detected. Course correction required. Warning, unknown objects encountered. Rear ring losing atmosphere..."

"Newton, turn off alarm and warning," Sedge yells. Silence ensues. He's left standing motionless, staring at nothing with a distant look in his eyes. He maintains his blank pose for several minutes, then begins to walk down the ringway toward sickbay. Upon arrival, he raids the medicine cabinet for the last bottle of pethidine, takes a tablet out and swallows it dry.

He walks back down the ringway to the viewing window just outside the Holo. Sedge sits on the floor, curled with his arms wrapped around his knees, just staring blankly into the darkness, watching the stars go round and round.

Part 3

Pictures of Phil Thacker's family keep flashing in a frame in front of Kendal as she patiently waits for him to get off a call. She looks out his corner window at the bright sun climbing into the morning sky. With the help of a little greenhouse effect, it warms the room. She continues facing the window, letting the warm light hit her face. Arriving at the tail end of a long cold winter, it not only feels good but also lifts her spirits.

"Sorry for that," Phil says after finishing his call.

"No worries," Kendal replies, snapping out of her sun-induced trance.

"I talked to Tim this weekend," Phil tells her, referring to the firm's other senior partner, Timothy Walcott. "Tim would like us to drop the Joy Rider case," he continues, cutting right to the chase.

"Oh," Kendal says.

"We never really agreed to take the case, only to look into it on a pro bono basis. We're two and a half months in and the story has all but faded in the news. Our client, if alive, doesn't seem to have much of a case, or an estate to even cover legal costs. We just can't afford to waste our time and resources on it."

"I can fully understand where Tim is coming from," Kendal replies. "I've got plenty of other matters I need to tend to as well. I would, however, encourage Tim to hold off on pulling the plug on this one for at least a few weeks."

"Why so?" Phil asks.

"For a few reasons," Kendall answers. "First, the legalities. Next week, this case moves into its discovery phase. GulfStar's lawyers will have to disclose whatever they've got, which I'm guessing isn't much. I had planned to propose a meeting with them soon after disclosures to offer a plea, asking them to drop all charges."

"Everything?" Phil asks. "On what grounds?"

"If I can show them they don't have a case for reckless endangerment, all they have left is theft," Kendal responds.

"Billions of dollars in theft," Phil replies.

"True," Kendal tells him; "but as you just pointed out, our client has next to nothing. Sure, they can drain whatever's in his paltry account, but keep in mind that public support is behind Sedge. GulfStar, despite being the only victims, has looked like the bad guys for coming after him. They have so little to gain and a lot to lose. Were they to even lose one contract over this matter, it would likely cost them far more than any gains."

"What about the half-million dollar grant?" Phil asks. "They've threatened further action if we don't reply."

"We shouldn't reply," Kendal answers. "I've looked into the injunction and it isn't worth its filing fee. They're really reaching on that one. The grant was applied for by, and awarded to NASA to do with as they see fit. NASA didn't steal GulfStar's ship. Their only option for further action is to lie on their backs, kick, and scream."

"Bold moves," Phil says.

"We have nothing to lose by going for full dismissal," Kendal responds.

"I like it," Phil answers.

"I'm not finished," Kendal adds. "Do you remember Holden Grant?" she asks.

"Sedge's partner?" Phil asks.

"Yes," she answers. "Anyway, I'm having lunch with him today. He wants to tell me about a crowdfunding campaign he set up on *fund-it* to help cover Sedge's legal costs. I don't know how successful it has been, but the way matters now stand legally, that money would likely cover this firm's legal costs. We don't even have to disclose it in discovery. It is a non-legal, clerical matter related to payment for our services. GulfStar doesn't have any legal claim to it."

"Very interesting," Phil tells her. "We've never been funded by charity."

"Yes," Kendal replies. "Holden is the legal fiduciary and may need our help ensuring he handles the funds in a non-fraudulent manner, but thus far, we are the only legal costs associated with this case."

"Good to hear," Phil says. "Well with that, let's continue forward with this case for now. I'll talk with Tim and let him know what you told me. Please keep me posted on any developments."

"Absolutely," Kendal replies. "I also think there will be a follow up in The Times on this at some point. Tina Moran mentioned wanting to keep the story alive and wanted me to contact her with any developments I could legally disclose. She may prove helpful."

"Thanks Kendal," Phil says; "nice work."

Kendal returns to her office eager to get back to work on the case. She spends an hour reading over the casefile and all of her notes, making sure she isn't missing anything. Realizing she has yet to get an affidavit from Stan Satterfield at Ground Control, she gives him a call.

"This is Stan Satterfield. How can I help you?" he answers.

"Stan, it's Kendal Benz with Thacker and Walcott. How are you today?" she asks.

"Good Kendal," Stan answers. "I've been meaning to get back to you. Does the affidavit need to be notarized?" he asks.

"No, but it would bolster its credibility," she answers. "If it's convenient for you to do so, we'd be happy to cover the cost."

"Sure, it's not a big deal," he replies. "We've got a notary in the building. I'm sorry if I seem to be dragging my feet on this. I've been a little busy."

"No problem," Kendal responds. "We are, however, moving forward with this case and it would help me if you could get the document to us this week."

"Absolutely," Stan says. "I'll do it today in fact. One other reason I've been a little hesitant is that I've still been trying to figure out what actually happened. I thought it might help your case if we could go a little further than simply explaining what the glitches weren't, and tell them what they were."

"Have you found anything?" Kendal asks.

"Nothing very rational," Stan answers. "I wondered if they may be extra-terrestrial, so I checked with SETI to see if there were any Sagittarius signals[1] received on the dates we discussed, or anything out of the ordinary, but they had nothing."

"That's interesting," Kendal replies. "Had they been alien, I don't know if that would help us or not in a legal case. They might think we're nuts."

"Maybe," Stan answers; "but if SETI had picked up the signals with their big ears, it would further indicate Sedge had nothing to do with their transmissions."

"That would be good," Kendal adds.

"I did, however, stumble on something equally mysterious when I did some research," Stan says.

"What?" Kendal asks.

"Well, I looked for other historical examples of signals transmitted without timestamps, and I came up on something interesting."

"What did you find?" Kendal asks with growing interest.

"There was a guy experimenting with time transmission sixty years ago, who claimed in his doctoral

---

[1] **Sagittarius Signals**: a series of narrow band radio transmissions received by SETI (Search for Extraterrestrial Intelligence) during the late 21st century, suspected of being alien in origin, possibly connected to the WOW Signal received from the same star group in 1977.

thesis to have sent a few messages without timestamps," Stan answers.

"What do you mean by time transmissions?" Kendal asks.

"There are some people in this industry who think it's theoretically possible to transmit messages through time," Stan replies. "Anyway, this guy thought he may have done it."

"Is the guy alive today?" Kendal asks.

"I don't know," Stan answers. "I just came across a summary of his thesis. It's all I could find. I'll beam it to you."

"I'd love to take a look at it," Kendal responds. "I've got an appointment I'd better get to, but thanks for all you've done and I look forward to getting the affidavit."

"It's my pleasure Ms. Benz," Stan politely responds. "It's an honor to be connected to this case. I hope the best for you and Sedge of course."

"Thanks Stan," Kendal replies. "I'll be sure to mention you in my reports."

3:2

Kendal leaves her office at a quarter to noon, giving herself enough time to walk to the *Siam* on 38th, where she has arranged a lunch meeting with Holden Grant. She recommended the place after they both discussed their love of Thai food over their previous Korean lunch and it's equal-distant to both of their places of work. As soon as she steps out of her building's door, she wishes she had brought a warmer jacket. The morning sun had fooled her into believing the day would be warmer than it is. Spring, after all, is only three hours away. A cold wind whips down the avenue. She zips her jacket to her chin and walks briskly to stay warm.

She arrives with two minutes to spare and is escorted to their reserved table. She sits and begins looking over the menu. Holden arrives a few minutes later, happy to see her. They've only messaged each other since their first lunch. Kendal is excited not only to see Holden, but also to fill him in on how well Sedge's case seems to be going. Holden takes off his jacket and takes a seat across from her.

"This place looks great," he tells her.

"Yeah, I love it," Kendal replies. "I come here fairly often. It's worth the walk."

"NASA has been in touch with me," Holden tells her.

"Really, why?" Kendal asks.

"They're expediting their next mission to Luna Nuevo, excited by the possibility of Sedge being there," Holden tells her.

"So why tell you?" Kendal goes on to ask.

"They wanted me to tell them a little more about Sedge's interests so they could prepare a supply package with things he may really appreciate," Holden answers. "They asked if I had any personal items they could send him that he might be really happy to get. I took a few things to them."

"What did you give them?" Kendal asks.

"Just what few things I had of his that he'd kill me for throwing out; his guitar, a small lockbox he kept, and his sextant," Holden answers. "I'm glad they took them. I'm tired of keeping them around and I really didn't know what to do with them."

"I hope he gets them," Kendal says. "By the way, things are beginning to look good for him here on Earth," she adds; "at least legally speaking."

"Really," Holden responds. "Good to hear. What can you tell me?" he asks.

"I don't think the reckless endangerment charge will stick,' Kendal answers. "It's looking flimsier by the day."

"So he really wasn't responsible for that glitch," Holden surmises.

"No, it seems he wasn't," Kendal responds. "If we can get that dropped, our plan is to ask GulfStar to dismiss all charges," she adds.

"Even the theft?" Holden asks.

"Even the theft," Kendal answers.

"How could you convince them to do that?" Holden asks. "It's pretty clear Sedge stole their ship."

"True," Kendal replies; "and I have no idea if they'll go for it, but I would advise them to if I were their attorney."

"Why?" Holden asks excitedly.

"Because they have more to gain by dismissing them," Kendal answers. "GulfStar is a large corporation with very little to gain by going after Sedge. They aren't getting their ship back anytime soon, and I doubt Sedge has enough in his bank accounts to risk the potential public backlash. By dismissing the charges, they go from being the bad guys, to being his sponsor."

"I love it," Holden exclaims.

"Well, let's not spike the ball yet," Kendal says. "Remember, we're dealing with lawyers who don't like to give in. They may choose to press forward with their charges."

"Are you guys ready to order?" a waiter asks.

"Oh, sorry," Kendal answers. "We got a little carried away in conversation."

"I'll give you a little more time," he tells them before moving to the next table.

"What do you recommend?" Holden asks.

"Everything here is awesome," Kendal tells him. "I can't seem to stay away from the noodle dishes."

"Sounds great," Holden says. "I'm starving."

"You mentioned opening a crowdfunding account for Sedge," Kendal says. "How is that going?"

"Very well, I think," Holden answers. "It's raised over three-hundred thousand dollars. How far will that go with his legal fees?" he asks.

"That's amazing," Kendal responds. "I don't know how much things will cost, unfortunately. Our firm is still working pro bono, but I don't think my bosses, the senior partners, will be willing to continue into discovery without charging. Honestly, our firm isn't cheap, but it will really depend on how willing GulfStar is to dismiss the charges. If so, your fund may more than cover it. It's really not up to me."

"I've worded the fund to include more than legal fees," Holden tells her; "so long as the money goes to help Sedge, it is not restricted to legal services."

"Good thinking," Kendal says. "So if the fund raises more than enough to pay our firm, it will go to help Sedge. That's brilliant."

"Thank you," Holden tells her. "I may need your help to make sure it's all legal."

"I'd be more than happy to help," Kendal replies. "Let me talk it over with my boss and see what he thinks. Just make sure not to spend any of that money on yourself or you could be in serious trouble."

"I won't," Holden says. "I know better."

They take a few silent minutes to make their choices, then give the waiter a nod to let him know they're ready to order.

"What are we having today?" he asks.

"I'll have the *phad see ew* with chicken," Kendal tells him. "Can I also get a side order of peanut sauce?" she asks. "I love that stuff."

"Sure," the waiter answers. "And for you sir?"

"I'll just get an order of *phad thai*," Holden tells him; "but I want to order a side of the cream cheese rolls? Do they come with a dipping sauce?" he asks.

"Yes, a plum sauce," the waiter answers. "Would either of you care for anything to drink?" he asks.

"Just water," Kendal and Holden both answer.

The waiter scurries away, leaving Kendal and Holden free to chat now that legal matters have been covered.

"So can I ask you a personal question?" Kendal asks.

"Sure, shoot," Holden replies.

"Why do you do all this for Sedge?' she asks. "Aren't you over him? It's been five years."

"I have been over the break-up for a while," he answers. "At least I think I have. I've never admired anyone more deeply, however. I still feel a strong connection to Sedge, emotionally though, a connection I don't want to sever."

"Have you been seeing anyone?' Kendal asks.

"I've dated," Holden says, "but nothing serious. I guess I'm enjoying my freedom, at least for the time being. I seem to get more done when I'm not in a relationship."

"I can understand that," Kendal says.

"How about you?" Holden asks her. "Are you seeing anyone?"

"No," Kendal answers. "I've been single since New Year's Eve."

"Dare I ask why New Year's Eve?" Holden asks. "Was it a resolution to break up?"

"No," Kendal answers with a laugh; "but you might say it became one in the New Year."

"Are you over him, her, or whomever?" Holden asks.

"Yes, I'm over him," she answers. "We haven't spoken since."

"Well good for you then, I guess," Holden tells her. "Sometimes it's time to move on."

"Do you want to go out with my girlfriend and me sometime?" Kendal asks. "We like to listen to live music sometimes and you're welcome to join us."

"That sounds fun," Holden says. "I'd love to. Where do you guys usually go?"

"Different places, but we typically stay in the Midtown area," Kendal answers. "Where do you live?" she asks.

"On Minetta Lane, just off MacDougal Street in the Village," Holden answers.

"Cool," Kendal says. "There's a lot going on around there. A lot of good looking guys."

"Yeah," Holden replies; "and some of them are straight too."

They laugh as the food arrives, happy at the prospect of their new friendship. They talk beyond the lunch hour, enjoying their meal, the conversation, and a few more laughs as they lose track of the hour. Finally, upon noticing the restaurant has largely cleared out, they split the bill and head happily back to their offices to take on Monday afternoon.

3:3

A small, blinking blue light in Kendal's office tells her she has voice messages. She plays them.

- "Good morning Ms. Benz," a woman's voice says. "My name is Trista Rybach and I'm the communications coordinator with NASA here in our New York satellite office. I understand that you are representing Sedge Nile and would appreciate it if you could return my call. I've included my direct contact line with this message. Thank you." A pong is heard.

- "Hi Kendal, it's me," Naya says. "I'm going to be in your area tonight and thought I'd see what you're up to. Do you wanna hang out and watch a movie?" There is another pong.
- "Hello Kendal, Stan Satterfield. Just letting you know I've beamed you the affidavit," Stan says. "You'll be pleased to know I had it notarized. Oh, and I sent a link to the time-transmission experiments that I mentioned earlier. Doubt they'll be of any use, but they are interesting."

Kendal calls Trista Rybach's line.

"This is Trista Rybach."

"Hi Trista, this is Kendal Benz returning your call."

"Yes Kendal, thanks for your prompt reply," Trista says. "How fascinating that you have the Sedge Nile case."

"I couldn't agree more," Kendal responds. "So you are with NASA?"

"Yes," Trista answers. "I called to let you know that we'd be pleased to transmit any messages you may have for Sedge if you'd like to update him on his case. We can do so confidentially as well, using a secured line. We wouldn't want to violate lawyer-client privilege."

"That's wonderful news," Kendal tells her. "I'd love to, in fact, as soon as possible. There's a lot happening with his case."

"Absolutely, let's schedule an appointment to record a message," Trista replies. "To assure confidentiality, we need you to come to our office though."

"That's no problem. Where is your office?" Kendal asks.

"We're in the Goddard Institute, all the way up here on the corner of Broadway and 112th West," Trista answers.

"I know right where you are," Kendal answers. "I'm a Columbia alum."

"Perfect," Trista replies. "We're on the ground floor, room one twenty-three. When are you free?" She asks.

"How's Friday morning?" Kendal asks in return.

"Friday works well," Trista tells her. "What time? We open at nine."

"How about nine-thirty?" Kendal suggests. "I'm kind of an early bird."

"Nine-thirty would be fine," Trista answers. "We'll see you on Friday."

"I'm looking forward to meeting you," Kendal responds.

Kendal pulls up her screen to see Stan's message. She opens the attached affidavit and reads it carefully. It's a powerful statement and should prove to be enough to get GulfStar to drop the endangerment charge. She, however, still doesn't know what GulfStar's attorneys are going to throw at her and feels it would only strengthen her case if she could better understand and explain the transmissions. Curious, she opens the other attachment Stan sent to her; the sixty-year-old study on time transmissions. It reads as follows:

Thesis: To When Did the Transmission Go?
By Cedric Davis
Submitted: November 23, 2069
Simon Fraser University / Department of Laser Communications

Thesis Summary

The principal objective of this thesis is to argue that through enhanced laser modification, radio signals are capable of breaking the light barrier and subsequently being transmitted through time. I aim to exhibit that such transmissions are not only theoretically feasible, but have been accomplished. It remains the most logical explanation for events outlined herein.

In the afternoon of July 10 of this year, 2069, I encountered my first successful transmission. Unfortunately, the success came inadvertently, thus limiting my documentation. On that date, I had been exhaustively conducting time-transmission trials. While taking a break, I had neglected to turn off both my transmitter and receiver. To my surprise, I heard a short series of events occur over my receiver - events which played out in real time moments later, as if my receiver had picked up audio from an event that had yet to occur in time. Though able to document the reception of this message, I was not able to accurately record its transmission's metadata, namely its time stamp. Hearing events occur over my receiver, then moments later with my own ears in real time, coupled with the transmission's lack of a time stamp, led me to conclude that the transmission had indeed traveled through time. The lapsed duration between events heard over the receiver and those which occurred in real time was roughly twenty seconds, but impossible for me to pinpoint without a timestamp.

Bewildered by the sudden success, I ran a cross reference of the successful trial with all others conducted. The primary difference between the successful transmission and all failed ones was that the successful transmission occurred during a downpour. I concluded that success was not due to the rain itself, but to the fact that rain, cloud mist, or water vapor had caused eclipses of laser-lines within the communication grid. This is not uncommon during storms. When such eclipses occur, laser lines mitigate broken connections via laser overriding, typically with the aid of satellites. Laser overriding, otherwise known as satellite overriding, though undetectable to the naked ear, adds significant length to signals; the length I needed to transmit through time.

Realizing the limits of my results, I asked an acquaintance of mine, Mr. Lennox Reed, whose work frequently takes him to the moon, to transmit a pre-programmed signal for me from Moondock, the moon's orbital station. Several weeks prior to this transmission and for several weeks afterward, I left my receiver on, prepared to receive any unsourced signals. Lennox transmitted the signal at 10:29 a.m. Pacific Standard Time, on August 27, 2069. The signal was directed at my receiver and should have easily been detected, yet my receiver detected nothing. To many, this would prove my trials inconclusive. This lack of reception, however, begs the question; to when did the signal go? If unable to verify, I aim to at least exhibit herein that the most logical answer to this question is through time, to another time.

Note: This thesis is kept on file at Simon Fraser University in the WAC Bennett library.

Kendal immediately looks up Simon Fraser University to find out where it is; Burnaby, British Columbia. She researches the name Cedric Davis and is mildly pleased to find a public listing for Dr. Cedric Davis in the Vancouver public registry. Why not give him a call? Who better to explain transmissions without timestamps? She puts on a headset for privacy, checks to see that it's not too early to call the west coast, and dials.

"Hello," a soft woman's voice answers.

"Hello," Kendal says turning up the volume to better hear her. "My name is Kendal Benz and I was hoping to speak with Dr. Cedric Davis if I may."

"Oh, I'm sorry, but Cedric passed away years ago," the woman says. "I'm his wife Nikki, Nikki Nova. We shared this line for years and I've never taken his name off the listing. You see, I used to be a local news reporter and I liked to remain unlisted. That was long ago though, and I doubt it matters today. Is there anything I can do for you?" she asks.

"I'm sorry to hear that," Kendal replies, getting a warm vibe from this woman. "You may be able to help me. Do I have the right Dr. Davis? Did your husband conduct experiments with lasers?"

"Oh yes," Nikki softly answers. "He was a laser-communication specialist, and a successful one at that," she proudly adds.

"It sounds like it," Kendal tells her. "I've read the summary to his doctoral thesis and if it's true, he was a real genius. He claims to have sent messages through time. Do you think he did it?" Kendal asks.

"I do," Nikki answers. "Cedric wasn't a guy who would make that up."

"I've never heard of such a thing," Kendal says. "It's amazing to me. Did he continue sending messages through time after he wrote his graduate thesis?" she asks.

"No, I'm afraid not," Nikki answers.

"Why did he stop trying?" Kendal asks.

"Because they weren't legal signals," Nikki answers; "and he wasn't able to use the same equipment after he finished his degree."

"Did anyone else continue where he left off?" Kendal asks.

"Several tried," Nikki says; "but you know, I think Cedric held out on them. He was so private with his work, and I've always questioned if he really shared everything or just enough to get the degree."

"That's so interesting," Kendal says.

"Are you a reporter?" Nikki asks.

"No, I'm a lawyer working for a New York firm," Kendal answers. "My client is Sedge Nile. Do you know who that is?" she asks.

"No, I'm sorry," Nikki answers.

"That's okay. He's the guy in the news who took the spaceship," Kendal says.

"Oh, yes, of course I know who that is," Nikki says excitedly. "So you're his lawyer."

"Yes I am," Kendal proudly responds.

"What does this have to do with Cedric?" Nikki asks in a kind tone.

"Nothing, I think," Kendal answers. "There were some radio signals received just prior to Sedge's departure that we can't explain. I was hoping to pick your husband's brain. I thought he might be able to explain them to me."

"Gee, I wish I could help you Ms. Benz," Nikki says; "but that's a little out of my area of expertise."

"Please, call me Kendal, and you've already been a great help. Feel free to keep my contact information and call me if you feel you have anything else to tell me," Kendal says, thrilled to meet Nikki.

"Okay," Nikki says after an awkward moment of silence.

"Did you ever do a story on Cedric?" Kendal asks.

"No, I wanted to but he was so private," Nikki says.

"I'm sure a lot of people would be interested in his work," Kendal adds.

"Thank you so much for your call," Nikki replies. "It's so nice to hear from you. I wish Cedric were still with us. I'm sure he'd be able to help answer your questions."

"So do I Nikki," Kendal kindly replies. "He sounds like a great guy. Please don't worry though, you've been helpful to me and it's truly been an honor and a pleasure to speak with you today."

"You too, please take care," Nikki says, sounding a little lonely.

"You as well," Kendal responds. "Bye now."

Kendal sits back in her chair smiling. What a kind woman. Though the conversation proved fruitless, she was pleased to have met Nikki just the same. She does a quick search on Nikki Nova and finds a short biography on Vancouver's DOT-5 news archive. She sees a picture of Nikki giving a newscast in the year 2070, sixty years ago. What a beautiful woman, she thinks, wondering how old she must now be.

3:4

Standing on her balcony, Kendal can see Orion's Belt along with several other stars brightly piercing her night sky. Could any of them be Centauri? She asks GIN, her voice-activated *Global Information Network*, only to learn that Centauri can't be seen in the Northern Hemisphere. The star system is out of sight to most people on this planet. She soon learns, however, that she's looking at the next closest visible star just over the horizon, Sirius, which tonight looks close enough to touch. To think, it would take twice as long to get there as it would Centauri; over eight and a half light years at the speed of light. It seems we're not really meant to travel this universe?

Her lights briefly brighten, then dim and her doorbell pongs, drawing her in from the cold evening air. It's Naya. Kendal invites her in.

"How are you?" Kendal asks.

"Good, Kay," Naya replies using a nickname from their childhood. "It's cold."

"Yeah, but nice to see the sun today," Kendal replies.

"Amen," Naya says in agreement. "The wind has died down too. Hopefully tomorrow will be a little warmer."

"What do you feel like watching tonight?" Kendal asks, digging through her kitchen cabinets for snacks.

"I'd love to see *Forbidden Island*," Naya answers; "but it's up to you. I'm flexible."

"Perfect," Kendal responds. "I've been dying to see that too. The preview looks good."

They grab popcorn from Kendal's cupboard, break up a chocolate bar and put it in a bowl, and get a few sparkling waters from the fridge before dimming the lights; a routine the two know well.

"So how is the big case coming along?" Naya asks.

"Really well, I'd say," Kendal answers. "I'm going to one of NASA's offices here in Manhattan Friday morning to record a case-update message to send to Sedge. This case is moving forward and I'm learning so many new things from it every day."

"That's awesome," Naya responds. "Like what?"

"A lot about stars, space travel, even communication," Kendal answers. "In fact, you won't believe this, but I talked to a sweet elderly woman today whose husband may have sent some messages through time."

"What do you mean?" Naya asks. "Like back in time?"

"Yes, I think," Kendal answers.

"Do you believe that?" Naya asks.

"I don't know, but she sounded so sincere," Kendal replies. "She was so kind. She used to be a news reporter back in her day. I looked up an old picture of her. She's beautiful. It really made me think about time, not only because of her husband's messages, but how we are two similar women, just stuck in different times."

"That's thought provoking," Naya says. "What does she and her husband have to do with your case, if you can tell me?"

"Nothing, I'm afraid," Kendal answers. "I was just following a dead-end lead. It was her husband I wanted to talk to, hoping to learn a little more about communication signals, but he died years ago. I felt sad for the woman. She sounded so happy to talk to me. I think she's lonely."

"Oh," Naya replies; "how sad."

"Yeah, I thought so too," Kendal replies. "On a happier note, I've invited someone to join us next time we go out for some live music."

"A guy?" Naya asks.

"Yes, a really handsome, intelligent guy," Kendal answers; "but he's not in the market to meet women. He's gay."

"Oh, just my luck," Naya replies. "Who is he?"

"His name is Holden. He's Sedge Nile's previous partner," Kendal answers. "He's been helping me with this case. You'll really like him. He's fun."

"Interesting, I'd love to meet him," Naya says. "I'm looking forward to it."

"Cool, so is he," Kendal replies, scanning channels for their movie.

After finding the movie, they turn their attention to the screen as Kendal hits the play button to start Forbidden Island.

3:5

Friday morning arrives with the serene sound of a koto being played over ocean waves. Seagulls can be heard far away. Kendal wakes again to the delight of ambient audio. Never one to spend much time in bed, she gets up and immediately makes her bed, a lifelong habit. To Kendal, an unmade bed is the beginning of a disheveled day.

After her workout and shower, she sits at her table watching morning news on a floating screen.

"The DOW dropped half a percent yesterday driven by weak earnings in the tech sector, while the NASDAQ managed to close the day a tenth of a percentage point ahead of its opening.

"NASA has announced the new launch date of its next mission to Luna Nuevo. The launch of *Pizarro*, originally planned for this summer, has been moved up to Saturday, May 27th due to the deep-probe spotting of Sedge Nile's stolen spacecraft. NASA made the announcement this morning, stating that until proven otherwise, the agency will work on the assumption that Mr. Nile is alive, and thus do everything within its power to assist him. In the event that he is not alive, provisions supplied will not go to waste. They can be stored on Luna Nuevo for future missions.

"Members of the UN General Assembly will meet here in New York today to..."

Kendal turns off the news, still thrilled to be so connected to one of the day's biggest headlines. The story had waned over recent weeks, but NASA's latest mission has given it new life. Speaking of which, she's got to get to her appointment.

Running later than usual, and given how far NASA's upper-Manhattan office is from her condo, Kendal decides to take a public pod. She steps out of her building and walks down 42nd toward 10th, which turns into Amsterdam Ave on the Upper West Side, taking her right where she needs to be. The sun is out and the morning noticeably warmer. Spring is now starting to really show up. She can feel the sun on her face. And it's Friday. She smiles uncontrollably.

She catches a pod on 10th, gets a seat by the window, and watches the city roll by. Others are obviously spirited as well. She can feel the energy. Her route takes her by some of the Upper West Side's more famous spots; Mt. Sinai Hospital, the Metropolitan Opera House, the Lincoln Center, and finally to her stop in front of the 111th Street People's Garden. From there, she finishes the last block and a half of her journey on foot, arriving at the Goddard Institute at ten past nine. Being back in familiar territory, she takes a reminiscent look around before going inside the building, enjoying a few college-day memories.

Kendal is pleasantly distracted upon entering the building, which has been newly renovated on the inside while maintaining its classic architectural façade on the out, compliant with New York's zoning laws for heritage buildings. Inside, she checks in with a guard at the reception desk, who gives Trista Rybach a call to let her know Kendal has arrived. He tells Kendal that Ms. Rybach is expecting her and directs her to room one twenty-three, just down the hall. Kendal has no problem finding it.

"Ms. Benz, I presume," Trista says as Kendal enters the room.

"Yes, but feel free to call me Kendal if you like," Kendal responds.

"It's nice to meet you," Trista says in return; "and you can call me Trista. Welcome to NASA's main New York office. Please come with me."

The two walk out of the room, down the hall, and into a smaller sound-proof room with recording equipment. Seemingly busy, Trista wastes no time with small talk. She shows Kendal how to start, stop, and erase a recording should she wish to start over. Then she leaves Kendal alone in the room, telling her she can take as long as she likes. Kendal takes a few moments to collect her thoughts, looks into the camera and hits record.

"Hello Sedge, this is your attorney Kendal Benz. I'm with the law offices of Thacker and Walcott. I truly hope that you receive this message. It's hard to believe how long it will take and far it will travel before reaching you. At any rate, it's both exciting and an honor to be representing you.

"First off, let me tell you that I've been working with someone you know; Holden Grant, who has been an enormous help both to me and to you. He has started a crowdfund that may very well cover your legal costs, and possibly more. We're doing what we can to ensure you receive the most from this fund. Furthermore, NASA has been awarded a half-a-million dollar grant to assist you with your survival. As you may already know, people on this planet are pulling for you, including me.

"Not everyone, however, has been on board. GulfStar has filed charges against you for reckless endangerment and grand theft. I guess they weren't thrilled that you helped yourself to one of their spacecraft. To let you know, they have also filed an injunction against the payout of NASA's federal grant. As your attorney, I'd advise you not to worry about the injunction. It's frivolous at best and I expect it to be tossed as soon as it goes in front of any judge. I am also confident that GulfStar's reckless endangerment charge will not stick. I've got a sworn, notarized affidavit from a guy named Stan Satterfield, who works for Allied Forces Ground Control. As it turns out, the glitch that GulfStar used as the basis for their endangerment charge happened twice more within a few weeks after your departure, from the same source according to Stan. We do not know what the glitches were, but we know what they weren't; sabotage on your part.

"This case is moving to discovery on Monday, a phase where we will see what GulfStar has and they will see what we have. I'm hoping to schedule a meeting with them as soon as possible, where I plan to suggest that they drop all charges against you, including the theft. I realize I have no legal grounds, but given that the world is publicly cheering for you, and that whatever remains in your accounts here on Earth is most likely a far cry from enough to replace their ship, I'm guessing it is within their best public interests to sponsor your mission rather than hamper it. I do not, however, know how this will go over when presented to them. We'll see and I will update you as soon as I know any more.

"I hope this is good news. We're doing all we can. Please take care of yourself as best you can and remember you have an entire planet behind you."

Pleased with her recording, Kendal hits the stop icon. She grabs her things and makes her way back to room one twenty-three, where Trista is waiting.

"That was quick," Trista says.

"Yeah, I got right to the point," Kendal answers. "I heard on the news today that NASA's going to be launching another mission to Luna Nuevo in May."

"Yes, we're excited," Trista says. "Your recording will arrive much sooner though. I'll have it transmitted today. It travels at the speed of light. Still, it'll take over four years."

"I realize that," Kendal replies. "I've been learning a lot about transmissions since I started this case."

"I'll bet," Trista says. "I really hope Sedge gets your message."

"So do I," Kendal responds; "so do I."

3:6

Back in her office by eleven, Kendal wonders if she can tie up her week's loose ends and slip out of work early. Why not? Both Thacker and Walcott have left for the weekend and the spring weather is reminding her that there's more to life than work. She checks her messages.

- "Hi Kendal, Stan Satterfield, just making sure you got the affidavit and that it's what you need."
- "Hi Kay, it's me," Naya says. "Just seeing what you are up to tonight. I'm in the mood for the Riparian. Give me a call."

Kendal calls Stan back first to get her work out of the way.

"Stan Satterfield," Stan answers.

"Hi Stan, Kendal Benz here."

"Yes Kendal," Stan replies. "I trust that you got the document."

"I did," Kendal answers; "and it looks great. I appreciate all you've done."

"It's the least I could do," Stan says. "I really hope it helps Sedge."

"I strongly believe it will," Kendal replies. "We'll know more next week and I'll keep you informed. I met with NASA officials this morning and transmitted a message to Sedge, which I hope he gets. I told him we don't know what the glitch was, just what it wasn't."

"Very good," Stan responds. "I hope he gets it."

"You know, I tried to call Dr. Davis, the guy who wrote the thesis summary you sent me. That was truly fascinating."

"Wasn't it?" Stan asks. "So were you able to get in touch?"

"I spoke with his wife Nikki, a sweet, elderly woman," Kendal answers. "Unfortunately, Dr. Davis is no longer alive. According to Nikki, he passed away years ago. I don't know when."

"Yes," Stan responds. "Those experiments were sixty years ago. I'm surprised you were even able to find his wife. Was she any help?"

"No," Kendal answers; "but an interesting woman just the same. She used to be a news reporter back in her day."

"Wow, good for her," Stan says. "Does she believe her husband's bold claims?"

"She does," Kendal answers.

"I'm glad she does," Stan replies; "because I don't."

"No?" Kendal asks.

"Not really, no," Stan answers. "He just didn't seem to have enough to go on, but hey, I haven't read his thesis, just the summary. What do I know?"

"Well you take the fun out of it," Kendal says jokingly. "I won't tell his wife."

"Sounds good," Stan says. "I'd better get off the horn. I've got a lot to do before the weekend."

"Well thanks again," Kendal says. "You've been more than helpful.

Kendal gives Naya a call.

"Hey Kay, what's going on?" Naya answers the call.

"Not much, just getting ready to get out of here," Kendal answers. "I like your idea. Let's grab a bite tonight at the Riparian."

"What about your friend Holden?" Naya asks. "Is he going to join us tonight?"

"I didn't ask," Kendal answers. "Let's wait another week on that, when we can go out to a live club or somewhere more exciting. Besides, we might have more to celebrate next week with this case."

"Okay..." Naya replies.

"Naya," Kendal interrupts. "I've got a call coming in I'd better take. How about meeting at the restaurant at seven."

"Sounds good," Naya answers.

Kendal cuts the connection, then answers her incoming call, identified only as *Vancouver*.

"Hello," Kendal answers.

"Hello Kendal, this is Nikki Nova again. We spoke on Monday about my husband Cedric."

"Yes Nikki, I really enjoyed our conversation," Kendal replies. "How are you?"

"I'm fine," Nikki tells her. "I enjoyed the conversation too."

"Is there anything I can help you with?" Kendal asks.

"Well, I've been thinking a lot about our conversation," Nikki says. "Anyway, I'd like to tell you more about my husband's work."

"Wonderful Nikki," Kendal says getting ready to take notes. "Go ahead, I'd like to hear what you have to say." There is a long moment of silence. "Nikki, are you there?"

"Yes," Nikki answers, "I'm just really hesitant to tell you what I want to say."

"Please don't worry," Kendal responds. "I'll keep it confidential."

"I appreciate that," Nikki kindly replies; "but it's more than that. It's something I've not told anyone in over sixty years."

"Okay," Kendal tells her, realizing how apprehensive she is. "Can you first just tell me why you haven't told anyone, if that makes you feel any better?"

"I don't want people to think I've lost my mind," Nikki answers.

"You come across as having a very sound mind to me," Kendal responds. "If you tell me, I promise to keep a very open mind to whatever it is."

"Thank you," Nikki replies. "You seem to be someone I can put my trust into."

"Thank you Nikki," Kendal responds. "Now what is it?"

"I don't know where to begin," Nikki says. "I guess it goes back to the day Cedric first told me that he had sent a message through time."

"Do you mean the day of the rainstorm mentioned in his thesis?" Kendal asks.

"Yes, thank you," Nikki answers. "I remember that day so clearly. I can't believe it's been sixty years. Anyway, I met Cedric in the park on that day and he told me that he had sent a message through time. I remember he said that he was able to boost the transmission to a speed where it would split, and at that point the message would travel through time."

"Was he certain?" Kendal asks.

"Very," Nikki answers; "but I was confused."

"Why?" Kendal goes on to ask.

"Because earlier that day, my station had asked me to travel to the moon to cover the Apollo 11 Centennial celebration," Nikki answers. "I had been in the public library with my two best friends who worked with me at the station just prior to meeting Cedric in the park, but after I'd been asked to travel to the moon. It was during the rainstorm, I remember. I dragged my girlfriends to the library to look up some information on the moon. I was afraid to go, but excited by the idea. I couldn't decide if I wanted to take the assignment. That's when something very strange happened that I can't explain."

"What happened?" Kendal asks. There is a pause.

"I was in the stacks, where they kept the old, actual physical books in the library. I was thumbing through a book on the moon," Nikki says, followed by a long period of silence.

"Don't be afraid to tell me," Kendal says, now very curious.

"I really haven't mentioned this in so long," Nikki says.

"It's okay," Kendal patiently tells her.

"Well, I came across a hand-written message to me in that book," Nikki replies.

"A message in the book?" Kendal asks. "What did it say?"

"It said that it was from a person, I think a guy who received a series of radio signals from Cedric in the year 2014," Nikki answers.

"When did this person claim Cedric sent the signals?" Kendal asks.

"He didn't, just that they were from the future," Nikki answers; "but the message also told me not to get on the flight to the moon, that it would crash. I know this all sounds so crazy," Nikki adds.

"No, it's alright," Kendal says to get her to relax. "How did he know you were going to the moon?"

"That's just it," Nikki responds. "He didn't. In fact, neither did Cedric at this point. I had only told my two best friends."

"So did you show them the message?" Kendal asks.

"I tried," Nikki answers. "I immediately went to where they were standing while I was still holding the book, but when I got to them, the message was gone."

"What do you mean gone?" Kendal asks.

"I mean gone," Nikki answers. "It was no longer in the book, nothing. I know how crazy this must sound. Now you see why I haven't told anyone for so many years."

"No, it's okay," Kendal replies. "What did your friends think?"

"At first, they trusted me, thinking maybe I had lost the page," Nikki answers; "but we looked and looked and there was nothing. I'm sure I had the right page. My thumb was still on it. Oh gee, I'm embarrassed to be telling you this."

"Not at all," Kendal tells her. "Did you tell Cedric?"

"I did," Nikki answers; "that day in the park; the very same day he told me about his successful experiment."

"Did he believe you?" Kendal asks.

"He really wanted to at first," Nikki answers, "but it just didn't make enough sense to him. I think he began to wonder if my mind had played a trick on me out of a fear of going to the moon. Although I know down inside he really wanted me to go, he was very understanding and never really thought of me as having any serious mental issues. In fact, Cedric had been experiencing strong episodes of Déjà vu himself around that time and told me how the mind is capable of projecting our fears. He also questioned if my friends might have somehow played a trick on me, maybe with disappearing ink or something, but that didn't make sense to me. I remember the message was written in ball point, and yet it left no trace, not even an indentation on the page. Still, a part of him wanted to believe it, especially since it involved his transmissions. Ultimately, however, he was just too skeptical to really accept it."

"So did you turn down the assignment?" Kendal asks.

"I did, and the station asked my friend Chara Luk to go in my stead," Nikki replies. "She was one of the two women with me in the library. She accepted the assignment. I remember how nervous I was for her. I tried to talk her out of it, but she couldn't say no. That's how I knew she really didn't believe me about the message in the book. Who could blame her?"

"Did Chara return safely from the moon?" Kendal asks, making a note of her name.

"She did," Nikki answers. "I was so relieved, though it definitely ended everyone's curiosity over the message in the book. There was no crash, thank God. I never brought it up again. Over time, it was simply forgotten by everyone, except for me that is."

"How could something so intense just be forgotten?" Kendal asks.

"Time keeps flowing," Nikki answers. "All great events simply fade into it. What else could be done?"

"Are you still in touch with your two friends from the library?" Kendal asks.

"I'm afraid not," Nikki answers. "Chara passed away back in 2116 of leukemia, the poor soul. Oriona, the other woman from the station died a few years later. She had a stroke and didn't live too long after that. We all remained friends until the very end. I still miss them both deeply to this day."

"I'm sorry to hear that," Kendal tells her, truly feeling for Nikki and all that she's been through. Is there anything more you can remember about any of this?" she asks.

"No, nothing I can think of," Nikki answers. "I guess I just wanted someone to know what happened. You know, I'm getting so old and as crazy as the story sounds, I don't want it to die with me."

"Well it won't," Kendal tells her; "rest assured. In fact, whenever I get a little time, I promise I'll do what I can to look further into it for you. Of course I can't promise anything. It happened so long ago," she adds.

"Oh, you're such a kind woman," Nikki tells her. "I really had a feeling I could trust you."

After ending their conversation, Kendal sits silently in her office pondering the story. Honestly, she isn't buying it and is now beginning to think Stan Satterfield is right. This Dr. Davis guy has truly triggered an avalanche of imagination. Nikki, nevertheless, had come across as being so thoughtful and articulate, so convincing. Her apparent love for her husband and respect for his work, however, had probably somehow seeped into her mind over time. Kendal wonders, however, if this lapse of perception came in the library, or later in Nikki's advancing years.

She calls up her computer screen and searches for the name Chara Luk. Instantly, she finds a short biography on the same Dot-5 site she saw earlier in the week. Sure enough, Chara was recognized as having covered the Apollo 11 Centennial for the station on July 20, 2069, and that she had passed away in 2116 of leukemia, just as Nikki had told her. Interesting that a story with such delusional twists to it would also be so accurate in detail. Kendal, however, simply has too much going on to deal with the diversion.

3:7

"What if it's all true?" Naya asks Kendal as they overlook the flow of pods down the FDR from the Riparian's bay windows.

"I wish it were," Kendal tells her. "She's such a sweet lady. I'd love to be able to tell her it was all true, even if it isn't. I just have no idea how anyone could verify it. Everybody involved, except her, has died. I think it's her way of clinging to her lost loved ones; creating an alternate reality to connect them, to add more meaning to her life."

"It certainly is a beautiful story," Naya says. "It makes me believe in true love."

"For all I know it is true," Kendal replies. "I'm just a lawyer. What do I know about time travel?"

Night has fallen over the East River. It's too dark to see the water itself, only shimmering reflections of light from the poles that line the docks. It's picturesque. The night is cool and getting cold as spring is still in its infancy. Below, people are enjoying the view as well, walking slowly along the terrace to take it in, some hand in hand.

"When did she say the message in the book was from?" Naya asks.

"From the year 2014," Kendal answers.

"And when did she receive it?" Naya asks.

"In 2069," Kendal replies.

"That's fifty-five years," Naya says after doing the math in her head.

A waitress approaches their table.

"Are we ready to order?" she asks.

"I think so," Naya responds. "I'm going to have the roast chicken."

"That comes with rice and your choice of potato," the waitress tells her. "We have mashed, baked, or fries."

"I'll take a baked potato," Naya says.

"A small, four-cheese pizza for me," Kendal tells her; "and I'd like a green salad as well, with blue cheese."

"Sounds good," the waitress replies taking down the order. "Would either of you like anything to drink?"

"A glass of your house merlot," Kendal answers.

"Me too," Naya adds.

"Let's just order a bottle then," Kendal suggests.

"Certainly," the waitress replies before moving to the next table.

"So how is the case coming along?" Naya asks.

"Great, but I'll know a lot more next week, when it moves into discovery," Kendal answers. "It will either be over really soon, or it won't be going so well."

"So what happens to Sedge's bank accounts if he gets to keep the money?" Naya asks.

"Usually in a situation like this, the accounts will go inactive, meaning they'll be dormant. The money would just sit there, however much it is, until he either returned or authorized someone to handle transactions for him. He could do that by granting someone power of attorney," Kendal answers. "It's difficult for him to do so from light years away, but it could be done."

"Do you think he's alive?" Naya asks.

"I do," Kendal answers; "but I have nothing to base that on. I guess it's just wishful thinking clouding my judgement. If he isn't alive, I'd be doing all this work on his behalf in vain."

"Have you heard from Brice?" Naya asks, knowing the relationship is far enough behind Kendal not to hit a sore spot.

"No, but that's like him," Kendal answers. "Not hearing from him reminds me why we needed to break up. His stubborn side is too unreasonable to bear."

"Do you think about him?" Naya goes on to ask.

"No, not really," Kendal answers. "I think this case has been a boost. I'm too busy to care about Brice. I'm happy it's over."

"I'm happy for you then," Naya tells her.

"How about you?" Kendal asks. "Is anything going on in your love life?"

"Nothing," Naya answers.

"What about that waiter you met here a few months ago?" Kendal inquires.

"He never called," Naya says.

"Why didn't you call him?" Kendal asks.

"I don't know," Naya tells her. "I guess I'm as stubborn as Brice. I wanted the guy to make the first move."

Kendal and Naya enjoy the night, again taking a trip down memory lane, recycling some of their old stories but laughing like they're new. After finishing their dinner and polishing off the bottle of wine, their busy week catches up with them. They decide to call it a night. Tired, they call a pod and share the ride.

3:8

How surreal, Kendal thinks, taking a moment to ponder her life as she looks out a sixty-first floor window at an eagle gargoyle from a boardroom window in the iconic Chrysler Building. The bird looks as if it's casing the Hudson River for fish. In all her years of coming to and living in this mighty city, she has never visited this world renowned, art deco architectural marvel. To think, now she's a part of its long history, here on official business.

The moment of wonder takes her away from the stress of her meeting. She's been summoned here by GulfStar's attorneys. Sedge Nile's case has moved into discovery, prompting them to waste no time in calling for this conference; a good sign but intimidating just the same. Phil offered to come along, but Kendal, inspired by Sedge's independence, has decided to go it alone, now questioning her own judgement.

Three men enter the room, all wearing suits. One of them is wearing a turban and has a long, black curly beard. Kendal stands to greet them. They all shake hands and have a seat with all three men sitting across the table from Kendal.

"Thank you for taking the time to meet with us today," the man in the center of the three tells her in an English accent. "I'm Ray Geldof from our London office. This is Mr. Yusuf Khan of our Muscat office," he says with an open-palm pointing to the man in the turban; "and this is Mr. Michael Reynolds of our office here on this floor."

"It's a pleasure meeting you gentlemen," Kendal tells them. They exchange cards across the table. "Now what can Thacker and Walcott do for you today?" she asks, shrewdly putting the ball in their court.

"We trust that you have seen our disclosures," Mr. Geldof tells her as Mr. Khan takes notes on a digital pad while Mr. Reynolds stares at her.

"I have," Kendal curtly replies.

"We're wondering what your thoughts are on the matter," Mr. Geldof continues.

"My thoughts are incidental," Kendal tells them. "What matters is what a judge would think, or moreover what a judge would rule."

"We trust that you have seen the injunction we filed," Mr. Geldof adds, remaining the spokesperson as the other two men sit silently.

"I have," Kendal says; "but I'm afraid you've misfiled it," she adds.

"Oh," Mr. Geldof responds. "What should we have done?"

"Frankly," Kendal tells them; "nothing. Any issues you have concerning the US government awarding a grant to NASA should be taken up with the US government or NASA, not my client. Honestly, I don't see any legal grounds for challenging it. I think you're out of luck."

"I see," Mr. Geldof replies as looks of surprise come over his two associates' faces.

"Have you given any thought to terms of a possible settlement?" Geldof goes on to ask her.

"I have," Kendal tells him, causing all three men to look hopeful. "I suggest that you drop all charges against my client," she adds. Their faces drop.

"Putting the injunction aside," Mr. Geldof tells her; "your client remains clearly guilty. Why would we want to drop all charges?" he asks.

"Look, we're all attorneys," Kendal says. "I'm going to be really straight with you guys."

"By all means," Mr. Khan says, adding a third voice to the conversation.

"This is not your ordinary case," Kendal says. "This is a case that will ultimately be tried in the court of public opinion. You saw the affidavit from Mr. Stan Satterfield. We all know the reckless endangerment charge won't stick, leaving you only with the grand theft of your company's spacecraft, which I'll readily admit will stick. I wouldn't even know where to begin defending that action. What it comes down to, however, is the aggregate loss versus the aggregate gain."

"We're listening," Mr. Geldof says in a moment of silence.

"From Sedge Nile's final recording, I gather he is a reasonable man. The world seems to support him," Kendal says. "Taking him to court to garner whatever's left in his bank account is a pittance of what your company wishes to regain. Furthermore, it paints GulfStar as the bad guy, and I don't think you guys are bad guys.

"On the other hand, if you were to drop all charges, you could go down in history as Sedge Nile's sponsor. The world would love your company. They'd view GulfStar as the bigger player. They already know your ship was stolen, yet they continue to support Sedge. Now you have a chance to be humane – to be the good guys."

"Do you understand how serious theft charges are in Oman?" Mr. Khan asks her.

"I do," Kendal replies; "but not to the extent that you do I'm sure." There is a long moment of silence. "Look guys, I understand. You do great legal work and you've explored all your options. This is a high-profile case though and the world is watching."

"We'll take this proposal up with the Sultan," Mr. Khan says after a long pause, apparently the one with the most direct line to him.

"That's' all I ask," Kendal tells them.

"Thank you, Ms. Benz," Mr. Geldof tells her. "We'll be in touch."

"Thank you gentlemen," Kendal tells them. "It was truly a pleasure."

Kendal kindly excuses herself, leaving the three men to plot their course forward. She remains completely composed until the elevator doors close. She presses the ground floor button really hard, releasing her tension. Regardless of the outcome, she knows she couldn't have laid out her case more clearly. She's done her job. Sedge's legal fate is now truly up to the Sultan of Oman.

3:9

Phil, anxious to hear how her meeting with GulfStar went, calls out to Kendal as she walks past his door, not even giving her the chance to make it to her office. She turns back and steps into his office.

"So how did everything go yesterday?" he asks.

"I think as well as can be expected," she answers; "at least on our end. I have no idea how the Sultan is going to react."

"Did you pitch the idea of dropping charges?" he asks.

"I did, and it seemed to go over well with the attorneys, but again I don't know," she replies.

"Well let's keep our fingers crossed," Phil suggests. "If they drop all charges, you'll be pleased to know we won't be charging Sedge for our legal services."

"So Tim has agreed to take this case pro bono," Kendal says.

"Only to this point," Phil tells her. "If it goes any further, we'll have to charge."

"What convinced him to be so generous?" Kendal asks.

"I told him you were proposing to drop all charges," Phil answers. "He was impressed. He thought that if GulfStar can pony up a ship for the cause, we could throw in some legal services."

"That's wonderful," Kendal replies. "Holden Grant will be pleased to hear it."

"Just remember to mention it next time you do any interviews with The Times," he tells her.

"I most certainly will," Kendal replies.

When she arrives at her office, she doesn't even have time to take off her jacket before a soft, sequential set of pongs alerts her to an incoming call. She takes it.

"Good morning, Kendal Benz."

"Hi Kendal, this is Ray Geldof with GulfStar."

"Yes Ray, I didn't expect to hear from you so soon," Kendal responds. "What can I do for you this morning?"

"I'm calling to let you know that I just got off the phone with Yusuf Khan," he replies. "Yusuf had a conference call with Sultan bin Saeed last night."

"How did it go?" Kendal asks.

"You'll be pleased to know that the Sultan has agreed to drop all charges," Mr. Geldof answers.

"That's wonderful news," Kendal says excitedly.

"Yes," Mr. Geldof replies. "The Sultan merely asks that you publicly mention GulfStar's generosity and willingness to support Sedge Nile's mission should you get the chance.

"Absolutely," Kendal tells him. "Please convey our thanks to the Sultan and thank all of you for being so willing to work with us. This is going to make a lot of people happy. Also, if there's anything more we can do for your company, let us know. There may be tax breaks you can take advantage of by charitably sponsoring Sedge's flight."

"Thank you Ms. Benz," Mr. Geldof tells her. "We'll keep that in mind. Have a lovely weekend."

Kendal, still with her jacket on, goes right back to Phil's office.

"They're dropping the charges," she tells him.

"Wow, that was fast," he answers with a smile. "Congratulations Kendal, great job."

She returns to her office and finally settles in. She checks her voice messages.

- "Hi Kendal, Tina Moran from The Times. Any updates on the Sedge Nile case?" she asks.

Kendal gives her a call.

"Tina Moran," Tina answers.

"Hi Tina, this is Kendal Benz returning your call."

"Yes Kendal, how are things going?" Tina asks.

"They couldn't be better, nor could your timing be more divine," Kendal answers. "I just got off the phone with a GulfStar attorney and they've agreed to drop all charges against Sedge Nile."

"You're kidding," Tina replies. "All charges?"

"Yes," Kendal answers. "They've now kindly agreed to support the mission, acting as Sedge's sponsor."

"That's amazing," Tina tells her.

"Furthermore," Kendal adds; "Thacker and Walcott are not going to charge Sedge for our legal services as our way of contributing to the mission. Legally speaking, it's like it never happened."

"That's astonishing," Tina replies. "Nice work on your end."

"Ultimately, the Sultan is to thank," Kendal says. "I wish there were more to tell, but this story is short and sweet."

"Has word been sent to Sedge Nile?" Tina asks.

"No, I'm glad you reminded me," Kendal answers. "With the help of NASA, I sent a transmission last week. I'm going to call them and schedule another one as soon as I get off this call. I'm sure we'll have word on the way soon."

"I'd like to include all of this in a follow up, if you don't mind," Tina tells Kendal.

"Absolutely, I'm looking forward to reading it," Kendal replies. "Please, if you can, put a kind word in for the Sultan and for Thacker and Walcott. Their generosity gives Sedge better odds of making it."

"I will," Tina tells her. "Have a nice weekend."

Kendal gives Trista Rybach a call.

"NASA communications, this is Trista Rybach."

"Hi Trista, it's Kendal Benz again."

"Kendal, how are you?" Trista asks.

"Never been better," Kendal answers. "Listen, I know I was just there, but I've got wonderful news for Sedge and I'd like to get another message to him as soon as possible."

"Sure, how does Monday morning work for you?" Trista asks.

"Perfect," Kendal answers. "Nine-thirty again?"

"That works for me," Trista replies.

"Great, I'll see you then," Kendal says.

Kendal then calls Holden Grant.

"Hi Kendal, what's new?" he answers.

"They're dropping all charges against Sedge," she tells him.

"Oh my God, are you serious?" Holden asks.

"Very," Kendal answers. "That's not all," she adds. "Our law firm isn't going to charge for this work either. It's our way of supporting Sedge. Your entire crowdfund can now be used to help him."

"I'm shocked," Holden tells her. "This is all so unreal."

"Let's celebrate. It's Friday. What are you doing tonight?" Kendal asks.

"I've got a company dinner party I can't get out of," he answers; "but I'm free tomorrow night."

"Sounds good," Kendal replies. "My friend Naya and I have been dying to try out the new CBGB. It's not far from you. What do you think?" she asks.

"I've been there," he answers; "and I loved it. I'd love to go again. Let's go!"

"Okay, do you want to just meet us there at seven?" she asks.

"We'd better make it six-thirty, so we're guaranteed a place to sit. It starts getting crowded around seven," Holden answers.

"Six-thirty it is," Kendal tells him. "I'll call Naya and let her know. I already know she's free tomorrow night though, so there shouldn't be a problem. She's excited to meet you."

"See you both at six-thirty," Holden says.

Kendal calls Naya,

"Hi Kay," Naya answers.

"We're meeting Holden at CBGB tomorrow night at six-thirty," Kendal tells her.

"Great, I've wanted to go there since they opened," she replies.

"Do you want to just meet there or come by my place earlier?" Kendal asks.

"I've got a lot to do during the day," Naya replies. "Let's just meet at the club."

Kendal checks the time. She feels like she's had a full day, but it's only nine-twenty. What a morning.

3:10

Right on time for their rendezvous, Kendal gets off the subway at Bleecker Street Station and makes her way up to the street, emerging on the corner of Bleecker and Lafayette. The second she walks onto the sidewalk, she finds herself face-to-face with not only Brice but also a tall, attractive woman holding onto his arm. Unfortunately, the confrontation is unavoidable.

"Brice," Kendal says surprised. "How are you?"

"Hi Kendal," he answers trying not to act as surprised as he obviously is. "Kendal, this is Simone. Simone, Kendal," he says to keep the situation cordial.

"Nice to meet you Simone," Kendal tells Brice's date with every morsel of honesty she can muster.

"It's a pleasure to meet you," Simone replies, followed by an awkward moment of silence.

"So where are you off to?" Brice asks, trying to keep it friendly.

"I'm meeting some friends at CBGB," Kendal answers, wishing she hadn't been so honest. She wants more than anything to tell him that she's also on a date, but has never been a good liar.

"I hear it's really nice in there," Brice replies.

"Yes, let's go there, next time," Simone tells Brice, causing Kendal to cringe.

"What are you guys up to tonight?" Kendal asks.

"We just had drinks at the Bleecker Street Bar, and now we're off to the Blue Note to listen to a little live music," Brice answers. There is another awkward moment of silence.

"Well, I'd better be going," Kendal tells them. "I don't want to be late."

"Have fun tonight," Brice says with a smile.

"Yes, it was nice meeting you," Simone adds.

"You too," Kendal says, now looking more calm and composed, as if she's accepted the situation. "See you later," she adds with a little wave before making her way down Bleecker Street without looking back.

Kendal arrives at CBGB at six twenty-five, five minutes early. She sees Holden sitting alone at a table, and Naya sitting at another just a few tables away. She grabs Naya and pulls her over to Holden's table.

"Holden, this is my friend Naya," she says as she introduces the two.

"Nice to meet you," Naya tells Holden. "I've heard good things about you."

"Oh thanks, you too," Holden answers. They sit and look over bar menus.

CBGB is part of a twenty-second century, neo Manhattan movement. Old, long-closed establishments are being resurrected, a trend that connects contemporary New Yorkers with the city's historical roots. The legend of CBGB has long outlived the original club, which went out of business well over a century ago. Frankly, the neo version is very little like the original. It's far trendier and more martini-bar like than the original darkwave rock bar. It remains, however, a live music club with pictures of the old club and bygone bands all over the walls. It's a fun place to hang just the same.

The server, a tall, long-haired woman in a very short skirt comes to their table and takes their order. They decide to share a carafe of merlot. There is no music yet - why they were able to so easily find a table. It's a perfect time for Naya to get to know Holden a little better.

"So Kendal has never told me what it is that you do," Naya tells Holden.

"Oh, well shame on Kendal," Holden says with a laugh. "I work at the New York Public Library."

"That's cool," Naya replies. "What do you do there?"

"I'm an information specialist," he answers. "It's really just another way to say librarian. I help people research their topics and give tours to school groups that visit."

"That sounds fun," Naya says.

"It can be," Holden replies. "So what do you do?" he asks.

"I'm an administrative assistant," she answers. "I work for Parker Research, an analytics firm in Soho, not far from here."

"Nice," Holden says. "Do you enjoy your work?" he asks.

"I do," Naya answers; "at least usually." There is a long moment of silence.

"Kendal, you seem quiet tonight," Holden observes.

"Oh, I ran into Brice just before I got here tonight," she replies.

"Oh Kendal, I'm sorry," Naya says. "Are you okay?" she asks.

"I'm fine," Kendal answers. "It's no big deal."

"Brice is your ex-boyfriend I take it," Holden observantly adds to the conversation.

"Yes," Kendal answers. "Running into him wasn't the issue," she adds. "What brought me down was that he was with someone."

"Oh Kendal," Naya says. "Was it a date?" she asks.

"Yes, it even looked like more," Kendal answers. "I think they're really together."

"You told me you haven't thought about him lately," Naya says trying to cheer her up.

"I haven't," Kendal replies; "but when he's got some woman hanging on his arm and I'm alone, it makes me feel like a fool."

"Forget about it girl," Holden tells her. "You need to jettison him. That was a concept Sedge always liked to bring up. He used rocket science as his example, especially the old Apollo Missions. With space flight, when something has already served its purpose, it becomes dead weight. Jettisoning it allows you to go further. It all calculates into a weight-to-thrust ratio."

"I like that," Naya says. "Yeah Kendal, time to jettison. Move on."

"I like it too," Kendal says. "I'll never get to Luna Nuevo dragging Brice around."

"There you go," Holden tells her.

"Speaking of Sedge," Naya says to pivot away from Brice; "it sounds like you really won your case."

"Yeah," Holden adds. "You must be a magic attorney."

"I guess we just got lucky," Kendal says with a smile.

"I don't think so," Holden tells her. "You were very convincing."

"I'm thrilled it turned out the way it did," Kendal says. "I've never had a case like this before. It was all new territory for me."

"How so?" Naya asks, pleased Kendal's spirits seem to be picking up.

"Well, of course all the science is new to me; the space travel and communications," Kendal answers. "It's really fascinating. Also, this is the first case where public relations played into it. Public opinion turned out to be our greatest leverage. I've seen plenty of high-profile cases where that has been the case, but never been involved in one. I was really surprised that it worked."

The waitress returns with their wine. They order an appetizer of potato skins to share and look over their menus for dinner options as she pours each of them a glass.

"The fettuccine alfredo looks good," Holden says.

"I was looking at that myself," Naya adds.

"I think we need a few more minutes," Kendal tells the waitress.

"So here's to Sedge," Kendal says, holding up her glass.

"To Sedge," both Naya and Holden say. They touch glasses and take a sip.

"So do you think he's alive?' Naya asks. "Sorry," she says to Holden. "I didn't mean to bring up such a touchy subject."

"No, not at all," Holden responds. "In fact, I feel comfortable talking about it with Kendal and you. I honestly don't know, however, if he's alive. I hope so."

"I do too," Kendal adds. "Down inside, I really hope he's alive and well."

"Did Kendal tell you about her friend who got a message from another time?" Naya asks Holden.

"No, she didn't," Holden answers. "What is she talking about?" he asks Kendal.

"Oh, it's nothing really," Kendal answers; "but it was through this case that I came into contact with her. I was trying to understand the glitch that Sedge mentioned. To make a long story short, I ended up calling this elderly woman in Vancouver BC, whose husband claimed to have sent messages through time using laser-beams."

"Fascinating," Holden says. "So who received the message from another time?" he asks.

"Ultimately and indirectly, she did," Kendal says with a smile. "The message was supposedly sent in or around 2069 from her husband to some other mystery person in the year 2014, who then warned her in a hand-written note inside a book not to take an ill-fated flight to the moon."

"Wait," Holden interjects. "What book? How did he get her to read it?" he asks.

"It was a book about the moon in a library," Kendal answers. "I don't know how he knew she would see it, but somehow he knew, allegedly. I don't think she knows how either. She only saw the message once, then it was gone."

"What do you mean by gone?" Holden asks, looking enthralled by the story.

"It disappeared," Naya jumps in to answer.

"It just disappeared?" Holden asks.

"Yes," Kendal answers. "It just disappeared."

"So I take it she didn't go to the moon," Holden speculates.

"No, she didn't," Kendal tells him.

"Well there you have it," Holden says. "That's why it disappeared."

"What do you mean?" Kendal asks.

"As soon as she had made up her mind not to go, time had jettisoned the message," he answers. "Her reality had changed, meaning she never went to the moon in the first place."

"I don't understand," Naya says.

"If she never went to the moon," Holden tells her; "there was never a message."

"Interesting," Kendal says. "You have a good point."

They spend a minute looking over their menus, then flag the waitress as she walks by.

"Are we ready?" the waitress asks.

"Yes, I think so," Naya says. "I'd like the seafood fettuccine alfredo," she says.

"Excellent choice," the waitress tells her. "I usually have that myself. It comes with garlic toast and a blend of wheat and spinach noodles with our own homemade sauce. You'll like it."

"I'd like the same," Holden says. "I'm sold."

"I'll have the grilled salmon with rice pilaf," Kendal orders.

"Excellent choice as well," the waitress tells her. "Would any of you care for anything else?" she asks.

"I'd like a glass of water," Kendal says.

"Me too," Holden adds.

"Make it three," Naya says.

"So do you believe this lady at all?" Holden asks as the waitress walks away. "Her story sounds so well-conceived. Did she just make this elaborate thing up?"

"I wouldn't say she made it up so much as she imagined it," Kendal answers.

"What's the difference?" Naya asks.

"I think she truly believes it happened," Kendal replies. "Her husband was an expert who got his PhD in laser communications. I read the summary of his thesis and he claimed to have transmitted radio signals through time."

"So do you believe that?" Holden asks.

"I don't know," Kendal answers. "The guy who sent the summary to me, also a communications specialist for the military, doesn't believe it. He knows a lot more about this kind of stuff than I do."

"Sedge would find all this interesting," Holden says. "He was also a communications expert."

"Yes," Kendal says. "We can thank Sedge for this story resurfacing."

"Sedge used to talk about the quantum mysteries of radio waves," Holden tells them. "He used to talk about how radio waves are electromagnetic, and how we don't fully understand how they relate to time."

"Really?" Naya asks.

"Yes," Holden says. "Quantum entanglement, or *spooky action at a distance* as Einstein called it, is a mysterious connection between particles where particles can instantly influence one another regardless of the distance between them. It's been demonstrated through experiments involving stars hundreds of light years away having different simultaneous, instantaneous effects on different observations, each at different locations here on Earth."

"Interesting," Kendal says, not fully grasping Holden's meaning.

"Yes," Holden says. "I don't really do the topic justice myself, but Sedge loved talking about it endlessly."

"Wow," Naya interjects; "that gets me thinking. If the message in the book turns out to be true, what are the odds of having a direct connection to both of these earth-moving events? It's you Kendal," Naya adds. "You are the connection. Your meticulous, thorough methodical mind has been the link to these two amazing stories. Had you not contacted this woman, she very well may have left her story buried deep in her mind to wilt with time – to die with her."

"How profound," Holden tells Naya with a look that's easy to read; he's intellectually tickled with the way her mind works.

The food arrives just as the first band kicks into their first set of songs. The place has filled in over the course of their conversation, leaving no empty table. Holden's suggested meeting time has proven to be wisely selected. They dine, converse, listen to music, and laugh the night away. Naya, like Kendal, doesn't take long to take to Holden. He's smart, charming, and makes for wonderful dinner conversation. Kendal and Naya have found a new friend, a friendship forged over a stolen spaceship now over four light years away. How bizarre.

3:11

Watching the city slide by block-by-block, Kendal finds herself once again on a public pod gliding down Amsterdam Avenue, through the Upper West Side on her way back to NASA's satellite office in the Goddard Institute. Unlike her last visit which fell on a Friday, it's now Monday morning, and the contrast is stark. Kendal, nevertheless, is feeling good this morning, still having a spring in her step from Friday's news of Sedge's charges being dropped, and the ensuing celebratory weekend. Now she's on her way to let Sedge in on the good news, or at least to get the good news on its way to the Centauri System.

She puts her headphones on and looks for any news of the case.

"...will be awaiting Sedge Nile when he reaches Luna Nuevo, if he reaches Luna Nuevo," she hears a morning show reporter say. "GulfStar, the company he worked for and from whom he stole the ship, in a shocking move has decided to drop all charges they filed against him. They have decided instead to sponsor his mission to the infamous moon around the planet Aureola, which orbits the star Alpha Centauri B."

"What made them change their minds Tom?" a second voice from the show asks.

"Word is that they couldn't have recovered their losses, so instead decided to jump on the bandwagon for favorable PR," Tom answers.

Kendal smiles almost to the point of laughter, then tries to hide it to avoid annoying fellow patrons. It is, after all, Monday morning. She's never heard someone talk directly about her case on a morning show. She puts her device away and presses the stop button as the bus nears her stop in front of Peace Fountain at Street People's Garden.

What a perfect morning, she thinks getting off the pod. The sun is out but it's neither hot nor cold. Tulips are blooming that weren't blooming just days ago. Spring is phasing in. Kendal takes the block-and-a-half walk to the Goddard Institute, arriving a few minutes before her appointment. Again, she checks in with the guard at the reception desk, who tells her to proceed back to Trista Rybach's office, room one twenty-three. They both seem to recognize each other this time.

"Hi Kendal," Trista immediately says as she enters the office.

"Good morning Trista," Kendal replies.

"I was just reading about your interview in The Times," Trista tells her. "You're a bit of a celebrity."

"I didn't know it was out," Kendal replies. "Is it Tina Moran's article?" she asks.

"Yes," Trista answers.

"She called me on Friday," Kendal tells her. "That was fast."

"I'm guessing this article has something to do with why you are here," Trista says.

"Yes, that's exactly why I'm here," Kendal responds. "There's not a lot left to hide. Sedge's legal issues are a thing of the past."

"That's wonderful news," Trista tells her. "I'm happy for Sedge and I'm sure he'll be happy as well to receive it."

"I hope he does," Kendal replies.

"Well I don't want to keep you from sending it," Trista says. "The room is set up. Do you need my help?" she asks.

"Not really," Kendal answers. "I remember the room and how to work the recorder."

"Then you're welcome to go on back," Trista says. "The door is open. Feel free to speak as openly as you like; the message is encoded. No one, not even I can listen to it, only Sedge. Just let me know when you've finished and I'll prepare the message for transmission."

"Thank you Trista," Kendal replies. "You've been a big help."

Kendal makes her way to the recording room, again excited to be sending a message across space. She gets to the room, closes the door behind her, takes off her sweater, and sits down in front of the microphone. She takes a moment to collect her thoughts and catch her breath, then presses record.

"Hi Sedge, it's me again, Kendal Benz. I realize that I just sent you a message days ago, but I have an update to your case. I have some great news. GulfStar has agreed to drop all charges against you. They've agreed to be your sponsor. Now I don't think that means you can expect more funding from them, but they're not going after you for the ship. You're legally free and clear, meaning whatever is in your bank accounts remains yours. Congratulations.

"On a personal note, I've become friends with your former partner Holden Grant. Again, he has been and continues to be a huge help with your case. His crowdfund should go a long way toward getting you better supplies. NASA is working on that as I'm sure they've probably briefed you. Holden is doing well and seems to be over what he would describe as being jettisoned, but he still harbors a great deal of admiration for you.

"Now that charges have been dropped, this will likely be the last time you hear from me. It's hard for me to believe I'm sending a message to another star. This experience has been both extremely exciting and enlightening for me. I really do hope you are alive and well out there, wherever you are, and that you're receiving these transmissions. A lot of people, including myself, have become fans of yours. Your actions, though criminal, have been inspiring. One day, I imagine, your name will be studied in history books along with other explorers. I look forward to the day, presumably in five years, when we receive your first transmissions from Luna Nuevo and hear of your experiences. The world is living vicariously through you. Good luck and stay safe."

Kendal puts her sweater back on as she walks back to Trista's office.

"I'm finished," she tells Trista.

"So soon," Trista responds. "You must be good at broadcasting. Most people feel like they have to erase and do over several times before getting it right."

"I guess I didn't really have that much to say," Kendal says. "It's really different when you're just communicating one way."

"Well, let us know if you need to transmit any further messages," Trista tells her. "We'll be glad to help."

"That's good to know," Kendal replies. "Who knows?"

They bid their goodbyes and Kendal exits the building. Instead of immediately catching a pod back to Midtown, she decides to walk a few blocks to her old stomping grounds; Columbia University. She is, after all, back in her old neighborhood and the day couldn't be nicer.

She strolls down Broadway to 116th and onto campus. She walks first to the sundial and tries in vain to determine the time, something she was never very good at doing. Students are hanging out, gathering on the

South Lawn, and enjoying the mid-morning sunshine. She takes a good look at the Alma-Mater Statue, arms extended, and ponders its meaning; Latin for *nourishing mother.*

A thousand memories race through her mind. It wasn't that many years ago that this school was her world. Now it seems like an eternity. The papers she had to write, the exams, the social pressures are all so long gone now. Everyone she knows has moved on, out into the real world. How small this collegiate world now seems, yet such a critical stone on which she had to step to get her further across her river. Time consumes. Now all these young minds around her are living in this microcosm, dealing with their own issues, while Kendal is sending messages to the stars.

Kendal walks past Kent Hall and over to the law school. With time to kill, she goes into the Arthur Diamond Law Library. She takes a good look around at a place she spent so many hours researching cases and preparing for mock trials. If these walls could only speak. A library assistant at the information desk asks her if she needs any help. Kendal tells him that she's a former student just reminiscing. He reminds her that former students have full access to the facilities, including the Ginsburg Research Center, if she wants to research any cases. He asks for her full name and finds her in the records. After checking her ID, he gives her an access code she can use throughout the facility, granting her access to Lexus-Nexus as well as all inter-library databases.

Kendal goes into the Ginsburg Center and takes a seat at one of their open research terminals. It's comfortable. They didn't have these snug stations when she was a student here. She decides to test out their floating-screen data system. When she enters her access code, three holographic screens appear, hovering over the desk in front of her.

Not really knowing what to research, Kendal decides to test the system anyway. She types the name Nikki Nova into the system. Immediately, she finds Dot-5 news report headlines flashing in front of her eyes. She is told the system cannot access Canadian criminal history, but shows that Nikki currently owns a condominium in downtown Vancouver.

Kendal wonders if she can do anything to research Nikki's claim, typing *message from future in a book*. Over three thousand listed examples appear containing this combination of words. She tries to refine her search, typing *message, book, transmission,* and *time*. The system produces four thousand listed examples. She clicks on an icon to search only published works then types, *message, library, back in time,* and *book.* The system produces three hundred and seventy-seven different works. Now I'm getting somewhere, she thinks. She scrolls through the list but doesn't really see anything. She thinks of how she can refine her search, then enters *transmission, moon, back in time,* and *2014.* This time three hundred and twenty results are produced, everything from movie and book titles, to song lyrics. Noticing an article on back pain, she realizes she needs to put *back in time* in quotation marks to prevent the system from treating each word independently. She tries again with moon, transmission, 2014, and "back in time." One result is produced, an obituary from the year 2072. It reads as follows.

In loving memory of Beau Hadley

Beau Hadley passed away peacefully on May 5, 2072 after complications due to Alzheimer's. After growing up in Kirkland, Washington, Beau attended the University of Washington, where in 2005, he earned a Bachelor of Science in Information Technology. He is survived by his former wife, Kendra Becket, whom he married in 2010, their son William Hadley, and daughter-in-law Alice Woods. In accordance with Beau's last wishes, there will be no service. He asked only that the following poem be printed with this obituary:

　　　She waits for me, across the sea, beneath a waning moon.
　　　She sent to me, across that sea, transmissions time consumed.
To 2014 from a time unseen, three bottles back in time.
　　　To set her free, I must unpiece this puzzle in my mind.
　　　She waits for me, across the sea, across a sea of time...

Kendal transfers a copy of the obituary to her device, then starts making her way out of the library, back to her office.

Part 4

Sedge sits in front of a communication terminal waiting for the interior lighting in the ringway to stop flickering. When it does, he takes a deep breath and hit's the record icon.

"I am pleased to report that I am alive and in orbit around Luna Nuevo," he says into the camera. "I've been incredibly fortunate. Following this ship's encounter with what I believe to be ice particles in the frost belt that sits on the outer reaches of this star system, with the aid of the ship's onboard computer, I was able to calculate and redirect the ship's course. To mitigate the damage done to the number three outboard engine, I had to put the ship on a trajectory that took it much closer to Beta Centauri than planned, thus using the star's gravity to assist in the slowing of this vessel. From there, I had to fly very close to the planet Aureola in order to deploy atmospheric anchors to further slow the ship. This was done over the planet's northern pole, given that an approach along the equatorial plane would have presented far too much risk of encountering debris from its ring system. I was, however, able to observe an aurora beautiful beyond words. Despite burning up all four anchors, I was successful in slowing the ship enough to get it into orbit around Luna Nuevo. I now travel at speeds well below the communication line and am able to transmit signals, including this one, to the Nina in orbit around Centauri B, signals that are sure to make it back to Earth one day.

"That, however, is the extent of my fortunate news. I now face many serious problems that significantly lower my chances of survival. The most immediate issue is the failing electrical system on this ship. Rounding Beta Centauri went as planned except for an unexpected coronal mass ejection, or solar flare, occurring just in front of the ship's path, forcing me to fly through a field of highly charged particles. The excessive radiation is what compromised the electrical system. It is functioning for the most part, but experiencing flickering failures that sometimes force system rebooting. It has also fried the communication system, particularly the receiver. I cannot seem to receive full transmissions, only fragments. All indicators suggest my transmissions are going out, however, so I believe someone will get my data bank of messages.

"Moreover, the orbit I am in is both unstable and highly elliptical. I'm in a decaying orbit around Luna Nuevo and the fried electrical system leaves me with limited control, unable to adjust it. You might say I was too successful slowing the ship. In short, this ship has only eight more orbits at best before it swings close enough to Luna Nuevo to be pulled into the moon. Whatever doesn't burn up in its atmosphere will crash onto its surface. So, my plans to spend a few years in orbit have been dashed. I am now faced with one option - to abandon ship. This Titanic is going down. My deepest apologies to the Sultan for this, but it is now beyond my control.

"I have been packing supplies into the seven functioning landing modules with the hope that they manage to safely make it to the surface, avoiding number three because of the damage it has already sustained. The modules, which will be released precisely at the point of perigee on this ship's next orbit, have been programed to touch down on the moon's surface as close as possible to the proposed coordinates of the bio-dome, which should have been put in place and begun functioning after the arrival of the Cortes. Again, I have no way of knowing this because of my damaged receivers, another hurdle I face. I plan to be aboard landing module number six, which I calculate to have the best chance of survival.

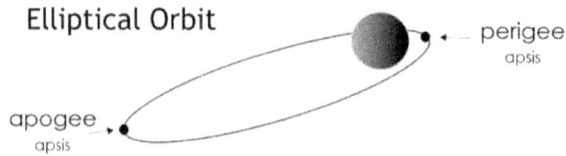

"Given my velocity upon entry and radical approach to the moon, touching down at the bio-dome site is a long shot. It is, however, my target. Luna Nuevo's stronger gravity and thinner upper atmosphere present unique problems for landers designed only for Earth and Mars. Assuming the heat shielding holds, which I think it will, I again will be approaching the surface at a dangerously high velocity. Should the chutes deploy and retro-rockets function perfectly, reaching zero KPH is feasible but cutting it extremely close, and that's not taking winds or weather patterns into account. Should my lander survive, my primary objective from there is getting to the bio-dome before my oxygen runs out, again assuming there is a bio-dome to which to get.

"I have eleven hours before my planned detachment from this ship, the only world I've known for the past five years. Achieving an escape velocity in this crippled craft is impossible, leaving no choice but to attempt a rebirth into the world below. I haven't slept in over thirty hours and I don't know how I can do so now. Given the odds, I feel as though I'm on the eve of my execution. How does one prepare for the gallows? Should I not survive, location beakers are activated on the landers which should transmit landing and or crash sites to the Cortes orbiter. If they fail, the orbiter will likely have the landers' last recorded trajectories, at least until the time of entry. God how I hope to survive. I've come this far. If, however, this proves to be my last transmission, let it be known I made it to Luna Nuevo, and I did so without the slightest regret. I've been staring at the moon since I achieved orbit around it and it's simply the single most beautiful object I've seen in my life," Sedge somberly concludes.

Sedge makes his way back to the central tube and into the kitchen supply room. He leaves the door open and begins throwing large boxes of dried food weightlessly down the tube, toward the back of the ship. They float effortlessly through the air. Retrieving them from their landers on the moon's surface will be back-breaking work. He spends a few hours finishing his packing, stuffing the landers to the gills with treasure, wondering if any of it will survive the journey to the surface. When finished, he takes a moment to sit in Lander Six.

"You're my only hope," he tells the vehicle. "You're going to take me either to the surface or to my grave."

Sedge drifts back down the central tube to the elevator, then returns to the front G-ring; his comfort zone. No longer feeling a need to use the ship's resources sparingly, he draws a hot bath in the presidential suite. After years of using a vacuum hose to shower, it's the first hot bath he's had since leaving Earth. It feels so good to climb into it. The landers are packed and programed, and the work is done. There's really nothing left for him to do but get in one and fly to that beautiful, ruddy ball in the window. He takes deep breaths as he watches Luna Nuevo continually roll in and out of view through the large overhead window. For the first time in a long time, he's able to relax as the lights again flicker. I'm alive, he thinks, sinking into hot suds.

"I'm alive," he says.

"How do you know?" Holden asks him.

"I'm breathing," Sedge tells him.

"Does a flower breathe?" Holden asks him.

"It has a respiratory system," Sedge replies.

"Is that how you define life?" Holden asks.

"It seems like one of the necessary characteristics," Sedge answers. "I'm happy to see that you're alive," Sedge tells Holden. "I'm sorry I left but I made it, you know. I made it to Luna Nuevo."

"Haven't you seen the news?" Holden asks. "There are dinosaurs on Luna Nuevo."

"What do you mean?" Sedge asks in return.

"Come out here onto the balcony and look for yourself," Holden says, motioning Sedge to step out onto a balcony he's never seen before. "Can you see them?" he asks pointing up.

"No," Sedge answers. "It's too far away."

"Look through the telescope," Holden says, pointing to a scope mounted to the balcony's railing.

"I'll be damned," Sedge says looking upward to the sky through the scope at what he can now make out to be a herd of dinosaurs on the surface. "I can see them."

"See," Holden says. "It's really dangerous down there."

Sedge opens his eyes to see Luna Nuevo still spinning outside the ship's window. The few short minutes of sleep seemed to help calm his nerves, though still leaving him far shy of refreshed. He watches Luna for a while, wondering what's down there, hoping he doesn't have to contend with dinosaurs.

After several minutes soaking, he dries himself, gets dressed, and returns to the Holo Café, hoping to harvest a little advice from Neil before his departure, or at least some encouragement. Inside the café, he makes himself a sparkling water and sits down at a bistro table with his friend.

"This is it, Neil," Sedge tells him. "I'm in the eleventh hour of my travels. Soon, I'll be on that beautiful moon below."

"Congratulations Sedge," Neil tells him. "What a feat, to travel all the way to the Centauri System. Thanks for taking me along as well," he adds.

"It's my pleasure," Sedge replies; "but I'm not finished with you. So I don't feel like you went down with this ship, I plan to shut you down before I detach. I'm planning, however, to see you again down on the surface. The bio-dome is set up to host astronauts, equipped I'm sure with a holo-projector. I don't know if it will be as good as the one on this ship, but I can't imagine Neil Armstrong won't be an option. I'll see you soon one way or another."

"What do you mean by one way or another?" Neil perceptively asks.

"If I don't survive the landing," Sedge answers; "then I too will most likely become an option on future holographic menus, at least I hope. If not immediately, then eventually. Technology only improves over time. So one way or another, I'll see you again."

"That's comforting to know," Neil tells Sedge. "In a way, these machines keep us alive."

"When existence is viewed as a continuum of processes, that's true," Sedge responds, feeling more philosophical in his sleep-deprived state. "I, for example, am looking at and listening to you, a process known as Neil Armstrong. Though you physically left us over a century ago, your existence is still reflecting through time. People are molecular societies, comprised of all that attracts to them. They are defined by these bonds, be it the shirts on their backs or the words that they write. Just as the paint that bonds to these walls defines this room, these are the things that define an entity. When subject to the perpetual process of time, these bonds are a society, and with time they will eventually rearrange into other societies. So even though I'm looking at a hologram of you, it remains a real part of your reflection through time, and thus you, a part of your ongoing presence."

"That's pretty deep," Neil says in thought.

"Do you think I'll make it to the surface alive?" Sedge asks.

"I don't know," Neil answers. "I certainly hope so, not just for your sake but for the human race."

"Thanks Neil," Sedge says. "I'm scared."

"Your fear is natural," Neil replies.

"You landed on carriers, got shot down in the Korean War, tested every flying machine they threw at you, regained control of that deadly Gemini 8 spin, all before even going to the moon," Sedge tells Neil. "You never seem to fear anything."

"I feared everything," Neil tells him; "just not as much as I was excited. You and I are a lot alike in this area."

"Thanks Neil," Sedge says. "That's the greatest compliment I've ever received."

Neil disappears and the room darkens. Seconds later, the lights come on but Neil is no longer there. The system has rebooted. Sedge runs to the closest communication terminal. Most of the precious little information from NASA transmissions he has thus far been able to garner has come in the wakes of reboots. He pulls up the screen. Sure enough, what appears to be a transmission from the Nina is coming in. He starts transferring the data to the ship's mainframe. Within seconds, the transfer abruptly stops. Among the transferred data, however, Sedge finds information on the bio-dome. Apparently, it was successfully deployed and done so to the location he had programed in the landers' coordinates, although he has no way of confirming the success of its deployment. Also transmitted is the security code for entering the dome, which Sedge had also already anticipated; five zeros. This is standard and widely known, just not by any alien races. Though the instructions in the transmission aren't news to Sedge, it's reassuring to receive them. Someone on Earth cared enough to inform him.

Also transmitted, Sedge finds an article from The Times written on December 13, 2124 entitled *Disgruntled Employee Takes Multi-Billion Dollar Ship on a Joy Ride*. It's the first news he's received since leaving Earth. He reads on:

Sedge Nile, communications specialist has stolen a ship from GulfStar Inc., the company for which he worked, a ship worth close to three and a half billion dollars. It appears that he has gotten away with both his crime and the ship. Timing his theft with the testing of Allied Forces ground-based Laser Propulsion System, Sedge managed to accelerate the stolen spacecraft to speeds beyond those reached by any human in history, though Allied Forces Ground Control was unable to ascertain the speed he was able to reach. One thing is for sure, he's gone and not coming back, at least not in the foreseeable future. Both GulfStar and Allied Forces Ground Control confirm that he did transmit a message just prior to his departure, but both claim the message is proprietary information and refuse to share it.

"He's on his way to the Centauri System," Mike Steed of NASA told us. "At least that's what his trajectory suggests. Hopefully he was able to get that ship going really fast, close to the speed of light, or he'll die enroute. We wish him the best."

"Thanks Mike, whoever you are," Sedge says aloud with a laugh. "I did manage to make it, at least that far."

Sedge begins to read another article, obviously singled out for him to see. This one is also from The Times; *NASA to Add Supplies to Cortes Mission for Joy Rider.* Sedge bursts into laughter with watering eyes as he reads the title.

"Joy Rider," he says. "Wow, I didn't even know I had a nickname."

It Reads:

"With speculative consensus betting on Luna Nuevo being Sedge Nile's destination, NASA has altered its original plans to supply the mission with only preliminary provisions, allowing more astronaut survival gear on board that was planned for later missions. This is being done out of compassion for Sedge Nile with the hope that he survives his ..." The transmission ends at that point.

"I'll just have to finish the article when I get to the bio-dome," Sedge says, talking to himself again. The transmission has given him a new sense of hope, knowing there are people back on Earth who care and are hoping he makes it. There are also, most likely, supplies awaiting him at the bio-dome if he can get to it. He looks out the window at the rotating moon aglow among the mighty rings of Aureola. It looks so peaceful. It's getting closer too, along with his moment of departure. The lights flicker again. Hopefully this ship holds together long enough for him to safely detach.

4:2

After taking a long look into the mirror, Sedge finishes fastening his extra-vehicular life support suit. He picks up the helmet and tests its lighting, then puts his gloves inside it. He smiles at himself in the mirror, looking like a real astronaut. It's his first time to ever wear the suit.

"T-minus twenty-five minutes to perigee," the ship's onboard system announces, set to warn every five minutes within the final hour.

Sedge walks down the ringway to the Holo and summons Neil one last time.

"How do I look?" he asks Neil.

"Like an astronaut," Neil answers.

"Thanks," Sedge tells him. "Do I look nervous?"

"Not particularly," Neil answers.

"Then I hide it well," Sedge tells him. "I'm sweating and shaking in my boots."

"Your course is plotted and programed. All you have to do is go for a ride," Neil tells him to calm his nerves.

"You always know just what to say," Sedge replies. "That's right, I'm just going for a ride."

"Frankly, I'm a little envious," Neil says. "There's a new world down there waiting to be explored, and it's all yours."

"I could wait one more orbit," Sedge responds.

"You'd be risking your life just to buy a few more hours," Neil replies. "This ship would be within its critical margin of error. It might survive one more lap, but it would be to a point where it also might not. Your window is now.'

"I think I'm getting sick to my stomach," Sedge tells Neil. "I don't have nerves of steel."

"It's probably the lack of sleep," Neil replies. "It will break you down. Soon you'll be in the bio-dome, getting a good night's sleep."

"A long night at that too," Sedge says. "That region is going to roll into darkness several hours after I touch down."

"That will give you ample time to rest," Neil tells him.

"I don't need to sleep for days," Sedge responds. "It will all be so new to me."

"That's the point, isn't it?" Neil asks rhetorically.

"I guess so," Sedge answers.

"Twenty minutes to perigee," comes over the central sound system.

"I'd better be on my way to my lander," Sedge tells Neil. "I need to run through my pre-flight checklist."

"Farewell Sedge, I'll be waiting for you in the bio-dome," Neil says.

"Farewell my friend," Sedge replies. "You've been a big help."

With nothing more to say, Sedge shuts down the holo-deck and slowly makes his way to the elevator. He takes one more, long look down the ringway before the doors to the elevator open. He gets in and lets it take him to the central tube. Using his arms to guide him, he drifts weightlessly down the tubular hallway to the ship's stern. Upon arriving, he drifts through the large landing ring to Lander Six, where he climbs into the lander and begins his pre-flight checklist. This close to perigee, from the lander, he has his clearest view yet of the red glowing atmosphere below, just before the ship glides out of Luna Nuevo's light-side view, entering the blackness of its far side. As the dark side comes into sight, Aureola's rings really stand out in the darkness, giving off just enough light to make out mountain ridges on Luna's otherwise lightless surface. He's so close, and yet so far.

"Ten minutes to perigee," the system announces.

Sedge can feel his heartrate increase and his sweat glands open. He hasn't been this nervous in a long time. He latches the hatch to his lander and turns on all control systems. All lights are green. He sees lights in the landing ring flicker again, but the lander remains steady; a good sign, another reminder that he needs to get off this sinking ship. He sees the engine on Lander One ignite as planned. It will be first to detach, followed by Two, Four, Five, then his, Seven, and finally Lander Eight, each timed one minute apart, leaving only crippled Lander Three.

"Five minutes to perigee," is heard as Lander One detaches and immediately begins to sink toward the dark moon. Sedge's engine fires. He puts on his helmet and fastens its ring-clip, then the gloves, and latches the safety straps to his seat harness. His hands begin to sweat and he starts to breathe heavily. Lander Two detaches and begins to sink, indicating three minutes to departure. He takes quick, deep breaths and stares at the fading light on Luna's horizon, trying to relax. It works for a few seconds. Lander Four detaches and begins to sink. Two minutes to go. So many thoughts begin to race across his mind, and so many questions. Did I pack everything I need? Lander Five detaches and sinks toward the surface.

"That was fast," he says out loud. "Damn, what have I done?" he questions.

"Prepare to detach," a calm, female voice says over Lander Six's interior system. Sedge can also hear it in his helmet com. "Detaching in ten, nine, eight, seven, six, five, four, three, two, one..."

Sedge initially feels his stomach drop with the vessel, then nothing as the deepliner rapidly rises above his head. All becomes so quiet and peaceful as the deepliner grows smaller and smaller. Aureola's rings stretch at a forty-five degree angle far beyond his field of vision, reaching into infinity. So many stars can be seen through the darkness, as well as the glow of the Milky Way. Sedge loses himself in the moment. He has re-entered Earth's atmosphere dozens of times, though never alone. He takes a really deep breath, forgetting about the imminent danger below. It's like Neil said, he's just along for the ride.

"This is Sedge Nile," he says into the lander's transmitter, knowing it's weak and extremely unlikely to be picked up. "Requesting landing on Luna's highlands, over." He laughs at himself, so alone but so alive, sinking into the great unknown.

"T plus five minutes into landing maneuver," the onboard system announces.

The first four landers remain in perfect formation in front of him. He turns on the rear-view cam and remotely tilts it slightly upward. There they are, landers Seven and Eight aligned perfectly. The scene is so serene, so placid. Sedge begins to laugh, overcome with bliss. All lights are green; all systems are go.

"Five minutes to atmospheric entry," comes over the sound system just as Sedge sees Lander One begin to glow from atmospheric drag. "Ground speed forty-seven point four thousand KPH."

"Oh shit," Sedge says aloud. "Here we go." He can hardly bear to watch. Within seconds, Lander Two begins to glow. The flames are clear and violent, but the landers in front of him look to be holding steady. He can see that Lander Two has closed some of the gap between it and Lander One. Suddenly Lander Four begins to glow so brightly and clearly, and finally Lander Five. Sedge knows he has one minute to entry. He takes one more look up to find the deepliner, but it's gone.

"T minus thirty seconds to atmospheric entry," another announcement warns. Sedge can see the moon's horizon growing wider. He tries to breathe deeply but finds himself again too nervous to relax.

"T minus ten, nine, eight, seven, six, five, four, three, two, one..." The window tints as it turns into a torch. The ship begins to vibrate violently. Sedge stares into the dancing flames, ignoring the vessel's shaking. His horizontal speed indicates he is now slowing, as hoped. The raging fire seems to go on and on, a steady reminder of how dangerous the universe is when you break its rules. Minutes seem like hours. The air conditioner powers up to mitigate the rising temperature in the cabin, which begins to shake more violently than before, causing Sedge to wonder if it can handle the heat. Is this thing going to burn up? He closes his eyes.

Suddenly, the shaking subsides considerably. Sedge opens his eyes to the sight of the first two landers. They have separated, no longer in such clear formation, an indication they have deviated from their courses during entry. They have survived nonetheless, as has Sedge. He laughs again, though still nervous as hell. Lander One's primary chute opens, causing it to slow. Within seconds, Lander Two's primary chute opens, followed by Lander Four, then Five. Sedge knows what's next and braces himself.

"Primary chute deployment in five, four, three, two, one," he hears just before his chute opens, causing him to slide firmly forward in his seat, held only by his safety belts. "Ground speed twenty-six point five thousand KPH and slowing," the onboard system says. Sedge can't see anything beneath him but darkness. Within seconds, however, the horizon appears far in front of the spacecraft, glowing red. The lander is traveling at a high speed toward Luna's light side; the dawn. It's beautiful to see Aureola's rings fade into its light.

Lander One deploys a secondary, larger chute. This two-stage parachute process is to avoid the neck-snapping danger of deploying the larger chute too early. Seconds later, Lander Two, and then Lander Four. It takes him a few seconds to find Lander Five, however, which has drifted well to his starboard side. There is no more visible formation. The landers are all on their own.

"Secondary chute in five, four, three, two, one," the system warns. Sedge feels the lander's sudden forward thrust from the abating of the primary chute's drag, only to be followed by a feeling of being slammed forward as the larger secondary chute deploys. "Ground speed twenty-one thousand KPH, tail wind detected at 47 KPH," something Sedge didn't want to hear.

Still ripping through the upper atmosphere, Sedge's lander enters Luna's twilight. He loses sight of Lander

One, and can still barely see Lander Four far off to his right. Lander Two remains on course in front of him. He can now see the terrain far below and just how fast he is still moving. His horizontal speed indicators suggest he's slowing, but hard to gage if the chute is getting the job done well enough to touch down. His altimeter is at seventy-six thousand meters and sinking, but its sea level is set to the average elevation of Luna's upper shelf. There's still no telling where he's going to land, or impact.

Then he sees it dead ahead; the Valles Grande canyon system, a sign that he's on course. He's not so sure about Landers One and Four though, or the ones behind him. Holy hell, he thinks, there it is. Its size is jaw-dropping, making the Grand Canyon look like a crack in the sidewalk. He's headed straight for it. If he is on course, the bio-dome should be on its far side, dead ahead. Sedge watches Lander Two glide over it. He stares at the high walls along the canyon edges. It's a vast area, stretching off to his port and starboard sides as far as he can see. He notices a continual reduction in speed as his lander begins to fly over the canyon.

"Hello Valles Grande," he yells, watching his horizontal speed decrease. He looks down through the vessel's front floorboard windows. He sees a multi-tiered system of canyon floors, with the deepest of them shroud in green vegetation. He sees sunlight reflect off lakes and what looks like a flowing river further down. The canyon's deepest sections are cloud covered, causing Sedge to smile widely. This moon has a water cycle.

"Horizontal speed, one thousand seven hundred seventy KPH," the computer warns. "Altimeter, twenty-two thousand six hundred meters. Approaching destination in seven hundred fifty-six kilometers."

Sedge studies the canyons as closely as he can, hoping to return with a quad-copter. He sees what he thinks to be a set of waterfalls, and what looks like caves in some of the walls. The far side is approaching fast. As he nears it, he notices an enormous impact crater on the far edge of the canyon valley, adjacent to the canyons, separated only by a tall, eroding, thin canyon wall. Damn, Sedge thinks, it's like the moon meets Mars. He's so excited to see solid ground beneath his feet, if only he can safely land on it.

"Destination two hundred ninety-six kilometers," the system warns. "Altimeter six thousand, two hundred twenty meters. Velocity one thousand, nine hundred KPH." The horizon is widening as sedge loses sight of Lander Two. He peels his eyes for the bio-dome as his lander nears the far side of the canyon system. Finally, he sees it coming up, sitting on the highland plain just beyond the canyon walls; a little geodesic dome, not far from the edge of the canyon.

"Destination thirty-six kilometers," the computer announces.

"Yes," Sedge yells.

"Altimeter three thousand, one hundred meters. Velocity four hundred twelve KPH."

Sedge watches the bio-dome increase in size. The lander seems to be pointed right at it. It gets closer and closer as the lander descends. Within seconds, however, the lander flies well over the dome.

"Slow down damn it!" Sedge yells.

"Velocity two hundred, seventy-two KPH," the computer says. "Altimeter, seven hundred meters. Releasing chute." The chute detaches from the lander as the ground moves swiftly below the craft. "Deploying retro-rockets." Sedge hears the rockets fire but doesn't feel much of an effect of slowing as the horizon rises.

"C'mon damn you," Sedge yells as the ground is rising. "Please, please slow down!"

"Velocity one hundred seventy two KPH," the computer warns. "Altimeter two hundred nineteen meters. Impact warning."

"Damn it, c'mon," Sedge yells, grabbing his armrests tightly.

"Velocity one hundred thirty-six KPH; altimeter seventy-nine meters. Prepare for impact," the computer warns as an impact warning light begins flashing.

"For God's sake, slow down," Sedge yells.

"Velocity ninety-nine KPH; altimeter twenty-two meters," sounds a final reading from the computer. "Prepare for impact."

"Shit," Sedge says to himself as he straightens up in his chair. He flips his armrests into their upright positions and puts his arms down by his sides. He can see the ground swiftly moving just beneath his feet in the floorboard window, much too fast.

"Warning," the onboard voice says. "Prepare for impact in five, four, three, two, one…"

4:3

It's a star, Sedge thinks, seeing the pinpoint light twinkle. No, it's getting closer. Why would a star be getting closer? His eyes close as he fades back into his subconscious mind. Am I alive? He wonders. His eyes open again. The light has grown brighter, more glaring. It's a tunnel, he thinks. I'm in a tunnel, but why? What happened? Where am I? He can't remember anything. The light is bouncing, dancing, and growing in brightness. He then remembers the fire. The flames were dancing. That's it, he thinks, I was in a fire. The fire was outside my window. Did I die in a fire? No, he remembers, it was a crash. I was in a... Suddenly, his short-term memory floods back into his brain. His eyes open wide as he gasps deeply for breath.

"I'm alive,' he says. He sees the light glaring off his helmet's visor; it's the sun, a new sun, Beta Centauri. "I'm alive," he yells; "ha-ha-ha-hahhhhh, I'm alive! Son of a bitch. I am ALIVE."

Slowly, he sits up to survey the scene. His legs are still entangled in deflated airbags. They must have worked. They had saved his life. He can hear a gust of wind whip through the broken clear shielding of the lander's flight-deck, or at least what's left of it. It's a ball, a sphere full of cracks and shards of polymer glass. The roll-cage worked, Sedge thinks to himself. It must have broken free on impact before rolling to a rest. The airbags must have kept him snug enough to absorb the impact, and packed tightly enough to keep his head from exploding from the centrifugal force of its roll.

"Houston," he says; "the eagle has landed."

Sedge unlatches his safety belts and frees himself from his seat. He has to slam on the side door of the roll-cage to get it to pop open. When it does, he gets his first ever look across the arid, red-rock landscape of Luna Nuevo's highland plains. The sky is bright with a hue at a perfect point between blue and purple, pierced only by a portion of Aureola and her rings just above the horizon. A second sun sits in the sky, just over the horizon; Alpha Centauri, just a few degrees lower and to the left of Beta Centauri. The land is so red. It's like a dream. He takes a little time, still letting oxygen reach his brain and the reality sink in. He's on the surface. He moves his arms around. Nothing seems to be broken. He begins to stand but abruptly stops to turn on his helmet cam to catch the historic moment.

"This is Sedge Nile," he announces as he prepares to stand. "I have just landed on Luna Nuevo, if you could call it a landing. Anyway, I am now stepping out of the lander." He looks down at the ground so his camera can capture his first step. With the aid of the door, he pulls his body out of the roll-cage. As he takes his first step onto the sandy ground, he speaks. "That's one small step for a man; one giant fuck my fucking back," he yells, grabbing the door to help him lean back against the lander. "Shit, this is bad," he says grimacing in severe pain, pressing both hands against his back. His fifth lumbar has failed him again. After a moment, he stands again, allowing it to stretch a little but being very careful not to twinge it. He's able to stand.

Where am I? He wonders. He looks at his wrist monitor but it's showing no signal from the Cortes' orbiter. He doesn't even know his coordinates. He surveys the ground. The roll-cage looks to be about a quarter of a kilometer from the rest of the lander wreckage. There doesn't look like there's much left of the lander. Debris is strewn in a straight line back to the lander. Sedge knows, that must be the direction in which he needs to go. The lander flew almost directly over the bio-dome. The dome must be that way. He finally takes that small step for a man but immediately feels a sharp pain shoot from his left hip to the center of his pelvis; the fifth lumbar. He takes another, then another and begins inching his way to the lander. Damn, he thinks, my back is really messed up this time. He remembers that he packed his last six pills of pethidine in the lander. He looks at his wrist monitor. His oxygen is at ninety-six percent. He has a backup pack in the lander, if it survived. He has no idea how far it is to the bio-dome, but he may very well need the extra oxygen, water, and whatever else he has packed in the lander. Each step he takes feels like a knife in the back left side of his pelvis, but he endures, step by step. Luna's nine percent stronger gravity isn't helping either.

It takes him twenty minutes to make it to the lander, though it feels like two hours. It's in pieces with parts and debris behind it, leading to a small crater obviously formed on impact. Wow, it's hard to believe he survived this, and in one piece. He finds his survival pack but has to really tug on it to release it from its pinched position inside what used to resemble a storage compartment, which causes him even more pain. His hands tremble in pain as he digs through the pack and finds the pethidine. Not since the first time he popped a pill on his way to this world has he been this justified in taking one. Besides, if he's going to die out here, he might as well go high. He checks his wrist monitor to make sure it's safe to take off his helmet. The atmosphere is safe, just much thinner.

He pulls off his helmet and tries to draw his first breath of air. The atmosphere feels cold and dry. He can hardly breathe. He quickly pops the pethidine pill with a swig from his hydration pack, puts his helmet back on for air, then leans back against the broken wreckage to rest.

I'm on Luna Nuevo, he thinks to himself. He stares around at the red rocks. The plain is completely barren, very Mars-like. The rocks look like iron-oxidized basalt, but what do I know, Sedge thinks. I'm a communications guy, not a geologist. Over the vast plain, he can begin to make out the curvature of Luna's surface, slightly smaller in size than Earth. He starts to laugh.

"I made it," he yells to himself. "Over four and a third light years from home. Ha-ha-hah! I made it."

Within minutes, the pain in his pelvis has eased. The pethidine is kicking in. Sedge reaches into the lander to pull out the quad-copter, nicely packed in its carry-case. "Oh hell no," he yells, feeling the pain as he tries to lift it. "I'll have to leave you for another day." The drone won't fly over the highlands anyway, not with the thin atmosphere and added weight. It should work, however, if he could ever get it to the collapsed shelves, to the canyons. His oxygen reads ninety-one percent. Feeling less pain, Sedge realizes he's going to run out of air if he can't get to the bio-dome. Still without a signal from the orbiter, he decides to go it on his own, without coordinates. He eyes a distant peak slightly to the left side of a direct line behind the lander's crash, a landmark he can use. It might not be that accurate, but it's a lot closer to the dome than this wreckage. Sedge grabs his survival pack, all he can manage to carry, thinking he'll make it back another time to retrieve the drone and whatever else he can salvage after he heals. With his new suns at his back, he sets off.

"The silk road," he says laughing to himself. "I'm Marco Polo. I'm Marco-fucking-Polo," he yells, walking slowly with a limp.

Walking presents a challenge. Not only does each step come with pain, the terrain seems either too soft, forcing Sedge to work harder to compensate for his feet sinking into the sand, or too rocky and jagged. The plain's rolling hills and endless impact craters, old and new, require further work to either climb over, through, or around. Ninety minutes in, he finally gets a signal from the Cortes Orbiter with coordinates of his current location as well as the bio-dome. He is still sixty-two kilometers away. "You have got to be kidding me," he yells into the sky. There are three signals mapped; Lunar One twenty kilometers north, Four twenty-nine kilometers northeast, and Seven a distant thirty-seven kilometers southeast. The others, including Sedge's have not been located by the orbiter. Sedge isn't able to gage how far he has already walked, but given his snail pace and the burdensome terrain, his best guess puts him at eight to ten kilometers. His heading is off but not by much. His oxygen, however, is down to seventy-nine percent. Fortunately, he's carrying a reserve tank in his survival pack, but may still be cutting it close. Feeling the greenhouse effect of the sun through his visor, he carries on.

Sedge encounters a huge crater. Its walls have eroded with wind and sand to the point that he thinks he can walk through it rather than around. He has to drop two meters, however into the crater to enter it, but should be able to walk all the way to the top of the opposite wall. The sand ramping up the walls looks soft. He sits on the crater's edge with his feet over the side for a moment, then slides off the wall into the sand beneath him. He sinks to his knees, loses balance, and begins tumbling down the embankment. Within seconds, he finds himself fifteen meters deep into the crater, in more pain than before. He rolls in the sand onto his feet, picks up his pack, and walks across the crater's basin. An eroded but massive conical shaped hill lies at the basin's center, at the point of impact. Sedge studies it closely as he walks by, wondering how long ago the impact occurred. Certainly, not a good place to be at the time, he thinks. Eventually, he reaches the crater's far side and works his way up the sandy ramp leading out. What a fascinating yet onerous task.

Sedge carries on for several hours, over hill, over dale, watching the suns slowly move toward the horizon and his oxygen deplete. Still high from the pethidine, he begins to feel the pain increase near the midpoint of his trek. Still days behind on sleep and no longer fueled by adrenaline, he feels himself weakening by the minute, both body and mind. In the middle of the red-rock terrain, he spots a large round, silver metallic boulder sitting in a smaller crater. Impact rays emanate in all directions from the crater, with one extending longer than all others. He can tell by the metallic boulder's texture that it has reached extremely high temperatures. He has discovered a meteorite. He veers off his path to take a little closer look at it. He stops to rest and take a drink of water on a red-rock shelf that overlooks another endless valley in front of him. His oxygen tank reads nine percent. He'll need to keep this pace, but should make it. He looks at the sun and the rings through the air. What a site. He feels too tired to carry on, but knows he can't stop here. His body aches.

Then he sees something afar in the cloudless sky; something moving. What could it be? Looking closer, he notices a green glow to it, then a tail behind it. It then disappears. It couldn't have been a lander. They're all down. It had to be a meteorite. Throughout his life, he has never seen one. How is it that he spots one here, on his first day on this moon? That can't be a good sign, he thinks. This moon may very well still be in its bombardment period. It is, after all, nestled into a ring system and pocked with craters. The level of Luna's meteorite activity remains unknown on Earth. There simply hasn't been time to study it. It's a risk Sedge hadn't anticipated and another reminder of how rash his decision was. This place seems so peaceful, but who knows the full extent of the dangers that lurk?

Sedge soon encounters another large crater, similar in size to the one through which he walked but deeper, with higher, more jagged walls. He sees no way in or out, forcing him to walk around it, adding three kilometers and twenty minutes to his journey. Just past it, his oxygen runs out. He stops to rest on a rock, still thirty-two kilometers from the dome. The suns are now slowly sinking just above the horizon behind him. He changes the tank, takes a drink from his now almost empty water bottle, and puts his helmet back on. Upon standing, his legs almost give out on him. He's exhausted. The pain has increased. He decides to double down on the pethidine. He sets his pack back down, finds the pill bottle and takes another tablet. He takes just a sip of water to wash it down, trying to conserve what little he has left. Hopefully the hydro-gills are functioning correctly at the dome. He's going to be thirsty when, or if, he arrives.

"I'm on my way Neil," he says to himself.

Ninety minutes later, the landscape turns to nothing but desert dunes. Sedge can't see beyond them. Each step takes the work of three, but there's no going around this land of sand. The wind has increased and the air is cloudy with dust. His oxygen reads seventy-four percent and his wrist computer indicates he's only nineteen kilometers away. He's come so far, but the pethidine is playing tricks on his mind. He sees water mirages and sometimes what looks like objects moving on the horizon. He's never crossed a desert and still unsure if this will be his first. Feeling short of breath, he stops to rest on the side of a dune for a minute, where he decides to slightly increase the flow of oxygen to his helmet. He lays on his back and looks up at the rings of Aureola, now starting to show clearer through a slightly darkening sky.

"What are you doing Sedge," Neil asks. Sedge opens his eyes to see Neil sitting next to him on the sand dune.

"I made it," Sedge says. "I crash-landed, but didn't die. I'm going to be alright."

"That's good to hear," Neil replies. "I'm pulling for you, you know."

"You've been with me all along," Sedge tells him. "I don't think I could have made it without you."

"I appreciate that," Neil says; "but are you sure?"

"Of course," Sedge answers. "Why wouldn't I be sure?" he asks. Neil remains silent. "Do you doubt me?" Sedge continues to ask.

"Are you sure?" Neil asks again.

"Of course I'm sure," Sedge answers. "I don't get why.... Wait a minute, you're trying to tell me something. There's no holo-deck on this sand dune."

Sedge opens his eyes to find himself alone under a much darker sky. The suns are well behind the horizon and stars are coming out. He looks at his oxygen level; thirty-seven percent with twenty-four kilometers to the bio-dome. Thirsty, he drinks the final few swallows of water in his bottle. Exhaustion, pethidine, and the increased oxygen flow had caused him to slip into a dangerous sleep, and most likely induced the dream. Had Neil just saved his life? He gets up, not only feeling muscle stiffness in addition to hip and back pain, but also a life or death shot of adrenaline. He's got to get to the dome, now in the darkness. He starts walking again, picking up where he left off.

It takes him almost another hour to get beyond the dunes. With his helmet lights being the only artificial light he has, he has a hard time with his footing. The ground is dark, rocky, and difficult to navigate. Fortunately, a portion of Aureola and her rings are still out, adding a little illumination to the ground.

Sedge comes to what appear to be ancient, dried river beds, a sign that he may be nearing the canyons. He follows one leading in his intended direction. The ground is harder with more fine gravel than sand, making it much easier to walk. He looks up at the endless stars as he walks. He stops for a second to marvel. He's never stood beneath so many. Maybe it's Luna's lack of light pollution, he thinks. He sees the three sisters in Orion's belt, then finds Betelgeuse burning brightly above them. It's hard to believe he had spent over five years traveling at a speed nearing that of light, only to end up getting nowhere according to the night sky. He's looking at essentially the same sky as he did growing up on Earth.

Sedge presses on, working his way through river beds. His elevation seems to be lowering. Looking down, he comes up on a small desert plant. "Hey little guy," he says to the dry weed-like plant. It's the first life-form he has encountered, and a sign he's getting closer to the canyons. His fatigue and pain are immense, but his excitement is growing. Unfortunately, his oxygen is now down to sixteen percent with thirteen kilometers left to the dome.

He encounters more desert plants as the river beds become shallow canyons. Looking up, he sees a satellite steadily cross the sky; the Cortes Orbiter. He's never felt such a unique combination of extreme sensations; pain, fatigue, excitement, wonder, fear, and solitude. His legs feel like they've been cut-off of their oxygen. He needs to rest but can't. His oxygen is now down to eight percent with only four kilometers to the dome. He seems to be burning oxygen at a rate of one percent per kilometer. God help him if the dome has failed to prepare any, or if anything prevents him from accessing it. His only hope then would be to try to descend into deep, dark, dangerous canyons with very little light and air to get him there. Knowing he wouldn't make it, he avoids the thought.

As luck would have it, he encounters another large crater, now within three kilometers of the dome. He finds a break in its edge where he can access it and makes his way to its basin, unable to see the far side or know if he'll be able to climb out of it. Fortune smiles on him as he finds a small canyon system leading out of the crater's far side in the direction he's traveling. He stays within the small canyon, looking up at the now incredibly endless field of stars above his head. The canyon walls occlude the glowing ground, really bringing the dark night sky into view. What an adventure, Sedge thinks as the canyon grows yet deeper. Wondering if he'll be able to climb out of it, he allows it to lead him further in the direction of the dome. His oxygen reads five percent.

His coordinates put him at one point two kilometers from his target. He tries to stay calm to conserve oxygen.

Half a kilometer further into the canyon, Sedge finds a passageway out of the canyon, which should be on the same side as the dome. He decides to take it, knowing it could be his only hope of getting out. It takes him to within a meter of the wall's top, then stops. Weakened and in pain, he pulls himself to the top of the crevice wall and rolls over, away from the small cliff. Weary, he stands, turns around, and there it is. Way off in the distance, he sees a blue light. He begins to laugh as he walks toward what must be the only light on this moon. Soon, the spherical structure comes into view.

"In Xanadu did Kublai Khan a pleasure dome decree," he says to himself as he nears the bio-dome. "Marco is home, baby."

Arriving at the dome with three percent oxygen, Sedge enters the series of zeros on the access pad. A green access light blinks. "Ah hah!" Sedge yells, eyes now watering. He enters the dome. He has to clear an airlock to enter the main area. There is no air. With his suit's oxygen still at three percent, he finds the ozone controller inside the dome. Its oxygen supply is full. He activates its flow. Generators fire up and the room immediately begins filling with air. The system is designed to handle just this scenario, and begins to flood the room quickly. He finds the lighting controls and turns lights on within the dome. Within five minutes, the air-flow turns to a low flow. The atmosphere indicator turns green. The room is livable. Sedge takes his helmet off and sets the thermostat to twenty-two degrees Celsius. He locates the water tap and fills his bottle, then guzzles it completely dry without pause, water pulled from Luna's upper atmosphere.

"Welcome to the Luna Nuevo Bio Inn," he says looking around the place. It's hard to believe how well robotics already have this place so well assembled. There are a series of smaller domes connected to the main dome. Sedge begins to explore them. He finds one with a communication station and a set of comfortable foam beds. This will be my room, he thinks, now selfishly hoping nobody ever shows up to share the place. He throws his pack on the floor and sits on one of the beds. A bed has never felt so good. Wanting so badly to further explore the dome, he decides to first rest a few minutes. He lies back on the bed smiling wide.

4:4

"You've been charged with the sabotage of a major public safety system, the endangerment of the public, and the theft of a multi-billion dollar spacecraft," the judge's voice is heard saying over an echoing microphone. The room is dark and the judge sits behind blinding lights that conceal her face.

"I didn't sabotage any systems, nor did I put anyone other than myself in danger," Sedge replies.

"Enough," the judge says. "Lying to this court will not help you."

"I'm not lying," Sedge replies. "Sure, I took the ship, but I didn't endanger anyone."

"Can you present any evidence to demonstrate your innocence?" the judge asks.

"What kind of evidence am I supposed to have?" Sedge asks in return. "That's absurd. Of course I don't have any evidence. Can you show any evidence I endangered lives?"

"Do you have any witnesses?' the judge asks.

"That's ridiculous," Sedge answers. "Witnesses to what? What are you even doing here?" he asks. "Aren't you out of your jurisdiction?"

Sedge opens his eyes to a dark room, awakened by his dream and a fierce windstorm. The walls of the dome tremble. It takes him a second to realize where he is. He looks around the room and sees an android sitting on a chair across from his bed, looking at him.

"Who are you and what do you want?" Sedge asks.

"Welcome to Luna Nuevo Sedge," the android answers in a semi-mechanical, masculine voice. "I've been hoping you would arrive. I'd love to introduce myself, but I don't have a name. I am waiting for you to give me one."

"How about bite me," Sedge tells the android. "I don't like you watching me sleep."

"*Bite Me* it is," the android answers; "or *Bite* for short if you wish. I have noted that I am not to watch you sleep. I am available to answer questions and assist you in any way that I can."

"Unless I tell you to enter, can you please stay out of this room?" Sedge requests.

"Noted," Bite answers. "Is this the room you consider to be your room?" the android asks.

"Yes," Sedge replies.

"Then I will leave," Bite replies.

"Wait," Sedge says. "Do you know how long I've been sleeping?"

"Eleven Earth hours," Bite replies.

"Eleven hours," Sedge responds surprised. "Are these windstorms common?" he asks.

"Yes, fairly," Bite responds; "more so on the highlands than in the Canyons."

"Do you have any female voice options?" Sedge asks.

"Yes, just stop me when you hear one that you like," Bite answers, shifting through multiple human voice samples.

"Go back to the one used on the word *hear*," Sedge requests.

"How does this voice sound?" Bite asks in a soft, woman's voice.

"Pleasing," Sedge answers; "much less mechanical."

"Very well then," Bite responds. "I'll get out of your room. If you need me, I'll be working in the greenhouse."

"Thank you," Sedge responds as Bite leaves the room.

Sedge is accustomed to working with androids at GulfStar, on various mechanical tasks. This one seems far more advanced. Though not very attractive physically, at least not this one, androids can be highly helpful. This one must have done the work around here. Feeling guilty for getting off on the wrong foot, Sedge now looks forward to finding the various ways Bite can be of assistance.

Sedge looks out a small window in his room to see darkness, to hear the wind howl like a ghost. He's again subject to weather, and violent weather on his first night is eerie. He searches comm stations, sifting through four-and-a-half-year-old information. It's all news to him. Happy to again be able to receive transmissions, he spends the next few hours catching up on old news. Still, the man has no idea of current events, who the president is, or even if Earth exists for that matter. It could have been taken out four years ago by a rogue planet and Sedge wouldn't have a clue. This is a price you pay to live on Luna Nuevo in the twenty-second century.

Once his need for news is satiated, Sedge goes into the dome's main area.

"Bite, I apologize for being a little testy with you earlier," he tells her.

"Please Sedge," Bite replies. "There's no need to apologize. You'll find that I'm pretty thick-skinned."

"Would you mind giving me a tour of this place?" Sedge asks.

"It would be my pleasure," Bite responds. "What would you like to see first?"

"How about your garden?" Sedge suggests.

"Come this way," Bite tells him.

They enter the greenhouse through a connected tube-way. Upon entering, Sedge is pleasantly surprised to find rows of sprouting cucumbers, tomatoes, carrots, peas, green beans, and various kinds of lettuce, all still in infancy but appearing to be very healthy.

"How long have these vegetables been growing?" Sedge asks.

"Just over six weeks," Bite answers.

"Impressive," Sedge tells her.

"Thank you," she replies. "I'm growing potatoes too, you just can't see them yet. All using Luna Nuevo's iron-rich soil."

"I look forward to trying them," Sedge says.

Bite shows him a kitchen area, equipped with a fridge, freezer, microwave, toaster, coffee maker, and sink with running water.

"Do we have coffee?" Sedge asks.

"Some, but we also have beans to plant more," Bite answers. "I haven't grown any yet because I didn't know if you were a coffee drinker or not."

"I don't have a daily habit of it," Sedge answers; "but I enjoy an occasional cup. I'm more of a tea drinker actually."

"Noted," Bite tells him.

She shows Sedge a small chemistry lab for testing Luna's plant samples, letting him know that she has been programed with the knowledge to advise if anything he finds on the moon is poisonous, or potentially edible.

Sedge asks about a washroom. Bite takes him to a restroom with a deep-basined Jacuzzi, a shower stall, and a toilet with a built in bidet. Next to it, there is a small utility room with a washer and dryer.

"These amenities are all heated and powered through a combination of our external solar cells and two wind-powered turbines here, just outside the dome," Bite says, pointing to a small window.

"They sure predicted the wind correctly," Sedge says laughing.

"The sunlight too," Bite tells him. "We haven't had much cloud cover here since I've arrived. There have only been a few mornings where clouds have risen above the canyon walls, and each time they burned off early in the day."

Bite shows Sedge the resource panel. It shows both wind and solar power at full capacity. Water, however, is only at thirty-one percent.

"Why is water so low?" Sedge asks.

"It's drawn from the air through the hydro-gills," Bite answers. "The air is simply too thin at this elevation for them to fill quickly."

"That may become a serious issue if we can't secure another source," Sedge tells her. "Still, I'd really like to grab a shower," he says. "Would you please excuse me?"

"Absolutely," Bite says. "You'll find clean towels on the counter next to the shower."

"Thank you," Sedge replies.

Sedge takes a long shower, noticing how the water slides off his skin and into the drain a little faster with the increased gravity. It feels so good. His back loosens up under the hot water. He sings another song he wrote on his way to this distant moon. He finally gets out before waterlogging and dries himself.

"Bite," he yells to get the android's attention. "Most of the things I packed are strewn all over the highlands, in different locations, and over fifty kilometers away. I only have the clothes I was wearing when I showed up. I don't suppose there is anything fresh to wear?" he asks.

"There are some duffle bags NASA has prepared for you," she answers; "with clothing, medicines, toiletries, and a few specialty food and beverage items. They are in the storage room next to the kitchen."

Sedge goes into the storage room, where he finds four hockey-sized duffle bags with his name on the ID inserts. He first opens the one labeled clothing to find ten four-packs of underwear, five pairs of athletic pants and shirts, five pairs of jeans, ten three-packs of t-shirts in various colors, bags of socks, two pairs of sneakers, two pairs of waterproof boots, a compact down vest, two compact down coats, a rain poncho, two pairs of gloves, and two knit caps all tightly packaged into the bag. He has to hold back tears, tickled that there are people back on Earth helping him survive despite his selfish acts. How could he have grown so angry at that world?

He opens another bag full of toothpaste, soap, shampoo, shaving cream, an electric razor with thirty packs of blades, razors, and all kinds of toiletries. A short hand-written note inside reads, "we are transmitting information on how to make many of these items from raw materials provided on Luna Nuevo, as well as 3-D print other items you may need." For Sedge, this is better than any Christmas.

The third bag is full of specialty food and beverage items. He finds beef jerky, cashews, macadamias, chocolate, and rare canned goods. He also finds alcohol; ten liters of whiskey in polyester film bags, ten liters of cabernet, and ten liters of chardonnay.

"Oh sweet nectar of the gods," Sedge says. "It's been too long."

In the final bag, he finds a first aid kit, extra bandages, gauze, wraps, cotton swabs, and all kinds of medicines. Included with the medicines, Sedge finds two bottles of pethidine. NASA obviously doesn't know his history with it. It has as much potential to kill him as to save his life, especially with alcohol now in the mix.

Sedge gets dressed in some of his new threads and brushes his teeth, feeling more refreshed than he has in years, still acclimating to his new world. He looks out the window. The wind has calmed somewhat but the night remains so dark, so deep.

"How many more hours until dawn?" he asks Bite.

"Forty-three hours and thirty-seven minutes," Bite answers.

"You have got to be kidding me," Sedge replies. "This is the longest night of my life."

"You'll grow accustomed to it," Bite tells him. "It's gotta be brighter than interstellar space. Besides, we can adjust the lighting any way you like to help."

"Have you installed the holo-deck yet?" Sedge asks.

"Yes, in the main room," Bite replies.

Sedge finds it and turns it on. He looks up the call numbers for Neil Armstrong and enters them into the control panel. Neil appears.

"Hello, I'm Neil Armstrong," he says to Sedge.

"I know who you are," Sedge answers. "Don't you know me?" he asks.

"I don't recall meeting," Neil says. "Why don't you refresh my memory?"

"I relayed the data from the ship before I left the deepliner," Sedge says to Bite. "Why hasn't it transferred?" he asks her.

"You may have to upload it from your account," she answers.

Sedge goes into his room and gets on the comm station. He signs onto his account. His messages indicate that they've been relayed back toward Earth, but not yet uploaded into the local mainframe. He begins to do so, but has to wait several minutes for the upload to finish. It finally does, giving Sedge access to everything he recorded on his way here – his full journals.

He returns to the holo-deck.

"Well hello Sedge," Neil says. "I see you made it to the bio-dome."

"That's more like it," Sedge says. "Yes Neil, I'm alive and well. It's good to see you."

"It's good to see you too," Neil replies. "How was your trip down?"

"It was hell," Sedge answers. "I almost died. Say, you don't recall meeting me in the desert, do you?" Sedge asks.

"In the desert?" Neil asks in return.

"Never mind," Sedge replies. "We've got to have a party, pick up where we left off the night the ship first encountered trouble."

"Say, now that's a good idea," Neil tells him. "We'll celebrate your arrival to this new world. I can't think of a better reason to toast."

"I've made history Neil," Sedge says; "and I have you to thank." Neil smiles, saying nothing.

Sedge signs off in a state of euphoric bliss. Feeling bored, he goes back into his room and sits at his communication terminal, where he records his first transmission back to Earth from the bio-dome.

"This is Sedge Nile reporting from the bio-dome. That's right, if you haven't already received my landing signals, I made it. I am alive and well, minus a stiff back. I am also well rested. I planned to send this message hours ago, but fell deeply asleep just after my arrival. I have explored the dome and am impressed. Thank you from the deepest depths of my heart for the supplies you have provided me. I can't begin to tell you how much they mean to me. I don't know if anything I packed from the deepliner survived entry. The landers are down but in different locations, all at least fifty kilometers from here, and if mine was any indication of their conditions, they're not in good shape. I may attempt future salvage trips when I feel stronger, but such missions are risky given the landers' locations and the lack of oxygen on the highlands. My journey to this dome, however, was scenic beyond belief.

"Though I have proven humans can survive travel to this moon, understand that I am very lucky to be alive. I know the Cortes Lander's entry involves a neck-snapping parachute deceleration that only machines are sure to survive. I did wake to a violent wind storm that if accurately predicted, may have been used as a counter-force for slowing upon atmospheric entry once weather is better known. By now, you guys probably understand weather patterns on this moon better than I do, but I would highly recommend installing a ground-based laser system here before attempting to land anyone else. I am available to help in any way that I can.

"I don't know how conducive Luna Nuevo is to the support of human life, but I'm anxious to find out. I arrived at the dome a few hours after nightfall and haven't had the opportunity to explore the vicinity. The highlands seem to provide ample resources, barring water. The hydro-gills don't appear to be drawing as much as anticipated, but I'm sure you guys have already seen the data. Upon entry, I was able to observe what appeared to be lakes and a river system deep within the canyons. I plan to set up rain traps as soon as I find opportune locations. I am very anxious to get down into the deep valleys, canyons, and onto the collapsed shelves. I will of course keep you posted.

"Thank you again for the provisions and all your help, including the android. I have a renewed sense of hope and feel like I have a real chance to survive here."

Sedge refills his depleted, portable oxygen tanks using the dome's central supply. He puts on his new down coat, hat and gloves, grabs a flashlight and an oxygen tank, and heads out into the endless night to have a look around the area. Once outside, he looks up at the deep sky full of stars, still amazed to find his feet on solid ground. He walks around the dome to have a look at the wind turbines and power cells. The wind is now much calmer but still moving the turbines steadily. He walks further, hoping to get a night view of Valles Grande. As he nears the canyon's edge, he slows his pace, making sure the canyon doesn't claim him on his first night on Luna. The desert sky is clear. All dust seems to have settled. He gets to what appears to be a sharp drop-off, unable to see anything beyond it. He feels a sense of dizziness as his vertigo kicks in, so he sits on a rock beside the canyon's edge.

Looking north over the dark, black canyon, Sedge notices a glow on the horizon. It begins to grow in surges, shifting from green to blue. Soon it starts to dance, moving like a flowing wave. It is Luna Nuevo's northern aurora, something Sedge knew about but never imagined he'd be able to see this far south. The bio-dome is not too far from Luna's equator. It must be the smaller curvature, or possibly stronger auroras. There remains so much unknown about this world, reminding Sedge of the importance of this journey. He scans the sky and finds what he believes to be Sol, Earth's star. It looks so small and insignificant from his new vantage point in the heavens, yet so clear, like you could reach out and touch it. To think, it took him over five years to travel from there to here, and all he has done is connect two little dots out of hundreds of billions, in one of over a hundred billion galaxies. Sedge sits under the stars for a few hours, gazing up at the sky, the aurora, and the rings of Aureola. What a view. This is my place in the universe, he thinks to himself. This is where I truly belong.

Upon finally returning to the dome, Sedge tells Bite that he wants to lie down again, but to prepare for a party after he awakens. What better cause to celebrate than his arrival on his first night on Luna Nuevo? Now tired again, feeling travel lagged, he turns off the lights and lies down on his new bed, in his new world.

Sedge awakens a few hours later, turns on his comm station and watches the first round of bobsledding in the 2126 Winter Olympic Games, almost four and a half years late but again new to him. He then spends a few hours reading news. With his new appreciation of information, to which he's been denied access for years, he's turning into a news junkie. After finally getting his fix, he goes into the main dome area and turns on the holo-deck. He summons Neil Armstrong.

"How are you Sedge?" Neil asks.

"Great, but anxious for morning," Sedge answers.

"Patience," Neil replies. "You're well into the latter half of the night."

"Bite, can you bring me a glass of cabernet?" Sedge asks. "It's time to let the party begin."

"One cabernet coming up," Bite answers.

When Bite returns with his drink, Sedge asks her to join. The more the merrier. Sedge takes his first sip of alcohol in over five years. A thousand memories cross his mind, all triggered by the taste of wine, a taste he'd all but forgotten. It doesn't take him long to finish his first glass. Feeling grateful to Bite, he fetches his own refill. He goes through holo-deck characters to see who else he can invite to his arrival party. The assortment of names is not as extensive as GulfStar's system, and more catered to education than entertainment, but Sedge manages to find an entertaining guest list just the same. Soon, laser projectors are at capacity as Marilyn Monroe dances on stage with Elvis singing Burning Love. Marco Polo argues politics with Thomas Jefferson while Galileo stands listening.   All three drink laser-generated mead. Sedge chats with Neil.

"You really know how to throw a party Sedge," Neil says.

"Thanks," Sedge replies. "Hopefully this one won't be interrupted with a calamity."

"You redirected that last misfortune toward success," Neil tells him.

"I'm glad I did too," Sedge says. "Had fate allowed me to follow through with my original plan, I'd be orbiting this moon right now, wondering if I'd ever survive entry. Now entry is behind me. Nothing ahead but lavender skies."

"Congratulations," Neil says raising his glass.

"Everybody, please listen," Sedge says between songs, now with a buzz on. "I'd like to propose a toast. Welcome all to the new world." They all raise their glasses. "Or should I say the newest world," Sedge adds, thinking of his distinguished, well-traveled guests. "We stand on the most distant land ever reached."

Sedge finishes his second glass, then goes into the kitchen to pour a third, moving pretty fast through the supply.

"We may run into an issue with this," he tells Bite as he returns to his guests. "There is only so much party fuel in the tanks. I don't suppose we have any yeast."

"We have bread yeast," Bite replies; "but no brewer's yeast."

"Bread yeast will ferment drinks," Sedge says in thought. "How much bread yeast do we have?" he asks.

"A limited supply," Bite answers; "but yeast can be cultured from yeast."

"I like how your mind works," Sedge says with a warm smile. "Robinson Crusoe is learning much from you. Say," he adds; "that's who we need to invite next time."

"It's unknown if he was even real," Neil points out.

"It's unknown if any of us are real," Sedge replies.

The party rages on for hours. The drinks flow, though Sedge is the only one truly draining the reserves. Finally, in a heavily intoxicated frame of mind, Sedge hatches a bad idea.

"Hey," he announces. "I know how to really get this party going."

"Oh yeah," Neil responds skeptically.

"Pethidine," Sedge says.

"I don't think that's such a good idea," Neil tells him. "You've had quite a bit to drink tonight and I don't think an opiate will mix well."

"Oh, relax," Sedge tells him. "This is the most special occasion of my life. We're on Luna Nuevo my friend. Besides, I've got a few pills left over from the ship. I don't even have to tap the dome's supply."

"That's not really a rationale for taking such a powerful narcotic," Neil says, watching out for his friend.

"I appreciate your concern Neil, but I know exactly, exactly what I'm doing," Sedge tells him, slightly slurring his speech.

Sedge goes into his room and digs through his pack to find the pethidine. He takes one of the final tablets from the pill bottle and washes it down with wine...

4:5

Sedge wakes up in the dark, stark naked with a splitting headache. His mouth is dry and his eyes are watering to the point of tears. He feels worse than when he crashed the lander. His back, however, seems to be on the mend. Sharp pain from dried mucus makes his eyes tear when he rubs them. It takes them a few minutes to adapt to the room's low light. He looks around the room but can't find where he left his clothes. He walks into the main dome, where his party guests all sit silently, doing nothing. Sedge turns the holo-deck off, finally declaring the party over. He sees his clothes strewn where the laser stage had been. He grabs his underwear, pants, and shirt and puts them on. Bite enters the room.

"Bite, what happened last night?" Sedge asks.

"Don't you remember?" she asks.

"I remember Elvis singing and the guests having a good time," Sedge answers; "then waking up on my bed without any clothes on. What is it with my clothes?" He scratches his head and back.

"You removed them while dancing," Bite answers. "You were challenging Voltaire to do the same, telling him it would free his mind."

"That doesn't ring a bell," Sedge replies.

"Do you remember disagreeing with Neil Armstrong?" Bite asks.

"What would I disagree with Neil about?" Sedge asks in return.

"Love," Bite answers.

"Really," Sedge responds. "In what way did we differ?"

"Neil mentioned his failed marriage," Bite says. "You didn't see it that way. Your point was that love is a complex bio-chemical bond that's strength should not be limited to the metric of time. Your point was that simply because a bond ends, doesn't mean that it wasn't strong, or had failed."

"That sounds like something I'd say," Sedge replies.

"It seemed to lift Neil's spirits actually," Bite tells him. "Then you carried on about Maslow's hierarchy of needs and how you had found the highest level of love, which you claimed are the higher faculties and pleasures of insatiable intellectual curiosities. You argued that such love is much greater than romantic, animal love."

"I don't recall," Sedge replies. "I'm drawing a blank. That all sounds like me though, except the naked dancing. It's been a long time since I've had any alcohol and I tend to make bad decisions when I drink."

"Were you drinking when you decided to take the spacecraft?" Bite asks, surprising Sedge with her curiosity.

"No," Sedge answers. "That was a rash but rational decision on my part. One I don't regret either. Taking pethidine last night, however, I do regret."

"The dosage instructions explicitly state that it should not be mixed with alcohol," Bite reminds him. "It could be lethal."

"I know Bite," Sedge answers. "I guess I just got too excited last night."

"And lucky," Bite tells him. "Drug abuse has reappeared throughout history, often among world leaders and explorers," Bite tells him. "It could be that the same thrill-seeking tendency that led you to this distant moon is also what fuels your narcotic curiosities."

"It could be," Sedge says; "or just that I like pethidine too much."

"Well congratulations on making it through your first night on Luna Nuevo," Bite tells him. "We're only about six hours from dawn."

"I don't know if I would really call this making it," Sedge replies; "but thank you."

He goes into the kitchen and fills his drink bottle with water. He drinks it all and fills it again. He drains his bladder in the washroom, grabs the water and returns to his room.

The excitement of the dawning of his first day on Luna helps burn off his hangover. This could be the most important day of his life; the first day anyone has set foot on the lower shelf. That is, of course, if he can find a way into the canyons. Thus far, he's seen only high, vertical walls. He takes an ibuprofen for his headache, then kicks back in his room to watch the second round of the 2126 Winter Games' bobsled, pondering time. In the time it took for this Olympic games feed to reach him, another winter Olympics has transpired and has already been transmitted to him; information most likely still making its way through the Oort Cloud.

Wide awake and anxious to see the suns, Sedge turns on a holographic projection of Valles Grande, based on orbital scans from the Cortes. It is lacking in some detail but may help him find a way into the vast canyon system. He notices arches in the eroding rock, reminding him of a trip he took with college friends to the Grand Canyon, driving through Wyoming and Southern Utah. He sees a coulee about four kilometers south of the dome that looks like a potential path into the canyons, at least to the next tier. Now more excited than ever, he wraps his waist for back support, then packs a bag with rice, bread, and water. His hangover has left him too nauseous to eat, but that will change. He may be gone for a long time. He packs a mapping scanner, oxygen, specimen bags for any samples, and his wrist computer to geo-mark his path. Ready to go, he watches the first two periods of a Russia vs. Sweden hockey game, eagerly awaiting dawn. During the second intermission, he notices the room getting its first phase of twilight as light from Beta Centauri begins to shed.

Not waiting for his new suns to crack the horizon, Sedge puts on his oxygen mask and sets out, now having enough natural light to guide him along the edge of the mighty Valles Grande. A shot of adrenaline drains down his spine as he takes a look at the high cliff walls just beyond where he sat in the dark hours earlier. He heads south, looking for the passage. How exciting, his first morning on Luna Nuevo. The long night was harder than expected. He thought his time on the ship would be similar, but it wasn't. He would have to find ways to cope, ways that hopefully don't require self-medication. Now he has a new issue, having to contend with the endless day. Sleep will obviously be required at some point. Would he ever adapt?

Beta Centauri breaks from behind distant hills on the horizon, taking the morning from a deep to a light purple just as Sedge reaches the coulee from the hologram. It looks much steeper in real life. There's an arch under which he'll have to climb, like a portal into another land. Through the arch, he can see green vegetation deep below, way down in the valley. Surely there must be breathable air down there. It looks so lush.

"There they are," Sedge says; "streams of wine, milk and honey."

Sedge carefully begins to descend into the coulee, one rock at a time, through the arch and into the canyon. The last thing he can afford is to fall and break a bone. There is no search and rescue here, only himself. He is careful not to jump off of anything that he cannot climb back out of, keeping in mind that he has to return. He can bring rope ladders on his next trip, whenever he returns, for the most difficult spots.

It takes him over two hours to reach the next tier down, a well-defined ledge obviously created millions of years ago, if not hundreds of millions of years. It's difficult for Sedge to know given that yearly cycles on Luna have different durations. It's amazing, however, how similar to Earth the upper canyon appears. Sedge rests on a rock still high up on the canyon wall, taking time to catch his breath and take in the view. He checks his computer. He has descended four hundred and eighty-four meters. From his new level, he begins to see the deep forested basin more clearly, still so far below. The trees are different than any he's ever seen, yet still too distant to clearly make out. The air is cool, almost cold and the sunlight is still far from reaching the canyon.

Sedge takes off his oxygen mask and draws a breath. He can breathe better but not well and soon runs out of breath. He puts it back on, gets up, and walks along the ledge to find passage further down. Before long, he comes to another coulee that looks passable. He begins his second stage of descent. Twenty meters down, however, he realizes there is nothing but vertical cliff wall beneath him. He spots another possible passageway but has to climb all the way up the coulee to the tier to reach it. It's a huge setback but one he'll be able to avoid next time – a lesson learned. Climbing back out gives him a good idea just how hard getting out of this canyon will be. When he reaches the tier, he's hit with a sudden sense of nausea. He barely gets his mask off in time to throw up. He feels a lot better when finished, except for the taste of regurgitated cabernet in his nose. Excessive drinking and rock climbing don't mix, he tells himself.

He takes a drink of water to kill the taste, spits, then makes his way toward the passage he spotted earlier. It is much easier than the first. It takes him ninety minutes, but he finds himself now over a thousand meters deep into the canyon, where he comes up on another ledge. He wonders what cataclysmic events separated these ledges from the other layers within the rocks. He videos them closely for geologists on Earth to see. The stone is changing color and becoming more compact than the bright red sandstone near the canyon rim. Descending into this canyon is like going back in time. Vegetation is now beginning to appear, especially in the coulees. His computer shows a green light on its atmospheric indicator. Sedge removes his oxygen mask to find that he can breathe the air.

"Yes," he yells. "I can breathe." The air at this level is dense enough to survive.

Fortunately, his new tier slants like a ramp downward, making the next stage of his descent considerably easier than the last two. He continues deeper into the canyon, eventually encountering trees unlike any on Earth. Their bark is very white and they are full of huge, lime green, spade-shaped leaves. There are more of them the further down Sedge goes. The natural pathway of the tier eventually comes to a rocky end. Fortunately, however, Sedge finds a dry stream bed that winds further downward, almost like a trail into the canyon. The walls are less steep too, making the journey much safer and more bearable. Thirteen hundred meters down, Sedge comes up on a waterfall coming out of the side of a rock wall, flowing downward into thick fern-like plants. He follows an adjacent dry stream bed until he comes to a cliff overlooking the valley basin. Sedge is awe-stricken, now able to clearly see the massive forest that fills the canyon's basin.

"It's the enchanted chasm," Sedge says to himself. "What riches lie here?"

The dry stream bed soon meets a flowing one. The water looks crystal clear. Not wanting to lug anything deeper, Sedge decides to wait until his return to the dome to gather samples. He follows the stream further down, deeper into the canyon. The terrain is no longer very steep at all, much easier to navigate, except for a few patches of thick vegetation. The spade trees have thinned as Sedge follows the growing stream into a large, green meadow of ferns, still losing elevation. There, he finds yet another kind of tree; a tree bearing bright blue fruit. The trees are low to the ground with bushy green leaves. Their fruit is shaped like fat bananas with a rounder bend. Further down, the stream meets another as the flowing water increases in volume. It's beautiful beyond compare. Before long, Sedge comes across a field of tall, purple flowers. As he walks along the field's edge, the faces of the flowers turn, as if they're watching him walk by. He avoids getting too close to any of them out of fear. This place may not have any animal life, but who knows the extent of the consciousness that resides in these plants, or their natural defense systems? It's nothing to take for granted, especially without further study.

At a depth of nineteen hundred meters, Sedge finally reaches the great forest below. The trees are neither leafy nor needled, but something else. Their trunks begin to take an inverted cone shape roughly halfway up their heights. Their branches do the same, extending upward at angles from the trees' main trunks. Their bark is thick and red with a large cell-like texture, forming a unique pattern unseen on Earth. They rise high into the air, most reaching at least seventy meters. Their trunks are massive, especially the deeper into the forest, some reaching fifteen meters in diameter.

Now several hours into his journey, Sedge follows the stream deep into the forest. The ground is damp but firm and easily managed. The stream reaches and drops off an inner cliff wall, deep within the forest.

"A sacred river flowing down to a sunless sea," Sedge says to himself.[2]

---

[2] Another of several references Sedge has made to the poem *Kubla Khan*, by Samuel Taylor Coleridge.

Tired, he rests where no man has rested before. Now hungry, he takes out his meal and dines at the top of the waterfall. Amazed, he looks around with wide eyes and laughs. The scene is untouched and so uniquely beautiful. The only thing missing is a damsel playing a dulcimer. It would have taken NASA decades to reach this place. He has not only stolen a ship, he has stolen fire from the gods as a gift to man. Upon finishing his food, he works his way down the side of the falls. Halfway down, he notices a second stream leading out of an opening - a cave in the cliff side contributing to the water's volume. There appears to be a rock ledge leading into the cave, though he has to climb back up to the top of the waterfall, cross the stream via stepping stones, then climb halfway back down to access it. He does so.

Entry into the cave is risky, but accessible. Sedge hangs on to rocks embedded within the cliff for balance as he side-steps his way between the falling water from above and the cliff wall. The mouth to the cave is fairly large but requires stooping to enter. There is a dry rock ledge leading alongside the water flowing out of the cave, providing a place to walk deeper into the opening. There are large, rock stalactites hanging from the cave's roof near the opening, apparently formed through years of minerals carried downward by moisture. They look like teeth, but get smaller the deeper Sedge goes into the cave. This is something no orbiting satellite would ever find, Sedge thinks as he takes out his flashlight. He's bedazzled when he turns on his light. The small opening leads to a vast system of massive caverns that go deep into the side of the slope. This valley has not only collapsed into the canyons, it has eroded beneath them as well. He begins videoing the underground caverns.

"Caverns measureless to man," he yells into the cave to hear his echo.

Suddenly, Sedge's breath is taken away, literally. He can't seem to draw oxygen. He pulls his oxygen mask out and takes a deep breath. His wrist computer is blinking red and flashing the word *argon*. He has encountered an argon pocket in the cave. Argon, the third most abundant gas in Earth's atmosphere is safe to breathe so long as too much of it doesn't accumulate in one area. Luna Nuevo has a higher percentage of it than Earth. It is denser than air and concentrated amounts can lead to asphyxia. This leaves Sedge with a dilemma, having used thirty-eight percent of his only oxygen supply descending into the canyons. To explore the caverns would risk his not making it back to the dome, though he's itching to go deeper into the caves. He ponders his dilemma just outside the mouth of the cave, behind the falls where he can breathe fresh air.

Though exhausted from the long hike, he decides to make his way back to the dome. It will take him longer to get back than it did to get here, but this long Luna day will still be in its morning phase. This will give him time to sleep, refresh, resupply, and make one more round trip into the canyon before nightfall. Sedge fills a small water sample from the falls, then begins his long climb back to the dome. There will be ample time to rest when this endless day turns into another endless night.

Sedge spends the next nine hours climbing over two thousand meters, up the stream, through the meadow, past the creepy purple flower field, along the ridges, and finally straight up the initial vertical phases to get out of the canyon. He stops frequently to collect samples and to catch his breath. He's able to backtrack his trail in from memory for most of the way out, only having to check his geo-map a few times. By the time he reaches the top, he can barely feel any energy in his body. The four kilometer walk back to the dome feels like a marathon. The two suns are high in the sky but still in the early phase of Luna's day. Having been awake now for over twenty-three hours, Sedge can feel a deep sleep approaching.

"Welcome back," Bite tells him as he enters the dome. "How was your hike?"

"There's so much down there," Sedge answers. "You wouldn't believe it. There's water, deep forests, flowers, trees, rivers, and massive caves."

"How fascinating," Bite replies. "Were you able to collect any samples?" Sedge hands her small phials of water samples and bags of various plant, fruit, and berry samples. "I'll test these ASAP," she tells him.

Sedge goes into his room. His muscles are as stiff as a board. He pulls the blackout shading over his windows and collapses on his bed. It was only yesterday, according to Luna time standards, that he had crashed his lander and made his way across the desert, and last night that he had partied like a rock star. Now, it's not even mid-day and he's been on a twenty-two-hour hike. He wonders if this world is killing him. He is sound asleep within seconds.

4:6

Sedge wakes in his room. Bright, direct sunlight beams through the sides of the blackout shades, rendering them ineffective. He looks at his clock. He has slept six hours.

When he stands, he realizes just how sore his muscles are. He goes into the main dome.

"Good morning Sedge," Bite says.

"Is it morning?" Sedge asks, entering the kitchen.

"Technically, yes," Bite answers; "at least for the next few hours. We're approaching mid-day. You'll be happy to know, I've recharged your oxygen tank and tested the samples you brought from the canyon."

"Anything interesting?" Sedge asks.

"Very," Bite answers. "I hope you didn't eat any of the ruby red berries. They will kill you."

"I didn't," Sedge replies. "In fact, I was careful to not even touch them."

"That's wise," Bite tells him. "The blue fruit, however..."

"You mean the blue bananas?" Sedge asks.

"Yes," Bite answers. "They are edible. You have discovered a food source. In fact, they're quite nutritious; high in fiber and full of vitamin C."

"Really," Sedge replies. "That's awesome. Can I try one?" Bite hands him a cut up sample. Sedge takes a bite. "Delicious," he says; "very sweet."

"Yes, they contain a lot of sugar," Bite tells him.

"Fermentable sugar?" Sedge asks.

"Certainly," Bite answers.

"We'll have to make some blue-banana wine," Sedge suggests.

"I'll work on a recipe," Bite tells him. "There's something else quite interesting," Bite says. "The spade leaves you brought are silicon based; the first non-carbon based life forms ever discovered."[3]

"That is interesting," Sedge replies. "I've got to get back down there. I need two rope ladders and a mapping drone," Sedge tells her.

"Are you going back today?" Bite asks.

"I am," Sedge answers.

"Are you sure that's such a good idea?" she asks. "You might not make it back before dark."

"I can do it," Sedge tells her. "I only need a little time in the cave with the drone. I can't bear the thought of waiting until another night has passed to return."

"Why the rush?" Bite asks. "You have years to explore the canyons."

---

[3] All life forms on Earth, plant and animal, are carbon-based. Scientists, however, have long known that Earth is capable of manipulating silicon. Hence, silicon-based life forms are bio-chemically feasible, although there are no such known forms on Earth.

"I didn't come here to sit in a dome," Sedge replies. "I'll have plenty of time for that tonight. You know, at some point in the future I want to camp a night in the canyon. First I need to set up a good base camp down there, with lots of lighting. I'd be too scared to get caught down there for an entire Luna night without lights."

"You took a ship into an infinite night, and you're afraid of the dark," Bite says sarcastically.

"You know Bite, you're the cleverest android I've ever met," Sedge tells her.

"Thank you," she replies.

Sedge wastes no time packing his things. He takes two oxygen tanks this time, just in case, the rope ladders, and more food and water.

"Are you sure you have enough food?" Bite asks.

"If I don't, I know where the blue banana trees are," he answers.

"The water is also potable," she tells him; "though I do recommend using sanitizing tablets just to be sure."

"I've got them," Sedge replies.

"Good luck, I'll be here when you get back," Bite tells him.

Sedge sets out again on what has thus far been the longest day of his life. The suns are high in the sky and the sky is bright. Only a portion of Aureola and her rings cut through it. What a life, he thinks, as he makes his way to the canyon rim and down the four kilometer stretch to the passage. This time, there will be no wrong turns. He knows exactly what he's doing.

Arriving at the coulee that leads into the canyon, Sedge notices that a layer of clouds has rolled into the valley far below, thin but increasing. He pays no heed. If anything, they'll give him a better idea of where to start setting rain traps on future visits. He envisions bringing a micro-dome down with solar panels, setting up his home away from dome in the canyon, but knows he's getting ahead of himself.

As he descends the first tier, he's reminded how depleted he is of energy. What he thought would go faster actually takes him more time. He does, however, get the rope ladders in place in the two hardest spots of the climb. A few hours later, he finds himself on the first tier below the rim, now just barely above the thickening cloud line. He questions the wisdom of his return, but presses on.

As he descends deeper yet into the great valley, he thinks back on his lander flight over this canyon, and the huge impact crater he spotted. He theorizes which of these canyon walls it shares, but that will have to be a quest for another day. As for right now, his goal is to expand on what he already knows. Within a few hours, he finds himself below the cloud line, no longer able to see the sky. He now questions if it might rain, but has his poncho rolled in his pack just in case. He continues on, finding the correct coulee to take him to the third tier, shaving a little time off his climb. His legs are weakening, however, and he has to stop often to rest them. Will he have the strength to make it out? Stubbornly, he presses forward, knowing how far he has already come.

Eventually, he reaches the third tier and again follows it downward until he reaches the dry river bed. It's funny, he thinks, how he's become familiar with an untrodden land light years from home. This is his world and his alone. For the next few hours, he follows the river bed, through the meadow and past the eerie flower patch. He films them turning as he walks by, a real botanical phenomenon. The clouds darken the day as Sedge finally reaches the flowing stream. Beta Centauri is barely visible through their filter. Rain now looks likely. Sedge follows the stream into the deep forest. His familiarity has helped him make up for time in the great basin. Again, he looks at the towering trees.

Finally, Sedge arrives at the waterfall several hours into his hike. He managed to shave almost two hours off his first descent, even as exhausted as he is. He takes a rest in his new sacred site. He has a drink of water, then makes his way into the cave, this time going deeper than before. He reaches a place where the cave becomes a large network of caverns, separated by large open areas. Sedge follows the stream to ensure he can find his way back out. Once deep inside, he pulls the mapping drone from his pack, programs it to explore for one hour, and releases it. It flies off scanning the cavern walls with lasers. Sedge sits silently by the stream, feeling fortunate to be in a cave where there are no reptiles, insects, or animals to fear. The cave is dark but his flashlight is in lantern mode, lighting up the large cavern. He takes the time to relax. Life could not sink any deeper, he thinks, having traveled deep into space, then deep into a canyon, and now deep into a cave within that canyon. It may not provide meaning, but it certainly has provided depth.

The drone returns at the end of its allotted hour. Had it finished earlier, it would have also returned earlier, a sign that there are more caverns than were mapped.

Checking the time, Sedge decides he should start back up the canyon walls to the dome. Night is still a ways away, but approaching and he is not equipped to be caught down here.

Reaching the mouth of the cave, however, Sedge sees rain, coming down quite hard. Hoping it to be short lived, he decides to try to wait it out inside the cave, at least for a little while. Exhausted, he lays on his back using his pack for a pillow. I'm this world's first caveman, he thinks. Just like Paleolithic Man, I use a cave for protection. The steady sound of falling rain is soothing. He feels sleepy.

Sedge bides in the mouth of the cave for over another hour, drifting in and out of sleep. The rain, however, doesn't let up. Water begins to rise in the caverns as the stream grows in strength. With the day fading and the cave near flooding, Sedge is faced with only one option; he has to brave the rain and head back up the canyon to the dome. He puts on his rain poncho and steps into the elements, almost losing his footing on the slickened rock ledge behind the waterfall. Feeling the rain on his face as he enters the open air, he wonders why he returned to this place on the same day.

Sedge face plants as he starts his way up the lower basin. What a mistake, he thinks. One thing they don't teach you in communications classes, to stay out of canyons during rainstorms. Soaked and now muddy, he gets back up and begins making his way out of the forest, moving carefully and slowly through torrential rain. Eventually, he's free of the forest and back in the meadows, which aren't much better. The poncho is doing little to keep him dry in these extreme conditions. Nevertheless, he presses onward, past the meadows. The river bed out of the meadows is no longer dry. A large torrent now flows, forcing Sedge to walk atop slick round stones to cross it. He notices it's getting gradually darker but can do little to expedite his climb. The coulee that leads into the meadow, which used to be an easy path, is now a small river. He has to climb out along its side, grabbing ferns to keep from falling in. Again, he slips and falls but manages not to tumble into the flowing water. The entire canyon is flooding.

Relieved, he finally makes the third tier. It too, however, is flooding, slowing Sedge's pace as he stays near the wall for safety. A huge mudslide wrecks the catwalk in a place he had fortunately just passed. He finds the pass to the second tier, but it too has become a waterway. Sedge has to wade through its fast flow to get to a spot where he can climb upward. He has just enough light to continue his climb to the second tier.

Night has fallen by the time Sedge reaches the second tier. The rain has become lighter the higher he has climbed, but he's soaked to the bone. Now rockier, his way remains slippery and dangerous. Worse, he has to travel by flashlight. Nevertheless, he eventually finds the coulee to the first tier. It is slick but there is no flowing water at this level. As he climbs, the clouds become thinner. He's relieved to see the blur of stars through the thin cloud layer as he nears the first tier. They become crystal clear by the time he reaches it. He has cleared the cloud line and the rain. The night sky is beautiful but hard to enjoy when you're soaked, exhausted, and your groin has been rubbed raw by wet jeans. He is alive, however, now taking a moment to catch his breath.

He finds the passage and starts his ascent to the rim, now back on oxygen. The difficulty of the climb is compounded by his having to hold the flashlight, only leaving one hand free. At least the rocks are dry. He makes it beyond the rope ladders, through the arch, and finally onto the canyon rim. Weary beyond word, he rests for a minute at the top of the canyon, trying to see into its darkness.

Just as he commences his four-kilometer home stretch, he sees it; an arrow of fire to the south, really high up in the atmosphere, racing across the sky. He first thinks it to be a meteor, but on second look pieces the puzzle together. It's the ship - the deepliner is going down. How amazing that he can actually see it. He watches it race across the night sky, finally disappearing over the distant horizon. It must be hundreds of kilometers away, he thinks, somewhere on the great plains of the highlands. Too tired to walk fully upright, Sedge staggers along the canyon's edge beneath the light of Aureola's rings, back to the bio-dome.

Back in the dome, Sedge finds Bite assembling gym equipment in one of the spare rooms.

"How was your trip?" she asks.

"I'm really lucky to be alive," Sedge answers. "I'm never going to make two trips into the canyon in a single day again. I'm also never returning ill-equipped either. Otherwise, the trip was great, Bite."

Sedge goes into his room and turns on his communication station. He finds a feed from the Cortes Orbiter, which managed to track the deepliner's entry. No location beacon is registering, but the orbiter is projecting an estimated crash site based on the ship's flightpath and last transmitted elevation. It lies twelve hundred and sixty-one kilometers southeast of the dome, a distance well beyond Sedge's current capabilities of reaching.

"Sorry Sultan," Sedge says once again. "If it's any consolation, your ship goes down on the vast highlands of history."

Part 5

Meanwhile, Kendal fights to keep her eyelids open in a small auditorium inside the Mandarin Oriental Hotel Events Center. She's inspired by the speaker, Dr. Roger Royce, but sinking deeper into her soft foam seat as his low voice echoes hypnotically over the sound system. Kendal has to be here. Dr. Royce's lecture is being sponsored by Thacker & Walcott. She welcomes the distraction nevertheless. It's a nice break from the office. It's relaxing, almost too relaxing. She snaps to, however, when Dr. Royce suddenly, sternly speaks out on the topic of zealous representation.[4]

"What does it truly mean," he loudly asks the room; "this zealous representation? What is this zeal which we must harbor? Must exhibit? Is it an act? A feeling? How do we display it, and do so professionally?

"To answer our question we must further examine what it means to represent," there is a pause in the speech. "To represent means just that, we must re-present our clients. We must act in our clients' stead. We must reflect them, and of course we must believe them. We must premise our arguments on their word. Ours is not to adjudicate; ours is to represent..."

Afterward, Kendal joins the after-lecture social, where she has the chance to meet Dr. Royce, introduced to him by a colleague as the lawyer representing Joy Rider. This leads to a lengthy discussion about Sedge Nile. Kendal doesn't mind, still loving the notoriety the case has bestowed upon her. Besides, it's a great ice-breaker. She fills Dr. Royce in on the legal details of the case. He thoughtfully takes in every word, enthralled by its uniqueness.

---

[4] Oaths attorneys are required to take often include a vow to provide their clients with **zealous representation**.

Thacker & Walcott reserved a hotel suite for Dr. Royce when the event was planned. Dr. Royce declined the room, however, opting to stay with extended family while in New York. Phil Thacker promised Kendal she could use the empty room as a bonus for the extra work she's done on Sedge Nile's case, if she wanted to. She seized the opportunity and has invited Naya to spend the night in the suite with her.

Naya arrives at the hotel excited for their slumber party. She gives Kendal a call to let her know she's in the lobby. Kendal excuses herself from the event and goes to meet her. They exit the hotel into the Time Warner Center, where they spend an hour shopping. Later, they sit down to have gelato in the food court.

"So what's our room like?" Naya asks.

"It's really nice," Kendal answers. "It has a view of the park, a baby-grand piano, sunken tub, and fruit baskets on every table. We're rock stars tonight girl."

"That's awesome, I can't wait to see it," Naya replies.

"Today's speaker was smart," Kendal tells Naya. "He's an astute guy. He projects a real presence. I'm sure he's an effective attorney."

"Is he handsome?" Naya asks.

"For his age I guess," Kendal answers. "He inspired me. He changed the way I look at zealous representation."

"That sounds good," Naya says; "though I've never questioned your zeal."

"It made me think about Nikki Nova," Kendal adds.

"You mean the elderly woman in Vancouver?" Naya asks. "The former newscaster?"

"Yes," Kendal answers; "but to truly represent, I shouldn't think of her as elderly, just as a woman, like me. It's easier to represent when we share ground."

"You weren't representing her anyway, were you?" Naya asks.

"No," Kendal answers; "but I was viewing her scenario very much like a case. It's just how I'm programmed. Anyway, were I to represent her zealously, I'd have to operate on the premise that the message in the library book was true, that it had indeed existed. If I were her lawyer, this would be the service that I'd be under oath to provide."

"So where would you go from there?" Naya asks.

"Somewhere I've already gone actually," Kendal answers; "to the library to search for answers."

"Did you find anything at the library?" Naya asks.

"I did," Kendal answers; "come to think of it. I found a poem."

"A poem? What did it say?" Naya asks.

Kendal scrolls through her saved documents and finds it; the poem within the obituary. She reads it to Naya. "Listen, then tell me what you think?

> "She waits for me, across the sea, beneath a waning moon.
> She sent to me, across that sea, transmissions time consumed.
> To 2014 from a time unseen, three bottles back in time.
> To set her free, I must unpiece this puzzle in my mind.
> She waits for me, across the sea, across a sea of time."

"It's not ground-shakenly profound," Naya says; "but it's got a certain ring to it."

"He specifically mentioned the year *2014*, *transmissions*, *back in time*, and *consumed by time*," Kendal says. "Nikki also mentioned 2014."

"Where did you get this poem?" Naya asks.

"I found it in an obituary from the year 2072," Kendal answers; "and get a load of this; the guy who died, the one who wrote it, lived in Seattle. How far is that from Vancouver?"

"I don't know, but pretty close," Naya answers. "Interesting, maybe there's a connection."

"I didn't think so at first," Kendal replies, "but the poem makes me wonder."

"Sounds like something you should follow up on," Naya suggests.

"I guess so," Kendal says. "I just don't know where to begin. The guy who wrote this has been dead for close to sixty years."

Kendal and Naya return to the Mandarin Oriental and check into their room. Excited, the young ladies explore the hotel's amenities.

"First, I want to take a hot bath," Naya says.

"Go for it," Kendal tells her. "Let's order room service for dinner."

As she waits for her bath to fill, Naya stares out at Central Park through the room's large window. The sun is setting on the park as the darkening sky turns pink. What a view, she thinks as Kendal kicks back on the bed and turns on some news.

"It's funny how value is perception," Naya tells Kendal. "In essence, this room is not very different from your apartment. It's about the same size. Your apartment doesn't have a Central Park view, granted, but it does have heat, AC, communications, and so on. The rate to rent this box for two nights, nevertheless, not only covers your entire month's mortgage, but also utilities."

"That's true," Kendal replies running numbers in her head; "but this one comes with much higher maintenance, labor, management, and assumed risk of vacancy."

The two women order a pizza from the kitchen for dinner. They eat it while watching back-to-back romantic comedies, keeping the night simple and relaxing.

5:2

After getting the morning off in exchange for attending the lecture, Kendal arrives at the office just after lunch.

"So how was the hotel room last night?" Phil asks her as she enters the office.

"It was wonderful," Kendal answers. "Thank you so much. My friend and I had a relaxing evening. We just stayed in, watched movies, and reminisced about old times, high school, and having the house to ourselves when our parents would leave town. It gave us that feeling."

"I'm glad you enjoyed it," Phil replies. "Are you on board for tonight's cruise? We've got a spectacular vessel this year."

"I wouldn't miss it," Kendal answers. "It will make for back to back nights of the high life. How decadent."

"You've earned it," Phil says.

Kendal ignores the stack of work on her desk, taking a few minutes to stare out her office window. She's well rested, just not in the mood to dive into her casefiles. She decides instead to spend a few minutes scanning news video feeds.

"The Pizarro will be on its way to Luna Nuevo on Saturday if all goes well," a news article in The Times reads; "on a mission which not only plans to further prepare for the arrival of future astronauts, but also to supply the one who may already be there; Sedge Nile. Not expected to arrive until late twenty-one thirty-five, the Pizarro will carry all kinds of clothing, foods, medicines, toiletries, and some personal items to help Sedge, or other future astronauts, survive.

"The Los Angeles Lakers advanced last night to the Western Semi-Finals..."

Kendal decides to take another look at Nikki Nova's claim, now acting under the assumption that the message in the library book is true. She reads the poem in Beau Hadley's obituary. What could it mean? If only she could ask him. The lawyer in her isn't ready to give up. She searches several current directories for the name Beau Hadley. To her surprise, she comes across the name Michael Beau Hadley, listed as an architect and co-owner of *Spatial Concepts*, an architectural firm in Portland, Oregon. Could there be a connection? How could there not? Her investigative nature won't leave this to wonder. She decides to give Michael a call.

"Spatial Concepts," a woman answers.

"Yes, my name is Kendal Benz and I'd like to speak with Michael Hadley if I may."

"Let me see if his line is busy," the woman replies. "He just got off a call. He'll be with you in one moment." Kendal waits, not really sure what to say.

"This is Michael Hadley," a voice is soon heard saying over the line.

"Yes Michael, my name is Kendal Benz," she tells him. "You wouldn't by any chance be related to Beau Hadley, who passed away in Seattle back in 2072, would you?"

"Yes, I think you're referring to my grandfather," Michael answers. "Why?" he asks.

"I came across his obituary," Kendal answers. "It contains a nice little poem and I was wondering if you could help me understand what the poem means."

"Ms. Benz, I didn't even know my grandfather. I don't know the poem you're talking about either," Michael tells her. "Do you have a copy of it?"

"Yes," Kendal answers. "It's short. Would you like me to read it to you?"

"Sure, why not?" Michael replies somewhat hesitantly.

Kendal begins reading:

"She waits for me, across the sea, beneath a waning moon..." She goes on to read the entire poem to him.

"You know," Michael says after she finishes, "I don't think I've even heard that poem, so I doubt I can be of much help."

"What can you tell me about your grandfather?" Kendal asks.

"Only what my father used to tell me," Michael answers. "My grandfather wasn't exactly right," he adds.

"What do you mean by that," Kendal inquires; "If I may ask?"

"He wasn't exactly all there mentally," Michael tells her. "I don't want to say he was mad, because according to my father he was perfectly normal most of the time. He suffered, however, from periodic *episodes* for lack of a better term."

"Really, how so?" Kendal asks.

"He was somewhat delusional," Michael tells her. "He had visions."

"What kind of visions?" Kendal carefully asks, now taking notes.

"He described them as lucid dreams while he was awake, similar to déjà vu but much longer and stronger," Michael answers.

"Really," Kendal says, remembering Nikki mentioning her husband's déjà vu.

"Yes," Michael says. "He believed someone, a woman, needed his help but he didn't have the information he needed to help her. He didn't know how. I'm sure that's who's waiting for him in the poem; the woman he can't set free."

"How did he know she needed help then?" Kendal asks.

"Through his visions," Michael answers. "He described them as clear glimpses through a veil of time. He had three that he thought were somehow projected, or sent to him over his radio, which I'm guessing to be the messages or transmissions he was referring to in the poem. He was really into radios."

"Radios, interesting," Kendal says.

"What is this all about?" Michael asks her.

"I'm doing research on a message that was allegedly sent through time," Kendal answers.

"You don't think my grandfather actually received something from another time, do you?" Michael asks.

"I don't know," Kendal answers. "Is there anything else you can tell me about your grandfather?"

"He was always looking for a treasure under stones in our park. He thought there was some kind of information buried under a rock that would lead him to a treasure. It was all part of his visions. Anyway, this strange obsession, at least according to my father, is likely what led my grandmother to divorce him."

"Can I speak with your father?" Kendal asks.

"No, he passed away in 2111," Michael tells her. "He always held my grandfather in high regard though, ignoring his visions, dismissing them as minor eccentricities. He always saw greatness in my grandfather, almost as if a part of him believed my grandfather's visions."

"Thanks, you've been helpful," Kendal says.

"You know, I have all of my grandfather's files," Michael tells her. "My grandfather kept extensive journals, mostly audio. He carried a memo recorder with him almost everywhere he went. I'm the guy left to shoulder our family's history, or our library of collected data, and I have his things."

"Anything you would like to share, I'd love to see or hear," Kendal replies.

"I'll dig through the archives," Michael tells her. "I can't promise anything will make sense, but I'm sure I have his journals. You now have my curiosity anyway," he adds.

"Great, I've just beamed you contact info," Kendal says. "I look forward to hearing from you again."

5:3

Kendal leaves the office a little early, giving herself enough time to run home and change clothes before heading to her company cruise. Slightly apprehensive to open her door after being away for thirty-six hours, she's calmed to see her place undisturbed. The Jack Pine bonsai she keeps in her kitchen window could use a drink but is surviving. She checks her voice-box.

- "Hi Kendal, it's me Holden. Just wanting to see if you and Naya wanted to join me for a walk on the High Line sometime this weekend. Saturday evening works best for me, but I'm flexible. Call or beam me anytime."

There are no further messages. With a little extra time on her hands, Kendal takes a brief shower before slipping into some shorts and a pair of Chucks for the boat. Her world couldn't be in higher gear, or more enshroud in mystery. Once dressed and ready, she calls for a private pod to take her to Pier 25. It arrives four minutes later to pick her up. Opposite the rush-hour flow, Kendal enjoys a pause-free pod ride to the pier, where she's quick to spot her law firm's staff gathered on the boardwalk, waiting for their ship to come in.

Within minutes, a deep foghorn blows as an approaching behemoth, four-story yacht slows to a soft sway. A deck-hand jumps from the vessel to tie it down as it softly presses up against the docks. Phil Thacker and Tim Walcott are already on board, enjoying themselves, waving from the top deck at people as they board. The night is warm, sticky, and ideal for a boat ride. Summer is now imminent. The days have gone from warm to hot. The city is alive and green this time of year with everything now in bloom. The moon is big and bright to boot, nearly full, just beginning to wane.

Kendal and her colleagues convene around the pool on the top deck. A reggae band kicks into its first set, helping everyone feel welcome and loose, like they've walked into a party already in motion. Cocktail servers can be found throughout the yacht, ready to cater to passengers' orders. Kendal does her best to pay attention to her group's dialogue, but her mind is adrift. The moon has lured her away, again into the past of Nikki Nova. She stares at it, for the first time truly wondering if Nikki has been there.

"I wouldn't want to pay them," Troy tells the group while smiling at Kendal, drawing her from her daydream.

"Pay who?" Kendal asks. The group grows silent as everyone realizes Kendal hasn't been listening.

"Oh," Troy says to break the silence; "we were just discussing the massive costs that must be associated with this yacht, leaving the price of the ship itself aside, like moorage, maintenance, and things like that. That was the *them* to which we were referring."

"Oh sorry I missed what you said," Kendal tells the group. "I was staring at the moon."

"No problem," Troy tells her, raising his cocktail. "We were talking about boring numbers. We should apologize for distracting you," he adds with a charming grin.

Kendal notices that she's being noticed, a sensation she hasn't felt in some time. The ship pulls away from the dock and glides north on the Hudson, leaving starboard passengers breathless at the Manhattan skyline. Kendal mixes with Troy for the first half hour or so, but distances herself from him a little later to maintain a professional posture. She gives herself an unaccompanied tour of the ship, exploring everywhere accessible, on every level, stem to stern. As she looks around this luxury vessel, she can't keep her mind off Sedge. To think, he stole something so much bigger and not just to go up the river. He's gone to a place so far from here that if he wakes, he wakes to different suns. The sheer magnitude of this ship invokes a sense of astonishment in Kendal for the raw courage of Sedge. Is he brave? Is he mad? Is he even alive?

On the edge of the sea and with the moon in wane, Kendal can't keep Beau's poem out of her mind; she waits for me, across the see, beneath a waning moon. What did Beau mean and was there a connection to Cedric's experiments?

Back on deck, Kendal notices Troy has outpaced the party on drinks. He's getting a little loud. She keeps Troy at an arm's length for now and diversifies her social interactions, spending the next few hours working her way through the party, enjoying herself while keeping her edge.

The ship returns to Lower Manhattan but doesn't dock. It swings by Liberty Island to give passengers a look at the Statue of Liberty, takes a wide turn toward Statin Island, giving the partying passengers a view of the mouth of the East River, and finally b-lines back to Pier 25.

Prior to docking, Kendal is pleasantly amused to find Matheus, the firm's newest, very popular junior-partner now giving her his undivided attention; talking and listening closely to her for the final leg of the cruise. He gives her a warm thank you and quick hug as the ship is tied down and the gangway extended. What a magic night, Kendal thinks, now anxious to talk to Naya, to tell her she may have more than one guy interested in her. Has her luck changed?

5:4

Kendal wipe's the train's interior window with her palm to get a view, but it's too wet with condensation. There doesn't appear to be much to see anyway, only darkness.

"Next stop Luna Nuevo," a voice says over the sound system.

"How can a train take us all the way to Luna Nuevo?" Kendal asks Holden.

"There are a lot of questions I'd like answered," Holden tells her. "Gather your things. We're slowing down. We can't miss this window."

Holden and Kendal grab their bags and move near the train's exit as it comes to a stop. The doors slide open. They step onto a platform. Kendal looks for windows to get a glimpse of Luna but there are none, only walkways filled with souvenir shops and restaurants. Holden sees Sedge looking for them at the end of the platform. He waves to him.

"Nice to finally meet you," Kendal tells Sedge. "I've heard so much about you." Sedge doesn't answer. Instead, he motions them to follow him, which they do, into a small, concrete meeting room where they take a seat around a table set within a cubbyhole, also completely made of concrete. Sedge closes the door, then joins them at the table. The place appears empty and completely private.

"How is this possible?" Kendal asks. "How is it that we are all here?"

"It's a singularity," Holden tells her. "We're in a moment outside of space and time."

"We are here for a higher purpose," Sedge tells them. "We're here because we're not finished."

"What does that mean?" Kendal asks.

"Just when you think it couldn't get any more connected," Sedge tells her; "there will be another dot to connect. Don't overlook it," he adds.

"Can we see Luna from here?" Holden asks Sedge.

"What do you mean?" Kendal asks. "Isn't this Luna? And how can we take a train here? There is no train," she says. "None of this makes any sense. Unless, this isn't really Luna Nuevo, is it?" She hears a pong. "Listen, can you hear that?" she asks.

The pong grows louder. Kendal wakes. It's four forty-seven a.m. She lies in bed thinking about her dream, now feeling like she's visited Luna Nuevo. It all seemed so real. Reality is, after all, perception. What purpose do these dreams serve? How seriously should we take them? Her mind kicks into motion.

Too awake to sleep, she checks her messages. She finds a text from Michael Hadley.

"Ms. Benz," it reads; "my grandfather recorded everything; phone messages, news headlines, even his dreams, usually on a memo recorder. I came across three unique recordings, however, that I believe might be the three messages, or *bottles back in time* he was talking about in his poem. Check them out, I'd be interested to hear anything you find. Mike Hadley."

Attached to the message are three audio files. Kendal, careful not to wake neighbors at this hour, puts on a pair of headphones to listen to them:

23:18 February 27, 2014 - duration: 00:33 – Vision

"Something just happened to me that has never happened before. I have just had some kind of vision," Beau's voice can be heard saying. He sounds genuinely bewildered. "It seemed to occur just as my radio cut out. I don't want to call it a lucid dream, hallucination, illusion, or déjà vu, because it was all of those, yet none of them can define it. I can think of no better word than vision. I think it came from another time. It was some kind of distress signal. Someone out there is trying to tell me something. Someone is breaking the laws of nature and I'm somehow involved. I know this."

22:57 March 11, 2014 – duration: 00:24 - Vision

"It happened again," Beau says stunned. "I could hear it this time over my radio, which oddly enough wasn't on at the time. I could see it too, in glimpses. There's a stone within the trees. I think it's in a park. I need to find that stone. There's something under it, some kind of vital information. There's a woman too, in distress. I can help her if I can find that stone."

22:40 April 06, 2014 – duration: 01:23 - Vision

"It happened again tonight. This is too weird. I told Kendra about it, but she just thinks unemployment has stressed me out. I know what I heard. It came over my radio speaker again tonight, and again, the radio was not on at the time. It's more than a radio signal, however. It triggers images in my mind that are more memory than imagination; memories sometimes of me, only in a different place and time, with a lot of money too. It's a profound, prolonged déjà vu. There's a woman out there, somewhere in time. She needs me to find the stone. I've seen it and would know it if I saw it again. Whatever this is all about, it's under that stone."

He sounds so serious, Kendal thinks as she stares through her window at a blinking green light in the deep morning twilight. It seems to be floating through the air over the Hudson River. Whoever this Beau guy was, he certainly believed these visions had real significance in his life. They were trying to tell him something. The mention of radio signals and the 2014 coincidence are interesting as well. Those, however, appear to be the only connections to Nikki Nova's story. These visions don't mention any lunar crashes or library books.

5:5

Kendal, Naya, and Holden meet at Think Coffee on 34th and 10th, where they get mochas in to-go cups. They climb up to the High Line, New York's historic elevated walkway and begin walking south, toward Lower Manhattan. The sun is out and the day is warm, somewhat sticky. The trees now all have green leaves. The walk above the street is beautiful, between endless condominiums, shops, and office towers. A Hoboken bound, lighter-than-air bus drifts across the Hudson.

"So how was the boat cruise?" Naya asks.

"It was fun," Kendal tells her.

"Did you meet anyone?" Naya asks, cutting to the chase.

"Two guys, believe it or not," Kendal answers. "I'll have to fill you in on it later."

"Oh, c'mon," Holden tells her. "Who am I going to tell?"

"Well, there's not really that much to tell," Kendal replies. "Two attractive guys did talk to me though, both very likable."

"Good for you," Holden says with a smile.

"It is good for you," Naya tells her as they continue their stroll down the walkway.

"I had a dream about you and Sedge," Kendal tells Holden.

"Really, what happened?" Holden asks.

"We went to Luna Nuevo to visit Sedge," Kendal answers. "Only we took a train."

"Okay, whatever," Holden replies.

"We didn't even really get to see the moon," Kendal tells them. "We were in some concrete room."

"Sounds strange," Naya says.

"It was," Kendal tells her.

"Do you think it has any meaning?" Naya asks.

"I don't know," Kendal answers. "Obviously dreams serve a purpose, but do the scenarios have any meaning?"

"They must," Holden tells them. "They're electro-magnetic, like radio waves. They probably have more significance than we'll ever know," he continues. "The alpha waves that dominate our brains in meditative or deep-thought states of mind have a trough or lower frequency of the alpha rhythm that is identical to Earth's electromagnetic wave. So, when relaxed, your alpha brain wave can actually go all the way around the world and come back to your brain between each peak of the wave's frequency, which happens over seven times per second. Dreams, like meditative states, must have electro-magnetic frequencies. Who knows the extent of these connections?"

"Do you think they can ever be tapped, or recorded?" Naya asks.

"Who knows?" Holden answers.

"I really feel like my dream was trying to tell me something," Kendal replies; "like it was a message of some kind."

They sit on a bench to finish their coffee. The day is really starting to heat up, already well above the late May average. The summer of 2030 is arriving early. The three of them just sit for a little while, enjoying the chance to be in the sunshine, watching people, and thinking. They're comfortable together, both in conversation and in silence. Eventually, they continue with their stroll.

"So have you heard anything new from your Vancouver news-reporter friend?" Naya asks Kendal.

"No, but I got a lot more from the Seattle guy who published the poem in his obituary," Kendal answers. "I got in touch with his grandson."

"Really, did he shed any light on the poem?" Naya asks.

"Yes," Kendal replies. "He sent me some audio files from his grandfather's journals that documented three visions the guy had in 2014. So I think we may have found the three messages sent back in time."

"Interesting," Holden says.

"Mildly," Kendal replies; "aside from the 2014 coincidence, there doesn't appear to be any connection between his visions and the warning written in Nikki Nova's library book."

"No," Holden asks; "are you sure?"

"Well," Kendal says; "he did talk about a woman from another time, in distress, who needs his help."

"Are you kidding?" Holden asks. "That's huge."

"Yes, but how would it go from there to a warning in a library book?" Kendal asks. "According to this guy's journal entries, these visions came only in glimpses. His visions came without any instructions. If they were mentioned in his obituary, I'm guessing he never fully knew how to act on them."

"Good point," Naya adds.

"Yes," Holden says; "but you're thinking like a lawyer."

"What do you mean?" Kendal asks.

"Right now, the three of us seem to share the same space and time," Holden tells them. "The laws of space and time appear to be the same for all three of us."

"Okay," Naya says, smiling attentively.

"Well that's Kendal's issue," Holden says. "She's looking for documentation that shouldn't exist here and now."

"How so?" Kendal asks.

"Assume the message in the library book worked. Let's say it served its purpose, thus altering space and time. If the tragedy no longer even occurred, neither did the events leading up to it, like the warning. We exist in Nikki Nova's altered reality, not her previous, supposedly ill-fated one. It is gone. Any instructions given on placing that message in the library book, should have faded out of time with the message itself the moment the course of history was redirected."

"So if Beau Hadley were no longer connected to the library book, what would his visions be?" Kendal asks.

"Good question," Holden replies. "Radio reflections, inter-dimensional memories, I don't know, but apparently some kind of residual echoes, maybe derived from the transmissions through time. It's peculiar," he adds.

"There's something else too," Kendal says.

"What?" both Naya and Holden ask in sync.

"Nikki Nova told me that her husband Cedric; the guy who wrote the thesis in 2069 claiming to transmit messages through time; the one who supposedly sent the warning back to this guy in 2014 asking him to deface a library book, also had unusually strong moments of déjà vu."

"Okay," Naya says.

"This guy Beau, the guy way back in 2014, described these three visions as déjà vu, though not precisely but for lack of better term."

"I'm starting to believe you're really onto something here," Holden tells Kendal.

"So am I, after you put it in perspective," Kendal replies.

"As am I," Naya adds. "It's exciting, isn't it?"

"It's a real rush," Kendal says. "It's still too funny to me that it all came about from Sedge's case. I mean here we are."

"It was meant to be," Holden remarks. "Here we are, solving a mystery that may have begun over sixty years ago with a transmission that went back yet another what, fifty-five years, then somehow sat in a library book for decades, assuming this tale is true."

"How romantic," Naya tells them. "It makes me believe in love."

"These dates and numbers Holden mentions," Kendal says; "they have something to do with the bigger picture. I get a strange sensation that I'm somehow linked to these stories; that they are somehow connected," she adds.

The three of them walk the High Line all the way down to Pier 53, where they continue their walk southward, down the Hudson River Greenway. Feeling energetic, they take the Sky-bridge Walkway to *Vessel*, where they ascend the spiral staircase to get a better view. Atop the structure, they snap the first ever picture of all three of them together. Back on the greenway, they stroll for hours through Rockefeller Park, eventually finishing their walk in Battery Park. They sit in the park for a while, staring out over the water at the Statue of Liberty before finally catching separate pods home.

5:6

In her bathtub, Kendal sinks deeply into foamy hot water, now a little stiff from the day's long walk. Could there really be a connection between Beau Hadley's dreams and the message left for Nikki Nova? She wonders. How is it that Sedge Nile's case led to this potential discovery? How could the stars have been so nicely aligned? She watches night fall over the city from the sliver of a skyline view she gets from her bathroom window. She cracks the window to vent a little steam and takes a sip of Chardonnay. Ambient sounds of nature softly play over her sound system.

After bathing, she towel-dries herself. Nude, she walks gracefully to her bedroom, conveying nothing but her glass of wine. Relaxed, she lies on her bed, above all bedding to cool after her hot bath. The moment is interrupted by the sound of five, consecutive soft staccato pongs, alerting Kendal to an incoming call.

"Take call," Kendal instructs. A single pong in another tone lets her know the connection is live. "Hello," she answers the call over the sound system.

"Hi Kay, it's me," Naya says.

"Hey Naya," Kendal replies. "I'm a little stiff from our walk."

"Me too," Naya says; "but I had a great time. Can you beam me the picture we took together at Vessel?"

"Sure," Kendal tells her.

"That's not why I called though," Naya says. "This is not a big deal. In fact, I debated if I should tell you this or not, but I knew you'd kill me for keeping it from you."

"What, Naya?" Kendal eagerly asks.

"I ran into Brice on my way home from our walk today," Naya answers.

"Oh really," Kendal reacts. "Did you talk to him?"

"No," Naya replies. "He was busy."

"Doing?" Kendal asks.

"Honestly, it looked like he was having a bad day. He appeared to be in an argument with a tall, wavy-haired woman," Naya tells her.

"Sounds like the same woman I saw him with," Kendal replies. "I believe her name is Simone."

"Did she have dark skin and streaks in her hair?" Naya asks.

"Yes," Kendal answers.

"Well, I hope I didn't spoil your day with this," Naya says in a concerned tone.

"No, not even," Kendall answers. "I had an awesome day."

"It's just that I know you're having a hard time believing in love," Naya says.

"Love, you're right I don't know," Kendal replies. "Now marriage, that is something I've completely lost belief in."

"Why?" Naya asks. "Don't you think it's a good way for couples to prove their love to each other?"

"No, at least not the lawyer in me," Kendal replies. "It's just as easy to argue that if they really loved each other, they wouldn't need marriage to prove it."

"Good point," Naya says. "You're so analytical."

"I suppose," Kendal replies.

"Don't forget to beam me the pic," Naya reminds Kendal before ending the call.

Kendal thinks of Brice and his new relationship. He's already fighting. He's come full circle with Simone. His romantic life is moving so much faster than hers. Is this good? Apparently not if he's fighting. In the back of her mind and off to one side, she's relieved not to be Simone, jealously taking some delight in the poor woman's displeasure, fully aware of the turbulence in front of her. Kendal's otherwise mature, responsible nature prevails, however. It's the reason she gleans more wisdom from her relationship with Brice than he does, at least she likes to tell herself. She dims the lights, then takes a drink of wine as ambient music continues to play in the background, pulling her far away.

"Hi Kendal."

Kendal turns to her side to see Brice standing beside her. They're atop Vessel, looking down at the people on the ground below.

"Hi Brice," she answers. "Are you here alone, or did you come with Simone?"

"She's still climbing," he answers. "She'll be here soon. I read about you in The Times," he adds. "I was amazed to hear that you are Joy Rider's lawyer."

"Yeah," Kendal answers. "It has been a fascinating case. I wonder how he's doing."

"Common sense will tell you," Brice replies.

"Common sense?" Kendal asks in return.

"Yes," Brice says. "Look beneath the surface, for the common sense," he tells her.

"What does that mean?" Kendal asks, just as Simone appears on the walkway.

"I'm sorry, I have to go," Brice says. "We never said goodbye," he tells her as Simone approaches.

"No, we didn't," Kendal replies.

Kendal awakens in sorrow, saddened by time's one-way directional flow. There was no goodbye with Brice. There is no going back; no moment can truly be relived. Is the wisdom gained really worth the innocence lost? She too has come full circle, no longer needing to deny her fond memories to protect her path. Though not entirely painless, she's reached a point where these obsolete walls may finally crumble. Cold, she puts on her nightgown and turns her wall screen on, setting the channel to Moondock's live lunar-surface camera. As she sits watching live feeds of the moon's surface roll by, her mind shifts back to Nikki Nova's claim.

Unable to drift back to sleep, Kendal opens her holographic workstation. Could her dreams be telling her something? Was there anything in the available data she'd missed? What common sense could she be overlooking?

"Time," she tells herself. "Time is the common denominator between Nikki Nova and Beau Hadley, particularly the year 2014. Had they both not mentioned this year, there would be no connection to ponder." Kendal stares at Davy Crater as Moondock flies over it. "Time is not, however, the common denominator between Sedge Nile's case and Nikki Nova," she continues. "I am." She stares at the moon. "Or am I?" she questions.

Acting on an idea, Kendal pulls up the affidavit submitted to her by Stan Satterfield and begins scanning the document for dates and times, jotting them down on her air-pad as she finds them. When she finishes with the affidavit, she enters all dates and times into a program she uses for legal analysis; a program which analyzes times and dates and looks for potential connections or patterns. What she discovers leaves her slack-jawed. There, in front of her eyes, she sees the dot that hadn't been connected. She immediately starts to laugh out loud, checks the time, and gives Holden a call. She gets his voice box.

"Holden, if you haven't gone to bed yet give me a call," she records; "this is huge."

Unable to contain herself, she calls Naya.

"Hi Kay," Naya answers.

"Naya, I think I've found it," Kendal says excitedly.

"Found what?" Naya asks.

"Wait a second, Holden is calling me back," Kendal answers. "I'm going to put us all on a conference holo-call. You'll want to see this."

Within seconds, Naya and Holden are sitting holographically in Kendal's condo, eager to hear why she has rattled their cages.

"I figured it out," Kendal tells them.

"What?" Holden asks.

"I'm not the common denominator between Sedge's case, Nikki Nova's library book, and Beau Hadley's dreams."

"Okay," Naya says, looking for more information.

"It's not me that connected these events. It was time, or in this case a lack thereof. The common denominator was Sedge's glitch, which turned out to be a series of glitches - the reason I contacted Nikki."

"So how are they connected?" Holden asks.

"They lacked time stamps," Kendal answers. "That's what prompted Stan Satterfield to discover Cedric Davis's experiments from 2069, which also lacked time stamps."

"I don't get it," Naya says.

"Let me explain," Kendal tells her. "I was always connecting A and B instead of A and C. I was looking for a connection between Beau Hadley's visions and Nikki Nova's message, when I should have been looking for a connection between those events and Sedge Nile."

"Is there a connection?" Naya asks.

"Yes," Kendal answers; "the glitches."

"How do you know?" Holden asks.

"They align in time," Kendal answers. "When I converted all the times to UTC and ran them into my legal analysis program, their times aligned precisely. I knew there was something about *fifty-five years* when I heard it. Get a load of this; the first glitch, the one that occurred just before Sedge took the ship, happened 40,462 days after Beau's first dream, or vision."

"Okay, so how does that align?" Holden asks.

"Bear with me," Kendal says. "The second glitch, according to military logs, occurred twelve days later, just as Beau's second vision occurred twelve days after his first, again 40,462 days apart."

"No way," Naya says.

"The third vision and the third glitch too, exactly 40,462 days apart," Kendal adds.

"Mind blowing," Holden says; "but still could be a wild coincidence."

"It gets better," Kendal tells them. "They align almost to the minute. The first two sets of visions and glitches are each 40,462 days, 22 hours, and 16 minutes apart. The duration between the third vision and third glitch, however, is one minute shorter. It's the only anomaly"

"How long are the vision audio recordings?" Holden asks.

"They're short," Kendal answers; "but I think the third one is a little longer than the first two."

"That could be it," Holden tells her. "The recordings, especially back then, may have been time stamped when the recording ended, meaning the vision may have begun slightly earlier."

"Yes, that makes sense," Kendal replies. "Holden, you're a genius. When you add the duration of the recordings to the interim time between the visions and the glitches, those durations equal out to the minute. The third recording was a little longer. I think it went over a minute."

"Clever Holden," Naya says.

"Yes, but weren't there four glitches?" Holden asks.

"Yes," Kendal answers, "but take a look at this. 40,462 days is equal to 110 years. There were a hundred and ten years between the visions and the glitches, to the minute. You have to divide those durations in half to find the midpoint between the visions and the glitches."

"Fifty-five years," Holden says.

"2069," Kendal adds; "and better yet, the midpoint between the first vision and the first glitch lands precisely on July 20, 2069, the day of the Apollo Centennial; the day Nikki's flight allegedly crashed on the moon. Is that a coincidence?"

Holden and Naya sit in shock.

"This leads me to the fourth glitch," Kendal says. "It may not have a corresponding vision, but using the same lapsed-time durations, its midpoint falls at the precise time Cedric claimed in his thesis to have had his test message transmitted, again to the minute. Is that a coincidence?" she asks.

All three of them sit in total silence, out of words. They soon begin to laugh, still in shock. Could it be that

Sedge's mad quest was triggered by a set of messages transmitted in the year 2069? Looking at the facts, how could it not? If true, Cedric's messages not only traveled back in time, but forward. Could these be the transmissions sent to warn Nikki Nova, in a library book, not to board her flight? This moment couldn't be more surreal.

After a good laugh and several minutes of shared astonishment, Naya and Holden sign off the call. Kendal, too excited to sleep, changes her channel from Moondock to Earthport's orbital camera. Immediately, she recognizes the Gulf of Mexico, Florida, and the eastern US coastline. Earthport is about to fly across her southern sky. She steps out onto her balcony to look for it. Sure enough, after a few short minutes, a bright light appears in the southwest, moving swiftly and steadily southeast. How cool. She can see the station from her balcony as well as a live feed of the lights of New York on her wall-screen, filmed from that station. What a memorable night.

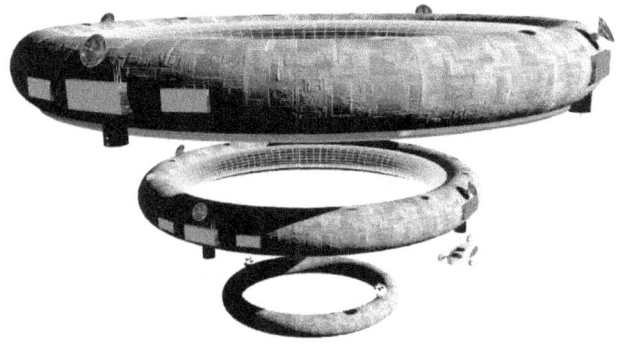

5:7

Having never been this alive, Kendal gets to her office early Monday morning, feeling more valuable than ever. She has the story of a lifetime to tell the world, but how? Where to start? Of course, where else? The Times and Tina Morgan would run it. It is, after all, highly relevant to her Joy Rider pieces. This story takes things into a whole new realm. Knowing it's a little early to call, Kendal takes a chance on Tina being in her office anyway. She dials her work number.

"Hi Kendal," Tina answers. "How are things?"

"Great Tina," Kendal replies. "Say, sorry to call so early,"

"No, not at all. I get an early start, especially on Mondays," Tina remarks. "Why? What's up?" she asks.

"I've got more to the Joy Rider story, and it's huge," Kendal tells her.

"What?" Tina asks. "Is it scandalous?"

"No, it's more romantic. It's astounding," Kendal tells her. "It involves time travel."

"Time travel," Tina says bewildered. "What are you talking about?"

"It's all conjecture but the overwhelming circumstantial evidence will blow you away. I'll tell you soon, and I have all the documentation to back me up. I just need a little more time to inform everyone I've worked with on this to ask if I can use their names."

"It sounds fascinating Kendal," Tina tells her. "As a reporter, I fully understand. I won't ask another question or tell another soul until you fill me in."

"You're awesome," Kendal replies. "I think this story will be big."

"Sounds like it," Tina says. "Looking forward to it."

Kendal smiles, watching a multi-tiered flow of traffic outside her window, pondering the profundity of the story on which she sits. Her next move, she thinks, is to tell Sedge. He is the end link of this chain. This story needs to go interstellar. Kendal checks the time; nine o'clock. Perfect. She calls Trista Rybach at NASA.

"NASA Communications Office," a young man's voice answers the phone.

"Is Trista Rybach in please?" Kendal asks.

"One moment, I'll connect you," the operator replies.

"Good morning, this is Trista Rybach," Trista answers.

"Hi Trista, this is Kendal Benz representing Sedge Nile," Kendal says.

"Hi Kendal, good to hear from you," Trista responds. "Do you need to transmit another message to Sedge?"

"You read my mind," Kendal answers. "I have news of some very interesting developments to his case."

"Sounds interesting, but I won't ask," Trista says. "When were you needing to send it?"

"As soon as possible," Kendal answers. "And I'd like to bring someone with me to join me in the message, if that's possible."

"Sure, they'll just need to scan and register with the desk when they come in," Trista tells her. "You know, I'll be gone for a week starting tomorrow, though I could leave instructions with my assistant. Or, if you wanted to come in today, I'm available just after lunch."

"The guy I want to include in the transmission is calling me right now," Kendal tells Trista. "Would you mind if I merged him into this call?" she asks.

"Not at all," Trista answers.

"Hi Kendal," Holden says. "Is there someone else on this call?"

"Yes Holden," Kendal answers. "We're talking with Trista Rybach at NASA."

"Hi Trista," Holden says.

"Hi Holden, nice to meet you." Trista tells him.

"Anyway Holden, I know you're off today," Kendal says. "Would you like to join me at the Goddard Institute this afternoon to send a message to Sedge, filling him in on the developments we discussed?"

"What time?" Holden asks.

"How about one?" Trista suggests. "We're on the corner of West 112th & Broadway."

"Sounds good," Holden says. "I'll be there."

"I'll meet you right inside the building," Kendal tells him.

Unable to hold her news in, Kendal next calls Stan Satterfield at Ground Control. He's the one, after all, who found Cedric Davis's thesis.

"Stan, how are you?" Kendal asks after he answers the call.

"Good Ms. Benz," he replies. "How are you?"

"I couldn't be better," Kendal answers. "I've got some seriously interesting news to share. Are you sitting down?"

"I'm usually sitting down," Stan answers with a chuckle. "What's so interesting?" he asks.

"The thesis you sent me from Cedric Davis, the guy transmitting messages through time..."

"Yeah," Stan says.

"Well I think not only did he do it, but we can prove it," Kendal answers.

"Who's we?" Stan asks.

"You and me," Kendal answers. "A big piece of the puzzle is in your affidavit."

"Really, how so?" Stan asks.

"In the times logged," Kendal replies. "They correspond perfectly with three dreams a guy had back in 2014."

"No offense Ms. Benz," Stan interrupts; "but you're not making a lot of sense."

"I know," Kendal says. "I prefer you to read the story that's going to come out in The Times which will detail it. I'd like to use your name though and the message times from the affidavit in the story, if you don't mind. I will get you a copy of the article in a few days and let you okay it before it's to be published."

"I don't mind at all, but it is a good idea to let me see it before it's published. The military can be sensitive sometimes," Stan says.

"You're going to like this," Kendal says. "I'll be sure they give you the credit you deserve too."

"If what you say is true," Stan tells her; "there will be a lot of renewed scientific interest in this field, including from me. I'm really looking forward to reading your story."

Kendal spends part of her morning writing out the story's timeline in point form for Tina. The rest of the morning she spends daydreaming. It's impossible for her to fully wrap her head around the interconnectedness of these events, or to comprehend her role in them. How did she stumble on this? Was she meant to?

Nearing noon, Kendal decides it's late enough to call Michael Beau Hadley in Oregon.

"Hello," he casually answers.

"Hi Michael. I got your recordings," Kendal tells him.

"Were they helpful in any way?" he asks.

"Extremely," Kendal answers. "In fact, you're not going to believe what I may have found."

"What?"

"I think your grandfather's visions may not have been just visions," Kendal tells him. "I think there really was a woman he needed to help."

"Really?" Michael responds.

"Yes," Kendal answers; "and I think he did help her. He just never knew it."

"How do you know all this?" Michael asks.

"It's going to come out in The Times in a matter of days," Kendal answers. "I'll beam you a link as soon as it does. It will explain everything clearly. I just wanted to ask if you thought it would be alright to publish and attribute the three audio recordings your grandfather made."

"Absolutely," Michael answers. "If this story backs his claims, it would be what he wanted. Please feel free."

"Awesome," Kendal replies. "Can I use your name too?"

"Why not?" Michael answers. "It'll be my fifteen minutes of fame."

"Others may contact you later wanting to know more," Kendal warns him.

"That's okay," Michael answers. "I'll be looking forward to the story.

5:8

On her pod ride back to Goddard, Kendal can hardly sit still. She's too excited. She can't stop smiling, even sometimes bursting into laughter, and then having to look around to make sure nobody has noticed. It's a high she's never felt, at least not on this level, and one that can't be described. This being her third time to visit NASA, the route is becoming quite familiar, every pod stop, every intersection, even some of the faces are beginning to look familiar. Again, she recognizes her stop in front of the Peace Fountain at the entrance to the

West 111th Street People's Garden. It's hard to miss. She hits the stop button to ensure her pod operator makes the stop.

Kendal gets off, stepping into another warm, sunny day. The city is so bright and green. She walks eastward on 111th to Broadway, hangs a right, and walks the final block to the Goddard Institute. She sees Holden standing on the corner outside the entrance, taking in the sunshine. They're both a little early. Holden has a youthful look of excitement on his face, energized to be a part of this ground-shaking discovery. He's also excited and kind of nervous to be sending his first message to Sedge. It's been over five years.

Holden follows Kendal into the building, where they check in at the security desk with the same guard Kendal has met twice before. The guard calls Trista's office, then motions Kendal and Holden that way. When they arrive, Trista is still eating lunch; take-out Chinese noodles. She sets the food aside.

"Welcome back," Trista greets them with a smile.

"Thank you Trista," Kendal replies. "This is Holden, a former partner and close friend of Sedge's."

"Nice to meet you," Holden tells Trista.

"Nice to meet you too," Trista replies. "I hope things are going well with Sedge's case."

"His case is closed," Kendal says. "It couldn't have gone better. We're here to fill him in on some fascinating follow-up details that are relevant to it."

"Sounds interesting," Trista says.

"It's incredibly interesting," Kendal tells her. "Do you believe in time travel?"

"I don't know," Trista answers. "I guess I haven't given it much thought."

"You will," Kendal responds. "I wish I could tell you more now, but there's a big story that will come out in The Times very soon. I'll make sure you see it. It will explain everything in detail."

"No kidding?" Trista asks, now looking really interested. "I look forward to reading it."

Trista escorts Kendal and Holden down the hall, to the communications room with the transmission equipment. She makes sure they're set up and ready to transmit, then leaves to allow them their privacy. Kendal places another chair in front of the camera for Holden. She adjusts the mic angle. Holden can see that she knows the drill.

"Are you ready, or do you need a little time?" she asks Holden.

"Do you want me to explain the whole story?" Holden asks.

"No, you don't have to," Kendal answers. "We can tell him as well to look for the article in The Times, which we can have Trista transmit the moment it's published."

"Okay, then I guess I am ready," Holden tells Kendal as he takes a deep breath.

"You'll do fine," Kendal tells him. She then counts down from three on her fingers and hits record on the touchscreen. A red light illuminates. "Hi Sedge, this is Kendal," she says into the camera. "I have some seriously fascinating news to tell you about your case, and I've brought someone with me today to help me tell you about it, someone you know."

"Hi Sedge," Holden says into the camera. "It's been a long time, and it's going to be a lot longer before you get this. I hope you are alive and well. In fact, billions of people hope so as well. I want you to know that I'm not angry for what you did. I was hurt but have healed. I'm actually proud of you," he adds with a smile. "That's not why I'm here though. I'm here because Kendal has uncovered..."

"We have uncovered," Kendal pipes in.

"Okay, we, though mostly Kendal, have uncovered what we strongly believe to be the source of the transmission glitch that GulfStar sought to pin on you. In a few days, we'll be sending you a Times article that will explain it all in detail, which will include the names of everybody involved. What we can tell you today, however, in a nutshell, is that the glitches appear to have been messages transmitted in the year 2069, sent from a telecommunications student in Vancouver BC. The messages appear to have traveled not only forward to us in time, but backward as well, where we believe they were received in the year 2014."

"It's true," Kendal adds. "You can read the whole story soon enough and judge for yourself. What Holden has just told you, however, is clearly the most rational explanation for the glitches, and we wouldn't have discovered this had you not taken GulfStar's ship. We couldn't have done it without you."

"That's right," Holden says. "Your actions have uncovered the story of the century." Holden looks at Kendal as if he has nothing to add. She nods.

"Like we mentioned, there's a story coming soon that will explain every detail," Kendal says. "Look for it. We just wanted to give you a heads up."

"I really hope you get this," Holden says, feeling like he should say more but not knowing how. "Goodbye and take care of yourself, Sedge."

Kendal and Holden bid a goodbye to Trista before leaving NASA's Goddard Institute. Too excited to return to work, they saunter up Broadway to 116th and walk through Columbia University's campus. Kendal gives Holden a brief campus tour as she strolls down memory lane. They grab juice and sandwiches at a kiosk set up in the Student Service Center before walking past the law school and over to Morningside Park, a sacred place for Kendal, where she had often gone to escape the stresses of law school. Excited, she shows Holden her favorite path to Morningside Pond. They find an available bench near the waterfall, where they rest for lunch. The sun is sitting high in the warm blue sky.

"It's hard to believe this is real, don't you think?" Holden asks Kendal as she takes the first bite of her turkey club.

"I've been having that same feeling a lot lately," Kendal replies. "It seems like we're in a dream."

"Do you think Sedge will get our message?" Holden asks.

"I do," Kendal replies. "It's what ties the meaning of all this together. It's what gives these events purpose. I think these events are somehow aligned on a plane we can't fully comprehend."

"Yes," Holden says. "It sure seems that way."

"That alignment includes Sedge," Kendal tells him. "Were he not out there going around or sitting on that distant moon, none of this would align."

"When is The Times going to run this story?" Holden asks.

"Within days, I hope," Kendal replies. "I've got to get in touch with Tina again, but before I do, there's one more person I need to talk to - someone I need to run this story by."

"I think I know who you're talking about," Holden tells Kendal smiling, nodding his head.

"I'm taking the rest of the week off," Kendal says. "This is something I feel I need to do face-to-face."

"I couldn't agree more," Holden says understandingly.

5:8

Mach three, Kendal thinks to herself; *three times the speed of sound*. She ponders the notion as she stares at a stream of endless clouds, flashing below. Using up some long-saved travel merits, she's got a stunning, half-dome, side bubble view seat in Deck Class. Sedge and his journeys come to mind. She activates her floating screen to see detailed flight analytics. To keep her brain exercised, she pulls up a calculator and conversion table to compare her flight's speed with Sedge's flight to Luna Nuevo.

If sound travels at 340.29 meters per second, or just over a third of a kilometer, Mach 3 equals 1020.87 meters, or just over a kilometer per second. To simplify, Kendal rounds down to calculate herself moving at one kilometer per second. Light travels at close to three-hundred thousand kilometers per second. Assuming Sedge reached three-quarters light speed, the speeds estimated by NASA's deep-space probes, then even though Kendal is soaring over Minnesota at three times the speed of sound, she's still only flying at roughly 1/300,000th of the speed Sedge attained to get to the Centauri System. What a daring flight he took. Speeds like that are simply unfathomable.

Kendal feels herself slide weightlessly toward the front of her seat, pulled forward as her plane initializes its descent. A pong sounds, followed with an announcement as the flight's airspeed indicator changes to Mach two.

"Good morning ladies and gentlemen, we've started our descent into Vancouver. We'll be touching down in nine minutes, and at the gate in sixteen. Please return to your seats and ensure your safety belts are secure. Thank you."

Objects grow clearer in Kendal's window as motion blur diminishes with the aircraft's speed. It's like time is slowing down with the plane, which it is, just not as much as it feels from the forward shift of deceleration. All windows go grey as the aircraft sinks into clouds, losing its visual perspective. Soon, however, it emerges from the clouds' underside. The Fraser Valley appears. The sky is overcast with thick, swirling high-speed clouds. They look like they hold a lot of moisture, but don't appear to be threatening rain, at least not at the moment. The view is jaw-dropping, like a painting. The mountain tops to the north of the city disappear into the cloud layers. The landscape is a lot like Kendal imagined it would be from pictures she's seen, having never been here. Her excitement grows as the plane slows, banking a slight turn to align with its designated runway.

"Ladies and Gentlemen, this is your captain," an announcement comes over the sound system. "If you haven't already, please return to your seats and buckle your harness for touchdown. The current temperature in Vancouver is twenty-four degrees Celsius. Winds are calm and skies are overcast. We'll be at your gate at YVR in a few minutes. Thank you for flying with us today."

Kendal's plane aligns with YVR's runway 26L and gently glides to a landing so softly that she can't feel when the craft actually touches down. From Mach 3 to zero; air travel has really come a long way. Within minutes, the plane is docked at its gate. Excited, Kendal deplanes and follows her fellow passengers to Customs & Immigration Services, where she's scanned as she walks through a short hallway. Inside the main terminal, she makes her way to the SkyBus platform, where she's able to walk directly onto the next bus for downtown Vancouver. Her timing is divine. She should be to her hotel by noon. It's hard to believe, given that she woke up in New York. With the three additional time-zone hours and supersonic flight, days can really feel long.

Six minutes after boarding, Kendal's lighter-than-air SkyBus closes its bay doors and begins its flight to the downtown. Though tethered with cables and pulleys to a main line, the bus floats ever-so smoothly above the buildings below, giving passengers an unforgettable approach to this world class city. Kendal can smell the ocean air. It feels so much colder than New York. She wonders how common this weather is. The city rises in front of snow-capped mountains as her SkyBus nears the downtown. It feels good to be here.

Kendal gets off the SkyBus at City Centre, where she connects to the Georgia Street Gondola, following some sound advice she'd read on her flight. This is how transportation should always be, she thinks as she reaches the Pinnacle, her towering hotel in Vancouver's West End. Her entire morning has flowed flawlessly, as if the world worked perfectly, at least for a morning.

Kendal's room is on the thirty-eighth floor, with a mostly obstructed, though partial view of Stanley Park in front of a high forested mountain backdrop. The low clouds ad to the picturesque scene, by which Kendal is too distracted to unpack. She sits on the edge of her bed, taking in a lush view that New York City lacks. She's startled to her senses, however, by a huge, white seagull that glides to a sudden rest on her balcony rail. It lets out a piercing call. She starts to unpack her things.

Too awake to nap, Kendal calls Nikki.

"Hello Kendal, I got your message," Nikki answers.

"Hi Nikki," Kendal replies.

"Did you get in alright?" Nikki asks.

"I did," Kendal answers. "I had a wonderful morning. Everything went smoothly. This city is so lovely,"

"Thank you," Nikki says. "I'm glad everything went well. Are you staying downtown?"

"Yes," Kendal answers; "I'm at the Pinnacle."

"Oh," Nikki responds; "I'm just a few blocks from there."

"Yes, that was my plan," Kendal says. "I knew you lived near Stanley Park. When they told me this hotel wasn't far from the park, I thought it would be convenient."

"Well I'm really looking forward to meeting you," Nikki tells Kendal. "I'm retired now, as you probably know, so my schedule is wide open. You're welcome to visit me here if you like."

"That sounds nice," Kendal says. "I tell you what. I just need a quick shower and to freshen up, then I can come right over. How does two sound?" she asks.

"Sounds good to me," Nikki answers excitedly.

"Have you eaten?" Kendal asks Nikki.

"Not lunch, no," Nikki answers.

"I could grab something along the way," Kendal suggests.

"That would be great," Nikki tells her.

"Any suggestions or restrictions?" Kendal asks.

"No, just get anything you like," Nikki says. "I can pay you back when you get here."

"No, please don't worry," Kendal replies. "I'll see you at two."

Showered and refreshed, Kendal walks out of her hotel and into the city. Aimlessly, she happens upon Bentall Centre's food court, where she combines some Indian take-out, butter chicken, saffron rice, and nan with a side-order of dolmades from the Greek restaurant next to it.

Kendal arrives at Nikki's building at five-after-two. After being let in, she takes an elevator to the 11th floor, a private floor with only a few residences. Nikki appears on screen as Kendal nears her door.

"Please just come in," Nikki says. "The door is unlatched. I'm on the balcony,"

Kendal lets herself into the entrance of the condominium and closes the door behind her. She takes off her shoes and enters the residence through an enchanting, spade-shaped, concrete entry-way. The place is cozy and warm, giving off strong vibes of a tenant with highly refined tastes.

Kendal spots Nikki sitting on her balcony, staring out over a much bigger part of Stanley Park than can be seen from her hotel room. Not wanting to make Nikki get up, Kendal makes herself at home, going directly to the balcony with the food. When Nikki sees Kendal, she starts to get up, but Kendal insists that it's not necessary. She places the food on plates with some bottled water on Nikki's balcony bistro table.

"I got mostly Indian food with a side of Greek dolmades," she tells Nikki.

"Wow, how kind of you," Nikki tells her. "You didn't have to bring lunch."

"It's my pleasure," Kendal says; "and it's my pleasure to meet you."

"I'm excited to meet you," Nikki says smiling, sitting quietly in the cool air with a blanket on her lap.

"Do you want any curry, dolmades, or rice?" Kendal asks.

"I'd like just a little of everything," Nikki tells her.

"Coming right up," Kendal replies smiling, overjoyed by the occasion. She dishes a small plate full of samples for Nikki and sets it beside her on the table. After serving Nikki, she helps herself to the same medley.

Not much is said as the two enjoy their lunch and the moment.

"That area there, just past those trees," Nikki tells Kendal, pointing toward the park; "that's where Cedric and I used to always go, over by Lost Lagoon." Kendal watches the trees sway ever-so-gently for just a moment, then stop. This city is enveloped with nature.

"He did it," Kendal tells Nikki. "He sent his transmissions through time."

"That's what your message said," Nikki replies. "Are you sure?"

"Nikki," Kendal says, squeezing her frail, thin hands; "it's why I'm here. I believe it with all my heart. It appears to be the most logical explanation for these documented events."

"Really," Nikki says with a smile; "and you say it has something to do with the Joy Rider case?"

"Yes, it does," Kendal says laughing. "There were four glitches in the communication system. The first glitch was blamed on Joy Rider, sending him running. NASA recorded the glitches too. Those glitches align perfectly in time with Beau Hadley's visions, having the exact same durations between them, to the minute.

"Even better, what makes it incontrovertible to me is the midpoints between those three visions and those four glitches; they all land in the summer of 2069. The first one falls on July 20, 2069, the date you would have broadcast the Apollo Centennial from the moon had you gone. The other really significant midpoint would be the one from the fourth glitch. It doesn't have a corresponding vision, but if you calculate the midpoint using the same transmission lengths, it falls to the exact minute of the transmission time mentioned in Cedric's thesis. Those glitches weren't glitches," Kendal adds. "They were Cedric's radio signals."

"It's amazing that you figured that out" Nikki remarks in astonishment.

"Yes," Kendal answers, dipping a dolma into some egg-lemon sauce. "To me, that's the calculation that connects this whole story. People can believe what they will. In fact, I sometimes have to run the dates again just to believe it. These numbers may not be telling us the full story, but they don't lie."

"This may sound a little crazy," Nikki tells Kendal...

"Nothing sounds crazy at this point," Kendal replies. "What is it? You can tell me."

"I've been having déjà vu since you first contacted me," Nikki says. "Sometimes, the feeling can be pretty strong, more like a memory, where I feel that my life is aligned with forces beyond my imagination."

"That doesn't sound crazy to me," Kendal tells her.

"Last night, the moon was so round and bright," Nikki says. "It happened again last night, when I was looking at the moon over the park. I knew there was something so familiar about the moon. Then I read your message, and how you had pieced all this together. The feeling intensified. It all made perfect sense, though just for a moment in time. It all made such clear sense," Nikki adds softly as tears slide down her cheeks.

"Are you okay?" Kendal asks, handing Nikki a tissue.

"I'm fine," Nikki answers. "I'm so happy. I only wish Cedric could be here to see his dream unfold."

"I'm sorry that he isn't. I wish I could meet him," Kendal tells her. "Though I wasn't meant to," she adds; "I take comfort in what I've learned from him."

"Oh," Nikki says with widening eyes.

"Yes Nikki," Kendal replies. "I've learned that he's out there, somewhere in time."

Nikki smiles warmly, staring out over the park.

Part 6

Lunita is so close tonight that Sedge can make out mountains, craters, and what looks to be a canyon on its surface, all with unaided eyes. It's brighter tonight too, combining with the rings' glow to give off almost enough light for Sedge to make out the landscape around him. He stops, cuts his flashlight, and takes a break to take in the night sky. More and more stars appear as his pupils dilate to adjust to the darkness. Nobody back on Earth would believe this sight. It's dreamy, like a poster for a sci-fi film.

A flash appears on a distant hill ahead when Sedge presses the solar-beacon locater on his wrist panel. There it is, the last beacon. He's following a course he knows well in the daylight but has never traveled by night; a course to the overlook. The course follows two ancient riverbeds, then crosses a large field of dunes to the rim of what he calls the Great Crater. The course itself is largely sandy and relatively safe. There are dangers present, however. The course remains in the highlands, where oxygen is needed. Furthermore, the crater's rim sits thousands of meters above its basin, all the way around it. Its walls are steep, practically vertical, rendering the crater inaccessible. Sedge, however, is convinced there must be a way in and obsessively determined to find it.

He presses on. Upon reaching the last beacon, he sees it; a dark void in the terrain where the ground disappears. He presses his locater again and a blue light appears on the edge of the void, marking the overlook. After reaching it, Sedge again cuts his lights and let's his eyes adjust to the darkness. Within a few minutes, he can see most of the crater's rim. He checks his oxygen supply. He still has twenty-six percent remaining on his first of two tanks. It took him forty-five minutes longer to get here in the dark than it usually does by day.

After catching his breath, Sedge makes his way eastward along the edge of the crater, hoping to get further than before, to a vantage point where he can get a glimpse of the crater's interior western wall. He has to tread slowly and carefully in the dark. One slip could easily be his last. It takes him another twenty minutes, but he finally reaches a cliff that extends into the crater like a small peninsula into water. Carefully, he walks out onto it, almost to its end. There, he sets up his camera on a tripod and begins taking long-exposure photos to see what he can't with the naked eye. Soon, he's looking at clear pictures of cliff walls below the overlook, angles never seen before. Further down, his photos reveal something he had hoped to find; a waterfall, flowing out of the wall of the crater.

"Eureka," he says to himself; "passage."

Satisfied, he makes his way back to the overlook, where he sits under a sky of endless stars, staring at the pictures he took.

"Oxygen at five percent," a voice inside his helmet warns.

Sedge changes his oxygen pack.

"Sedge to base camp," he says into his radio. "Are you receiving this Bite?"

"Loud and clear Sedge," Bite replies.

"Wow, this is the furthest out this radio has worked," Sedge replies. "The comm relays must be working. Anyway, I'm at the overlook. I've got what I came for and am now starting back."

"Roger that," Bite responds. "You're due for your filling."

"My tooth has been reminding me," Sedge responds. "I should be at the dome in a little over two hours."

Taking one last look over the deep crater, Sedge sees it; a clear glimpse of the future. This very overlook will one day be a tourist spot after this moon is colonized. Lights will blanket this land. It's inevitable. The human race not only knows what's here, but how to get here. There really is no stopping it. This moment's worth cannot be gauged, sitting here alone between a violent, catastrophic impact that occurred millions of years ago, and a colonization of a species from the next star, over the next few centuries.

A slight westerly wind begins to blow as Sedge sets out again toward what is now the first beacon on his journey home. High overhead, he sees the light of the Cortes Orbiter glide steadily by. He can't take his mind off the crater, convinced he may have found a way into it. That's probably its allure, he thinks; it's inaccessibility. It taps something deep within him. It's the same passion that brought him to this forbidden moon; the thrill of just knowing it's off limits. It is, after all, the prime motive of any conquest.

An hour into his return, Sedge comes to the most difficult stretch of the course, an area of rugged, rocky terrain between the two sandy riverbeds. He crosses the ground carefully, but slips and falls on his side as he climbs down an embankment into the second riverbed. He stands up and brushes himself off, fortunately without injury. With still over an hour's walk back to the dome, a broken bone could prove deadly if suffered while on life support. He can feel his back, however, gradually beginning to stiffen as he walks further along. It reminds him of his first day on this moon. If he could survive that, tonight should be a walk in the park.

Winds have really picked up by the time the dome comes into view. Dust is stirring. Sedge's oxygen reads thirty-two percent, with five percent still remaining in his original tank. A sensation that he's crossing a lifeless, ancient ocean floor overtakes him as he makes it back to the bio-dome.

6:2

"Welcome back," Bite tells Sedge as he enters the dome. "How was your night hike?"

"Great," Sedge answers. "It went better than expected. It feels good to now have more options on these endless nights."

"Did you run into any problems?" Bite asks.

"I fell on my hip coming back," Sedge answers. "I'm alright, though I think I'll put my back-brace on for a while."

"Are you ready for your filling?" Bite asks.

"Yeah, actually," Sedge replies. "Just give me a minute to put my things away."

Several minutes later Sedge sits back on a recliner while Bite prepares the dental equipment.

"I discovered a waterfall on the inner wall of the crater," Sedge tells Bite.

"Really, how interesting," she responds.

"It bolsters my theory," Sedge adds. "I think I know the source of those falls. I suspect they flow from the same caverns found on the northeastern side of the canyons. I'm guessing there's a way into the crater through those caverns. There must be."

"Why are you so obsessed with this crater?" Bite asks.

"Primordial urges," Sedge answers; "difficult to explain. You see it in children, and how they love to build tree houses or forts. We came from caves. It's in our blood. This crater is the peak of these urges. You should see it. It's truly entrancing to behold. It's unique. In fact, I first noticed it when I flew almost over it during my entry and approach the day I crash-landed. It's difficult to imagine anything more scenic."

"It sounds beautiful," Bite says.

"Immensely," Sedge replies. "I'll never forget the first day I made it to the overlook. It was dry and windy on the highlands, but foggy and gray deep down in the crater. I could only see the higher-elevation trees climb above the fog line, unique trees. Sitting bull's eye, dead center of the crater like an island in the fog was the mighty tower. It made me feel like I was in a Chinese painting. This is an entire world within itself; a unique environment nestled in the hollowed remnants of a massive, catastrophic event. It's harmony in the wake of chaos, untouched by time."

"You seem really happy on Luna Nuevo, even being so alone," Bite says.

"I am happy," Sedge replies. "I do miss things, but I've never been one to live in the past."

"Will you ever go back to Earth?" Bite inquires.

"I doubt the opportunity will arise," Sedge replies.

"What if it does?" Bite asks.

"I'm an outlaw," Sedge answers; "a wanted man. Remember, I'm on the run."

"Would you return if you had assurances that you wouldn't face any legal consequences for your actions?"

"I don't know," Sedge answers. "I would miss this place so deeply. I still feel like I have unfinished business here. It will take NASA years to advance technology to the point of returning crew, or anything for that matter. It won't be until they robotically build and launch the ground-based laser system here with the Ponce de Leon mission."

"What if they moved up their mission plans to get you back?" Bite asks.

"I wouldn't go," Sedge answers; "not across that deep, dark sea cooped up on whatever they're sending, not anytime soon at least."

"How about eventually?" Bite asks.

"I don't know," Sedge answers.

"Open wide," Bite tells him.

Bite gives Sedge a shot of procaine to each side of his lower right molar, number thirty. Within seconds, he feels nothing on the right side of his mouth.

"I have some good news," Bite tells Sedge.

"Oh, what?" Sedge asks, now slightly slurring his speech.

"The first batch of Banana Blue wine has reached maturity," she answers. "It's drinkable."

"That calls for a party," Sedge says. "Let's have a Banana Blue party tonight, before I go into my final sleep."

"Very well, a Banana Blue party it is. How is your jaw feeling? Are you numb?" Bite asks.

"Yes, Sedge says, almost slobbering.

Half an hour later, Sedge sits at his desk, still numb from the filling.

"This is Sedge Nile," he records into his comm station's camera. "I've just returned from the edge of the crater, this time in the dark. I discovered a waterfall, which I think could be coming from the same caverns I've discovered in the canyons. I'm going to attempt entry tomorrow, via the caverns in the canyons. Proxima Centauri has been wandering further from her sisters in the sky, making the days here longer and the nights shorter, with much longer, purple twilights. It's not easy to adjust to these really long days, psychologically or physiologically. My sleep patterns are still subject to change with the position of this moon.

"Otherwise, I'm doing really well. I'm looking forward to exploring the caverns, and hopefully soon the crater. I'll live feed the greatest moments to the Cortes.

"Sedge out."

6:3

Sedge taps his baton in the air, prompting the kettle drums to soften. This helps bring out the high note in Muddy Waters' blues harp solo. The strings quiet as the song, Blown Away, decrescendos. Sedge, having worked on this for weeks, couldn't look more serious. The ensemble is tight tonight as they finish with an intense, unified power chord. A loud ovation from energetic partygoers ensues.

"I'll be taking a short break," Muddy announces. "In the meantime, please continue to enjoy the classical sounds of the London Philharmonic Orchestra."

"Attention everyone," Bite announces to the lively room, taking advantage of the brief silence. "Tonight is special."

"How so? Is Sedge going to drop his pants again?" Voltaire yells out with a chuckle, holding a tall glass of Canyon Vineyard's first batch of Banana Blue.

"No," Sedge interrupts. "That's the good news."

"Actually, the good news is that all of you will be able to taste the food and drinks at tonight's party," Bite announces.

"How is that possible?" Neil asks.

"Through an algorithm," Bite answers; "I can tap my material sensors, cherry pick your memory banks, reorganize them, and thus create unique tastes."

"We can now all experience this bountiful feast," Sedge adds, pointing to the table full of food harvested both from the canyon and the garden. "It's our Plymouth Rock moment, so please enjoy."

The orchestra kicks in to a contemporary version of Four Seasons. Neil carries on his conversation with Amelia Earhart, comparing stories of their times at Purdue University. Sedge joins Marco and Voltaire.

"You tend to exaggerate a lot," Voltaire tells Polo.

"Marco often speaks in metaphor," Sedge says to defend him. "He's known as one who can paint pictures with words. It's how he survived the barbarianism of the thirteenth century, if I recall reading."

"Yes, so I've heard," Voltaire replies.

"Sedge," Marco says; "if you don't mind my asking, why did you do it?"

"Do what?" Sedge asks.

"Take the ship," Marco answers.

"You don't have to answer that," Voltaire tells Sedge, rolling his eyes at Marco's audacity.

"No, it's okay," Sedge replies. "It was a crime of opportunity for me," he tells them. You see I knew well which buttons to push. I had played the scenario out so many times in my mind that when the moment actually arrived, I just acted on impulse."

"Interesting," Marco replies. "Opportunity knocks in many forms."

"Indeed," Sedge says, raising his glass to Marco's for a quick toast. "There's something I've been meaning to ask you," Sedge goes on to mention.

"Anything," Marco responds.

"You eventually returned to Venice from the Far East," Sedge points out.

"I did," Marco replies.

"Didn't you miss it after returning?" Sedge asks him.

"Deeply," Marco answers; "but as you say, the grass is always greener on the other side."

"True," Sedge affirms.

"I can see your dilemma," Marco tells him. "You, even more than I, have lived in two worlds. Where one is, the other is not."

"Hey everyone, gather around," Sedge announces. "I want to show you my latest quest. Bite, can you cue my 3D crater?" A rotating 3D hologram of the impact crater Sedge has been obsessing over fills the center of the room. Sedge stops the model's rotation with his hand and zooms in on their current location, the bio-dome. "The crater I'm talking about is here," he says, scrolling the terrain along his beacon-marked trail to the crater's overlook. There, sedge activates a textured mode that applies imaging from his trips to the crater. Once the satellite-generated, topographical mapping is activated, the site looks breathtakingly real, similar to the crater, as well as the highlands around the dome. Earth should love this model. It has to be the most distant land ever to be so accurately mapped.

"There it is," Sedge tells his guests, pointing to the crater. "That's where I'm going after sun up."

"It's huge," Neil says.

"Incredibly," Sedge replies. "Look how beautiful it is. It's inaccessible too, untouched by man, but I think I've found a way in."

"How," Amelia asks. "It looks like an impenetrable fortress."

"Yes it does," Sedge replies. "Here," he says, pointing to his recently discovered waterfall. "Look how thin the wall is behind the waterfall, the same wall that separates the canyon from the crater."

"Okay," Marco says.

"I know the other side of that wall from my trips to the canyon," Sedge tells them. "It's cavernous with running water. I'm guessing the same water source that feeds that waterfall."

"I can see why it's calling to you," Marco says.

"I told you so," Sedge tells Bite. "The crater sits deep in the ground," Sedge adds; "as deep as the canyons, if not deeper. It's full of flowing water, vegetation, trees, all kinds of plant life, and oxygen."

"Look at the tower in the center," Neil points out.

"Isn't it awesome?" Sedge asks. "It looks like there may be a way to scale it from its northern side, assuming I can get to it."

"The top looks like it has an oasis of its own," Voltaire points out. "Is that a cave?"

"Most likely, they're everywhere. I won't be satisfied until I reach the top of that tower," Sedge tells them. "It's my Shangri-La."

"Based on my travels, it sounds more like *Alamut* to me," Marco says.

"Alamut?" Neil asks.

"The Persian mountain fortress where young assassins were trained," Marco replies. "They were drugged with opiates before being brought into or out of the high mountain grounds, concealing its entrance and exit. Once inside, their every pleasure was indulged; wine, damsels trained in the arts of amorous allurement, you name it. When they woke days later from another opium induced sleep to find themselves cast out, into the real world, they were told they'd been to paradise and that the only way back was through their servitude, which in their case meant to carry out assassinations."

"Fascinating," Sedge says. "I knew Marco had a lot to add to this party."

"One question," Voltaire asks Marco; "did they wake up from their opium highs wearing pants?" A brief, collective laughter rumbles through the room.

"Ha hah," Sedge tells Voltaire. "I'll have you know I haven't had any pethidine since the last party, and I don't intend to take any more. I've kicked that habit."

"Probably wise," Voltaire tells Sedge. "You were a bit out of control."

"Those were extreme times," Sedge replies. "Besides, we've got Banana Blue wine now. Who needs opium?"

A powerful feeling of euphoria takes over Sedge's senses. Out of the blue, he begins laughing. Soon, he finds he can't stop, now laughing hysterically. Neil joins in.

Moments later, so does Marco, Amelia, and soon all guests, all provoked by Sedge.

"It's the Banana Blue," Sedge says after catching his breath. There's something in here that really tickles the liver."

Sedge mingles among friends, drinking. Though Bite and the holographic guests can taste the food and drinks, they can't consume them. The entire food supply is really for Sedge, whose life now seems to be free of peril. His stars are so aligned.

"Neil definitely seems to have caught a buzz on the wine," Sedge tells Bite.

"Yes," she replies. "Like his sense of taste, his frame of mind too can be altered based on current stimuli being interpreted according to his past experiences."

"So had he never drunk in his lifetime, would he be able to feel intoxicated?" Sedge asks.

"No, he wouldn't," Bite answers; "at least not accurately."

"These people, especially Neil, have become true friends of mine," Sedge tells Bite.

"What makes you say so?" Bite asks.

"Their personalities continue to evolve," Sedge answers; "now not only based on their lifetime experiences, but also their time spent interacting with the holo-deck, and with me."

"That's true," Bite replies.

"They're developing post-mortem, derivative personalities," Sedge adds; "personalities unique to this day and age, to this situation, and unique to our group."

"Yes," Bite replies. "I can see how your friendships have developed."

"*Our* friendships Bite," Sedge says. "You're just as much a part of this as anyone."

"Thank you Sedge," Bite responds.

"Thank you Bite," Sedge says.

"For what?" Bite asks.

"For everything," Sedge answers; "the new filling, the food, the Banana Blue beverages. It's all so perfect. You've made my life here so perfect."

"It's my pleasure," Bite replies.

Two hours later, Sedge can feel it all catching up with him; the wine, the day, and the increased gravity. Staying true to his gentleman form, he excuses himself from the party, allowing his guests to carry on. Laughing to himself, he makes his way back to his room, where he lies on his bed, smiling, listening to music from the party over the sound of wind outside the dome.

6:4

The screen to Sedge's comm station suddenly lights up. Sedge sits up from his bed. The screen begins to flash pictures of Earth. Then a man in a police uniform appears. He looks like he's saying something, giving some kind of warning, but the volume on the transmission is too low to hear. The screen shifts to a fleet of ships approaching what looks to be Luna Nuevo. Sedge scrambles to find the volume but the option is oddly missing from his screen.

Suddenly, bright light appears outside his window. Sedge steps out of his room, walks out of the dome and into the windy night. One by one, ships fly overhead, descending over the highlands. One of the ship's search lights lock on to Sedge. An announcement can be heard over its PA system.

"Sedge Nile," it says. "You are being put under arrest. Do not attempt to evade arrest."

"This all seems a little overboard, don't you think?" Sedge yells to the ship. "I need a drink of water."

Sedge opens his eyes to a room filled with darkness. There are no ships outside his window, no police officers. The wind, however, is real. It has increased significantly, rattling the dome. Sedge's mouth is so dry that he can't even open it. He rises from his bed to realize that dehydration isn't his only issue; his back has stiffened and his head feels like it's been axe driven. He stumbles in the dark to the main room. It too is dark. The party obviously must have come to an end. He feels his way to the kitchen, grabs a tall glass of water, and puts it up to his arid mouth. It's the Banana Blue, he thinks. He's never been this parched in his life. Once the water has separated his lips, and his tongue from the roof of his mouth, he finishes the full glass within seconds. Talk about hitting the spot. He takes two ibuprofen with his second glass of water. Outside, he can see the sky has turned from black to a deep purple. Proxima will soon make its way over the horizon. Sedge considers his condition and wonders if he'll have to postpone his crater quest another day. With every fiber of his being, however, he wants to go. These nights are too long to wait another one out. He goes back to bed, this time dressed for it, under the covers. He has a few more hours to get the sleep he needs before he has to decide.

At least, he thinks, I'm not on a ship back to Earth to stand trial.

6:5

Sedge awakens a few hours later to a lighter sky. Proxima is cracking the horizon, dimly lighting the plains. Soon, Alpha and Beta Centauri would rise. He gets up and shakes his head to see if it still aches. To his surprise, it doesn't. He's feeling a lot better than he did a few hours earlier and glad he woke in the night to hydrate. His back, however, still has a stiffness to it, so he puts on his brace for a little extra support. Its compression always seems to keep his rogue lumbar in place, where it needs to be to heal.

In the main room, Bite is cleaning up after last night's party.

"Did you sleep well?" she asks.

"I've slept better," Sedge answers; "but I'm rested."

"That was quite a party last night," Bite adds.

"Yeah, anything happen after I crashed?" Sedge asks.

"Not really," Bite answers. "Sigmund ended up giving the group a lecture on obsessive-compulsive disorders. Things just kind of faded away from there."

"Obsessive-compulsive disorders," Sedge asks; "how did that come up?"

"Everybody was still looking at your 3D crater model, discussing your obsession with reaching its tower," Bite replies.

"I see," Sedge says; "but that only explains obsession. Psychology tends to lump it together with compulsion."

"What could be more compulsive than stealing a ship?" Bite asks rhetorically.

"Good point," Sedge answers. "So it sounds like everybody was psycho-analyzing me behind my back," he replies.

"A little," Bite answers. "They're all jealous of you."

"Of me?" Sedge asks in flattery. "Why me?"

"Because their days have come and gone," Bite answers. "You're still living in yours, taking it all in. They can only experience vicariously, through you."

"That's ironic," Sedge says to himself laughing.

"What is ironic?" Bite asks, having overheard.

"We envy each other for the same reasons," Sedge answers. "A part of me envies them for being dead. They've all reached their great craters."

"Don't wish your life away," Bite tells him. "It's too short."

"I don't," Sedge replies. "In fact, I love life, it just gets tiring sometimes. Have I ever told you that I'm jealous of you?" he asks Bite.

"Jealous of me?" Bite asks. "No, you haven't."

"It's true," Sedge responds. "I've been jealous since we met."

"Why are you jealous of me?" Bite asks.

"Because you beat me to Luna Nuevo," Sedge answers. "I realize that I'm the first person to walk on this moon, but still a little envious just the same."

"I'm sorry if I've made you jealous," Bite replies.

"No need to be sorry," Sedge tells her. "I'm also proud of you."

"Thanks," Bite says.

"I'm going for it," Sedge tells her.

"The crater?" Bite asks.

"The crater," Sedge answers. "If water can find access, so can I."

"I thought you would," Bite replies. "So I've charged your battery packs and replenished your oxygen tanks."

"How thoughtful," Sedge tells her.

Sedge has breakfast, grabs a shower, and packs his pack.

"My back is a little stiff," he tells Bite. "I'm going to wear my brace."

"Good idea," she replies. "Don't forget to pack the first-aid kit too. Even with the additional comm relays you put in place, there's nobody to help you if you have a medical emergency."

"True," Sedge replies; "but there's been nobody to help me since I left Earth."

"What am I?" Bite asks; "chopped liver?"

"No human, I should say," Sedge clarifies.

Sedge sets out under a dark purple sky. Days dawn ever-so slowly on Luna, especially since Proxima drifted into its current position, but the wind is dying with the darkness. It seems that every day presents a new picture, each uniquely scenic. Out of the dome, Sedge feels alone. All this beauty and no one with whom to share it.

It seems that his Luna honeymoon is fading, and for the first time on this moon, he's feeling lonely.

The sky brightens to a dark pinkish hue by the time he reaches the canyon rim. Clouds have accumulated in the canyon, blanketing its entire floor. This is typical, and they often burn off by mid-day. Sedge observes them as they swiftly flow through the canyon like a river. Soon, he reaches the coulee and begins his descent beneath the arch, into the mighty fissure. For Sedge, this never grows old.

With rope ladders in strategic locations and even a small bridge constructed over what used to be an impassible crevasse, Sedge is to the first tier's ledge in half the time it took him the first time he'd ever entered the canyon. Repetition leads naturally to proficiency. Just above the cloud-line, Sedge walks along the tier's ledge, thinking about Bite's question; will he ever return to Earth? He could only imagine doing so under the assurance that he would not face trial. Given that assurance, however, he can now see himself returning one day. Why not? Marco made it back to Venice, Columbus returned to Spain, and of course Neil got back to Earth. It seems to be a pattern among explorers.

Eventually, Sedge reaches the coulee to the second tier. He follows it down, deeper into the canyon, into the clouds. Like most mornings on Luna, at least the windless ones, this morning is quiet. There are no sirens, dogs barking, or birds in the sky. There aren't even crickets. This moon is quiet, a great place to get some sleep so long as you don't overdo it on Banana Blue.

Vegetation in the canyon seems to be changing seasonally. This is fascinating for Sedge to observe. Luna's three suns and its gravitational lock around Aureola make for seasonal cycles that are vastly different from those on Earth.

Alpha Centauri has dawned on the plains but has yet to reach the canyon by the time Sedge makes it to the second tier. Again, he has made great time. He stops amidst the clouds to stare at the silhouetted treeline. He is nearing the forest, but he's not going there this time. His plan is to stay on the second tier, past the river to a set of caverns that sit on the eastern wall of the canyon, a place he's only reached once. Those caverns, he believes, provide passage to the crater.

The second tier catwalk grows frighteningly narrow in places, but eventually leads Sedge to the canyon wall.

Shaded, it's much cooler, dimmer, and filled with caves. Logically, Sedge enters the largest one. It has a stream flowing out of it. Knowing odds are high of encountering argon pockets, he puts on his oxygen mask and turns on his lighting system. He follows the stream into the rock wall. It has a smooth bank running alongside, obviously formed from a previously greater flow of water. This place probably floods heavily during rainstorms.

Eventually, much deeper into the caverns, the stream forks. Water now flows from two sources. Sedge is beyond where he's ever been and doesn't have the aid of his mapping drone. He already packed too much with his auxiliary oxygen tank to bring it, though it sure would come in handy at this point. Following his instincts, he continues along the stream with the greater flow of water, deeper into these catacomb-like caverns.

Well beyond the fork in the stream, Sedge encounters the base of a high underground cliff wall. It has an enormous waterfall flowing over its edge, feeding the stream he's been following. It's an incredible sight. How could such a large waterfall be underground? Where does all this water end up? His mind fills with wonder.

The falls, unfortunately, are a dead end. He can't scale that wall and doesn't want to anyway. His hope is to work his way further down, meaning he'll have to turn around. Before doing so, he sits at the base of the falls. What a find - a place which he and only he knows. How could he ever go back to Earth knowing he would never return to this moon?

After photographing the waterfall extensively, Sedge works his way back along the stream to its fork, where he changes course. Following the smaller stream, he eventually comes to a series of round, hemispherical, underground rock slopes. To navigate his way through them, he winds between them, geo-marking every step he takes to ensure he won't repeat any wrong turns. They seem endless, but eventually do come to an end. The stream has widened, giving Sedge greater hope that it will lead to his desired passage.

The stream eventually guides Sedge to a small underground lake. The cave's ceilings are low, and covered with small stalactites. The breadth of the cave, however, is remarkably wide. Sedge works his way around the underground lake to a separate stream that it feeds. This is what he'd hoped to find, since the stream he had been following up till now flowed into the canyon. Could this one feed the crater? He presses forth.

His newly discovered stream flows into a set of bankless narrows. Sedge can see a wide bank along the right side, just past the narrows, but has no way of reaching it without getting wet. Unprepared, he decides to take off his clothes, at least everything from the waist down, and pack them in his waterproof pack so he can walk through the narrows. He does so. The water is cold and flowing fast. He steps carefully, not knowing what lies beneath. Fortunately, it's only smooth rock. The water, however, runs deeper than he gauged, getting the lower half of his shirt and back brace wet. Upon reaching the bank, he takes a moment to dress and rest. What an unexpected adventure.

Half a kilometer deeper downstream the narrows prove to be worth their risk. Sedge sees natural light entering the cave. He's too far into the caverns for the light to be coming from the canyon, and too deep for it to be from the plains. It has to be coming from the crater. To go to it, he abandons the stream to follow yet another interior cave. His excitement is short lived, however, when he encounters a series of deep cracks. He's able to easily jump over the first two, but the third is wider. He walks along its edge to what appears to be its most narrow point, where he's confident he can jump over it. He takes a few moments to psyche himself up, but not enough time to talk himself out of it. He gets a two-step jump on the jump and goes for it, leaping with all he's got for the other side. His landing, however, cracks and crumbles the edge, forcing Sedge to grab hold of a stalagmite on the other side to keep from sliding into the bottomless abyss. Luckily, he's able to quickly pull himself up to safety.

"Damn, I just cracked the crack," he says with a huge sigh of relief, not expecting such a brush with death.

Getting up, Sedge feels a pain he knows all too well. He stays down, knowing that any wrong movement could make that fifth lumbar slip. He tightens his back brace to minimize his spine's motion, knowing his circumstances aren't good. Just meters in front of him, he can see sunlight and the opening. It has to be the crater, and here he sits, partially wet and structurally screwed. He knows what's to come; the inflammation and hip pain.

Sedge digs in his pack for his first aid kit. In it, he pulls out his pethidine pills. Tempted, he opts instead for a double dose of ibuprofen, remembering his conversation with Voltaire. He wants to enter Alamut without the opiates, and with his pants on.

6:6

Waiting for the anti-inflammatories to kick in, Sedge stares at the red sandstone wall. Were he to die here, would he ever be found? Then it dawns on him. Here, deep, deep within these caverns is the perfect place to draw this world's first petroglyph. Who knows when anyone else will be here?

He picks up a sharp stone and begins carving images onto the red sandstone walls. He carves a map of the Earth, the moon and the planets all going around the sun. It's crude but conveys information effectively. He then draws Alpha, Beta, and Proxima Centauri, along with Aureola, Lunita, and finally Luna Nuevo. Between the stars, he draws a deepliner in flight and arrows from Earth to Luna Nuevo. Staring at the illustrated story, he starts to laugh really hard, a laughter heard throughout the cave. Sedge then draws a human figure, Da Vinci's *Vitruvian Man* next to the spacecraft, only this time with a mammoth male organ.

Sedge has entertained himself. He can't stop laughing. Sure, the cave drawing is funny but this laughter also indicates the pain relievers are kicking in. He lies on his side in the cave, now loosening up. After finally catching his breath, he decides to test out his back. Sure enough, there is less pain. In fact, he feels surprisingly good. He stands, though he has to stoop under a low ceiling. Feeling okay, he makes his way to the light.

When he reaches the opening, Sedge stands stunned. The cave sits about halfway up the inner wall of the crater. The scene is surreal, overlooking the enormous meteor-made valley. Clouds flow along its floor without covering it. Many have burned off. This view is far more spectacular than the overlook. Sedge can see the waterfall off to his right, lush vegetation, and trees everywhere. Clouds of venting steam rise from various points within the crater. Far below, a river flows around the central tower, like a mote.

"Alamut!" Sedge shouts, triggering an echo across the crater. "Marco, I'm in!"

The inner wall is steep, slowing Sedge's descent into the crater. Like the canyons, the lower he gets, the less steep the grade. It takes him over an hour to reach the safety of the crater floor. The temperature is really warm, almost hot. The southern wall receives little direct sunlight, however. Further north, the trees and vegetation really change. Things look much different than they do in the canyon. The trees here are dryer and have needles, similar to pine trees on Earth but with far different colors and shapes. They're almost cartoon like.

The crater is enormous, estimated to be over eighty kilometers in diameter, covering over a five-thousand square kilometer area. Sedge follows the stream from the falls, knowing it eventually leads to the central tower. An hour into his trek, he reaches a dense forest. He follows the widening stream into it. Two hours into the forest, he reaches the crater's inner river, which flows around the base of the mighty tower. His excitement grows.

After walking along the river for a few kilometers, Sedge finds a place where the stream takes a series of steep winds. It's a perfect place to cross. At the closest crossing, he realizes he has the same issue he had in the narrows. He has to strip again. He does so, this time stark naked, putting all his clothes into his watertight bag. The water is cold but invigorating, flowing chest high. He holds his bag over his head, taking slow secure steps. The riverbed is full of stones, round and smooth from millions of years of flowing water. Though slippery, they actually feel nice beneath his feet. Sedge tosses his bag onto the ground ahead of him before taking his final steps onto the inner riverbank.

Only one hurdle remains now; the tower. There it stands.
Scattered clouds gliding just above it cast shadows on its
walls, adding to its majestic presence. Utterly thrilled,
Sedge gradually makes his way around the tower's base
in search of the point where he'd theorized it could be
scaled. Sure enough, the far side of the tower has a
series of roundly eroded rocks full of caves. Sedge
begins his climb.

As rugged as Luna Nuevo has proven, through its water-
cycle it has carved some smooth trails in places where
water has flown over centuries. Fortunately, this tower
too has a smooth streambed running down its side,
carved over time. Again, not the best place to be during
a rainstorm, but on a day like today seems custom-made
for Sedge's arrival. Unfortunately, it only runs to the
tower's navel. From there, Sedge has to climb up a
series of rounded stones, most of which are not difficult
to scale but time consuming and laborious. Sedge,
nevertheless, has no better place to be. A passing cloud
in a brightening sky tells him he's gaining elevation,
lighting a fire under him. Rhapsody rises with every step.
He must be getting close to the top.

It's near the top where the tower gets most interesting. It
becomes too steep for its face to be scaled without
serious equipment, but also much more porous, filled

with caves. Sedge, anticipating these caves, having plotted this course on his 3D model, follows his plan and enters the cave with the most oval opening. As he'd hoped, it opens to a membranous labyrinth of tunnels, all softly carpeted with sand. It's a landscape he has never seen on Earth. He works his way upward, through the unknown part of his model, following any glimpses of daylight he gets. This had better work. The thought of turning back now, so close to the top, sends adrenaline down his spine.

Sedge sees a light much brighter than those along the way. It's really bright. He goes to it. It's direct sunlight, coming straight from the Centauri star trio. Never has it looked so good. The opening is to a ledge. The tower walls are steep but the ledge is wide, flat, and cat-tracks around the tower's outer face, further upward. There are trees and shrub-like plants growing off the tower walls. The ledge leads between two, lower jagged peaks, around to a small waterfall. Only clouds can be seen above the waterfall's edge. It must be flowing from the top, from that little valley Sedge has stared so long at on his model.

The ledge levels off onto a small, flat area near the top of the falls. It's the first tier of the top of the tower. Here, Sedge takes a few minutes to catch his breath, get a drink of water, and takes in a two-hundred sixty-degree view of the crater. It's humbling, reminding him how miniscule he is.

Another yet smaller cave system leads to the second tier. It's the largest and main tier. Sedge's euphoria heightens as he steps onto the small, heavily forested valley in the sky, tucked snugly between scenic, rounded mountain peaks. A small lake sits in the land's interior. It flows into a stream that feeds the falls. Geothermal steam vents within the forest add aesthetic pleasure to the dreamy landscape. The even greater, three-hundred and ten degree view of the crater from the edges of this tier are chilling. Again, the future flashes before Sedge's eyes. What will the value of this real estate one day be? He sits on a stone, looking out over the vast land. He made it. He's standing at the top of the tower. He calls Bite.

"Hey Sedge," Bite answers.

"Take a wild guess where I am," Sedge suggests.

"On the central tower," Bite answers.

"What makes you say so?" Sedge asks.

"My calculations for one," she answers. "Your elevation as well. This signal is too strong to have come from the canyon or crater floor."

"Clever Bite," Sedge says. "I like how you think."

"Thank you," Bite answers.

"Let's move here," Sedge suggests.

"Are you serious?" Bite asks.

"Why not?" Sedge answers. "It's going to be known in history and we have a chance to be its first inhabitants."

"Sounds nice," Bite replies.

Right then, while talking to Bite, Sedge sees them; the caves just beneath the tower's highest peak. One stands out above the others, prominently overlooking virtually the entire crater. That, Sedge thinks, has primordial allure. It's like a master penthouse, naturally carved by wind and rain over millions of years.

"Even an android would be blown away by this scene," he tells Bite. "Anyway, I'm going to check a cave out, relax a few short hours, maybe get a nap, then I'm going to start back to the dome. I'll still be a while."

"Be safe Sedge," Bite replies. "See you back here later."

Staring up at the alluring cave, as tired as Sedge is, he knows he's not going to rest until he explores it. It represents the grand prize in his quest; the chalice. It looks like the best place to rest anyway. Sedge crosses through the small forest and walks along the lake side. Just beyond the waterfall's crest, he climbs up the hill to a flat space in front of the outside entrance of the enchanting cave. There, he takes a good look around at the awe-inspiring view. It's dizzying from this height. A sudden, dry breeze whips through the air.

Sedge enters the cave. Just inside, protected from the elements, he sees something that leaves him weak at the knees. He kneels in front of it. Questions race across his mind. How did it get here? When? Who put it here? In shock, he sits mesmerized by what could easily be the most profound discovery in human history; an almost two-meter stack of patiently, meticulously balanced stones.

Though his questions lack answers, Sedge can now clearly understand why he has been drawn across a sea of time.

Author's Note

All characters in this story are fictional. Any likenesses or similarities to actual people are unintentional. Astronomical information, however, is factual except for the planet Aureola (to the best of our knowledge) and its moons.

Alluring Echoes is a continuation of the story set forth in Moonliner. To those who take the time to read either or both of these books, thank you.